UN/COMMON GROUND

by

Allan Kolski Horwitz

Illustrations by Patrick Rorke

First published in 2002 by

Botsotso Publishing
Box 30952
Braamfontein
2017

botsotso@artslink.co.za

Second reprinting – 2012

ISBN 0-620-29725-5

Cover, layout and design – James de Villiers

CONTENTS

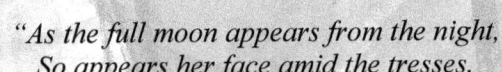

"As the full moon appears from the night,
So appears her face amid the tresses.

From sorrow comes the perception of her;
The eye crying on the cheek
Like the black narcissus
Shedding tears upon a rose."

From 'The Special Love'
Ibn El Arabi

GEMORS

"Claudia!"

Where was she? Why was she doing this to him?

"Claudia, I need you, man! Stop your nonsense!"

His key didn't fit - she must have changed the locks while he was out playing pool in Klein Street – so he'd spent the night on a bench in Park Station. How he'd cursed her! His mind jagged in the stale vastness of the station concourse; solitary, furtive men, who made pass after pass, forcing him to lie stiff as if he was dead. At two o'clock he had checked the flat for the last time, praying she would open for him, but his knocking and shouts only woke the neighbours, the old ones who smelt of samp and beans. They had yelled abuse and told him to leave. He'd limped back to the station, bought another pack of cigarettes and dossed down near the Rotunda. More mangled hours. Afterwards, just before sunrise, propped against a rubbish bin in Noord Street, near the Art Gallery, he had dozed while a blur of bodies drifted by on their way to the six o'clock shift. Now it was morning and he was exhausted, his stomach rumbled and every few minutes he farted.

Yesterday, while he was sleeping, she had thrown this note onto the kitchen table, and left for work.

Daniel, I can't go on like this. It's true I loved you in the beginning but since you moved in things have gone bad. You only think of yourself. For all our sakes it will be better when you leave. I'm not saying I don't want to see you again, but we musn't live together. Please take your clothes. Take all your stuff. Come and see me in a few days. Now I'm too mad. I'm sorry but I can't go on with you. Think why, ja, think. I don't want to find you here when I come back. Please! I don't want more trouble. Good bye.

The megaphone in his mouth aggravated the pounding in his head.

He stood up on the tiled floor and walked out of the concourse past the ticket offices, the Kentucky Fried Chicken outlet and the liquor stores. Running his fingers over the knife tucked into one of his socks, he stepped into Wanderers Street. Thick pieces of wors were frying in portable braai stands on the pavement. He passed the TWO SHOES FOR THE PRICE OF ONE sign in the window of the Indian shop and headed down towards a kaffie near the Cathedral.

"Hoosit, my china?"

"Hoosit, jou mal vark."

That last pipe he'd hit in the station toilet had really blown him.

The Sowetan headline read: VOLCANO IN JOUBERT PARK: MAN BLOWN UP BY BLOUETJIE ON THE REEF

She's got a surprise coming if she thinks I'm going to get a job to support her brat. Mal varke. His mind turned to Eddie and his killer girl, a juicy number he'd picked up in Elders.

"Hoosit, jou vark."

The morning was melting.

In the kaffie he ordered a packet of chips. He watched the long, off-white slivers of potato sizzle in oil, then slither as they were tossed into a paper bag. He slipped one into the mouth of the drunk who was sprawled outside the door. Vinegar soaked through the bag.

"Waar's die curry powder?"

A dark woman with a trace of a moustache stooped over the cash register.

"Stop messing around!"

She shoved it across.

"Waar's djou old man?"

She looked at him without smiling, but while he pretended to search for money, she looked down at his pants. Years ago he'd naaied one of these hairy women in Riversdale. Stuck at night by a garage, while her father counted the takings, they had groped each other in a storeroom near the fridges.

"Claudia, where the hell are you? That Eddie sold me kak the other day, the day before yesterday, the day before the lunar eclipse, before we became raving button spiders."

Ja, that last pilletjie had fractured his skull. It was blowing out. The counter was full of his bright red madness. He ran out of the shop with the packet of hot chips burning his hand. The woman at the cash register called to him. He ran as fast as he could. Sies! Why were his pants not covering his cock? He could feel his cock quivering like a slap chip.

Sit, boy. Sit in the gutter, the only place to sit in King George's Street in the shade of plane trees next to Joubert Park, and centre yourself.

The chips wriggled all over the pavement.

Good for nothing, drug addict.

"Daniel Adams!" Two dark brown breasts spilled out of a blue overall. "Come suck, my boy. Come suck."

The woman began opening her buttons. Behind her was a metal tub piled with dry ice; propped against it was a broken cardboard sign advertising ice-cream prices. A man with a yellow woollen cap squashed

2

on his head stood near the tub.

"Daniel Adams, come sign up for the Workers Revolutionary Party! Buy our paper! Enter the ranks!"

The man drifted off, stopping others.

"Claudia! What the hell is going on? Why are you doing this to me?"

He badly needed to make a new move that would get him back inside the flat; back inside her. Her skin coated him, the snugness of her tongue permanently warming his mouth. What subtle secretion had she been infusing into him?

MAN BLOWN UP BY BEAUTY QUEEN IN JOUBERT PARK

The big-breasted woman bent over him.

"He's sick."

Next to her was an elderly man dressed in khaki; the green and black badge of the Zionist Church pinned to his white shirt.

"I've never seen him this bad. He looks like a zombie. He's naughty, this one. You see him here all times of the day and night. He likes to take chances."

"But he's got a good heart! He carried lollies for me once, all the way from my boss's van." The ice-cream seller covered her face with her hands and laughed. "Hau! He's got wandering hands!"

Daniel remembered those long sweet lollies - summer afternoons, overheated women chatting, legs stretched out in front of them on the grass.

The Zionist took her arm.

"I know this clever! He stole from my bag last year. Now he's doing the Devil's work again." The Zionist spat, a thick white glob that covered Daniel's cheek. Then, abruptly, the old man bent down to check his breathing. "These tsotsis, they survive anything." He scratched his chin. "He doesn't deserve kindness but we must do right by everybody in their time of need. We must save each other from Damnation."

The old man's eyes shone. Daniel's head rolled.

"Sisi, let us put him in the park."

*

They picked him up from the gutter and carried him through the iron gates of the park, his legs trailing against the photographers' boards of portraits, the hawkers plates piled with fruit and sweets alongside the rim of the small green fountain. Then they laid him down on the Post Office side near the banana trees and the hothouse. Daniel kept his eyes closed. From far away he heard a low chant. There were car sounds beyond the park railings. He did not wish to speak. Foulness clogged his throat till suddenly a cascade of water splashed his face and a gentle hand wiped his lips so that he could feel the cracks piece together. More water sprinkled onto his forehead. The ice-cream seller cradled him to her bosom. She squeezed his hand as he drank.

The Zionist said, "There is nothing more to be done. I must go now, Sisi."

She smiled. "Thank you, my Brother. God be with you on your journey."

Daniel shivered, remembering the Zionist's voice. Months before he had been beaten; a mob had chased him into the courtyard of a block of flats, an enraged mob armed with sticks and knives. And out of this mob, this same voice had shouted out that he was a thieving Boesman witch who spirited wallets out of locked metal trunks. Daniel had begged for mercy, waved a handful of R50 notes in the air till the Zionist had grabbed the money, and walked off leaving him to stew in that hot, yellow day, its thickness of trees, the mass of taunting, jeering men and women still ready to draw his blood.

Bladdy liar, causing shit. I don't play with nonsense. I buy and sell. I'm no cheap dief.

The ice cream woman wiped his forehead with her sleeve.

"You stay here and rest. I must go back to my stand. I left my cousin there and she doesn't know the prices."

The palpitations in his chest eased. He lay on the grass near the hothouse while she was swallowed up in the streams of people thronging the pathways. The morning rolled on, stretching up into the ether; pure stratosphere where everything is sweet nothing.

"Jesus, Claudia! Where are you?"

He had still been asleep, as usual, while she had dressed for work, getting the kid ready for crèche. After they had left, mid-morning, waking briefly, he had tried to warm the cold space beside him, then slept on. Soon it was noon. He was fresh, free to stroll over to Bertrams where he and Hendricks broke a pipe in the backyard of Koos's broken-down house. There was a fig tree, full of ripe, purplish fruit. He had plucked a fig, and splitting opening the skin with his fingernails, licked the white sap; he had split open a ripe fig and buried his face in it.

Daniel felt in his pants pocket. The plastic bank bag holding the tabs was there. He took one out and swallowed it. Then he closed his eyes, and lay back. Within minutes his head began revolving. Dammit! What was up and what was down?

He rolled over towards the hothouse. It glowed with a green radiance that made every other object seem pale, even colourless. Then he sat up. There was a flash of pinkish-white. Sticking out through the side of the glass door was a hand. Following this hand, he saw a black albino man wearing a suit of lotus leaves. On his head was a diadem of pearl; his whole being glowed with energy and light.

"Daniel! At last! You don't know how excited I am! All this time, years and years, stuck in the Gemors! How could you? You've been so battered and abused." A cloud of fireflies, wings shimmering, hovered about. "Come, inside, my boy. Come inside for a little refreshment."

The man waved, making a circle in the air, and suddenly, before he could think of how to respond, Daniel found himself standing in front of the hothouse door, a stream of warm air, moist and cloying, enveloping him.

"I can't tell you how pleased I am! This is such a terribly overdue meeting!"

The albino clasped his hand, kissed his cheek lightly. Daniel felt a shiver of pleasure. Then the man sprayed him with rosewater, and taking his greasy head in his hands, massaged it.

Daniel sighed. What a welcome - for someone all smeared and brooding, made cunning and hard! Then said, "It's true I can't give a good account of myself but I haven't had it easy. You see, I was never taught right or wrong. Now all I want is a crust, a little crust of your kindness." The fireflies glinted. "Just a drop of your loving kindness." The fireflies flashed.

"Only a drop, my friend?" The man embraced him. "Is that all you want? You're very modest. After everything you've been through. You certainly deserve more than a morsel . . . I'll see to that. Yes, I'll see to that."

Daniel breathed in the scent that rose from his body; a scent of untamed wilderness and manicured voluptuousness, of passion and calm. And while the strong, sensitive fingers drained out the pressure hammering in his head, he observed a small pond at the entrance to the hothouse.

In the middle of the pond stood a concrete statue of a boy kneeling with a bucket. Several paths led off from this centre point and along these paths, in raised platforms of rich black earth, planted in all the available space, brilliant flowers of every description flourished. Daniel felt the pulsation of growth. It was as if he was instantaneously seeing buds take shape, expand, swell out and bloom.

"Ja . . ."

Lotus leaves quivering, the albino man released him.

"Don't be shy. Tell me about 'out there'. How are things, my dear boy? Is there peace? A little plenty?"

"Its mal," Daniel said, "real bladdy hectic."

"Even more gemors?" The albino spoke sadly. His grip on Daniel's hand tightened. "How much more? Why does it go on and on? Have you tried with all your heart? Are you all so inadequate? Are you?" His voice rang out, then dropped. "Anyway . . . you're here now. Let's go inside, I can't take too much cold." He shivered as he spoke. "I don't know how anyone does." He drew Daniel over the threshold. "Welcome, my boy, welcome to this holy house."

Daniel closed the door with his foot. "Hell, thanks, mister. Look, I've messed up badly but I didn't have a chance. You see, in the orphanage I had no one to care for me except this one kid called Cherry. He was the only one. The other boys and the masters used to bugger me up. There wasn't enough food. Jesus, man, you can't blame me . . ."

Daniel stopped. Why was the man detaching himself, withdrawing from him? Especially his warm, understanding eyes that had now become hard and remote.

"Please! Don't leave me! It isn't my fault . . ." The albino stared into the hothouse's misty glass.

"Why is it all our visitors say that? There's always a story, a long, drawn out excuse, a million reasons and half-baked explanations! At some point I'll give you an opportunity to go into history but right now let me rather show you our beauties." His eyes were again soft and absorbing. "I'm sorry. I shouldn't be angry. I know how difficult it is to be on your own and be forced to carve out a space." He touched Daniel's cheek lightly. "Just leave your shoes outside on the step."

Daniel kicked off his tackies. They were grimy and split, stains covered the purple fabric, the laces were frayed.

"I don't usually smell like this but last night I had to kip at Park Station. Claudia locked me out. She didn't come home." The tackies landed next to a fern. "She was out screwing some arsehole churrah. I know she was jiving at Boobs while I was thick in dogshit in the bushes opposite the flat. Bladdy whore, messing around while I was dead on my feet and starving and all these fokken moffies trying to get into my pants . . ."

6

As he peeled off his socks, the knife taped to his ankle clattered onto the paving.

The albino man shook his head. "Oh, Daniel, how terrible . . ." Then he stiffened. "If you dare speak like that again about her I'll see you drown in the fountain! I'll push you under myself! She's half of you, the better part, no doubt! And as for the moffies . . ." Sliding his palm across Daniel's cheek, he hissed, "Now pick up that knife and throw it out of here before I lose the last drop of my patience!"

Daniel rocked back on his feet. "Jesus, I didn't mean to bring it in, sir! I forgot!" The nausea returned, he felt weak and pale. "I need to sit down."

"Yes, you'd better! Sit down and think before you gaan aan." Still glaring, the man gave him his hand and led him to a small bench. "Stay here. I'll bring you something to drink." He touched Daniel's shoulder, before disappearing down a path overgrown with hanging plants.

Daniel slumped back.

The hothouse was saturated with swollen drops of water that hung from the glass with the rounded succulence of larvae. Slowly, one by one, these drops gathered moisture to the point when their weightiness caused them to fall gracefully onto the already very wet soil. But despite the calm and restful atmosphere, Daniel felt worse. The churning inside his stomach and the spinning in his head rushed back. He stood up, almost falling.

"Where's that idiot? He's got to help me!"

He ran down one of the paths but the albino was nowhere to be seen.

"I can't take this! Where are you?" He thrashed about, scattering leaves. "Dammit, why you doing this, Claudia!"

*

Claudia and Isabel, her best friend, were sitting at *The Three Sisters* on Pretorius Street. Each had ordered an Irish coffee. Claudia was talking.

There was the landlord's ultimatum - rent was three months in arrears. If she didn't pay by tomorrow, they would throw her out. There were also four court summonses. Folded in manila envelopes, they lay on the red plastic restaurant table: one from Truworths for five dresses; one from Edgars for jerseys and shoes; one from Russels for a lounge suite, a dresser and a double bed. The last one was from the local bottle store. Years before, she had been arrested in PE after failing to appear in court on a similar charge. From that time, when applying for credit, she had never given her real address. So what had gotten into her now? Had it been some lunatic sense of security because she was living with a man again? The summonses could be sorted out, slipped out of, but the rent had to be found.

While the two women sipped their drinks, Daniel returned to the hothouse entrance and sat down next to the pond. The water was filled with a mass of lilies and darting goldfish. On all sides, murmurings gushed from the dark, dank soil; flowers glowed and throbbed along the veils of vegetation. He sat back against the bench and closed his eyes. Ja, it was rough, so rough that sometimes he didn't want to get up. Every day, more shit. But what could you do? There were always surprises. He breathed in deeply, gulping down the soothing scents. At last, a chance to gather himself and reflect. But, as he was about to close his eyes, there was a rustling behind him - the swish of delicate materials.

Daniel turned round.

A large brown horn spiraling out of the centre of a pale but glistening forehead, the forehead of a squat plump, white man dressed in a bright orange robe, loomed over him. Daniel squinted. In one hand, the man held a glass flask which glittered with a silvery liquid; the other hand held a tray on which balanced a single glazed goblet.

"Here, my friend. Enjoy this refreshment."

The horn thrust out into the air, firm but trembling.

Daniel nodded.

"I know you."

He laughed. The man was one of those shaven-headed Hare Krishnas who paraded through Hillbrow on Saturday afternoons, beating drums and bells and giving out free bowls of rice to street kids and hobos.

"Hey! Where's your manners? Don't grab!"

The orange robe drew back and the liquid almost spilt, but lunging forward, Daniel grabbed the goblet.

"I'm fucking thirsty!"

The silver liquid tasted strong and fruity. He drained the goblet. Within seconds he found himself gliding through the hothouse, the air rich with scents, subtle and intense. And while he floated along the narrow paths, the Hare Krishna followed behind, a gravelly but not unpleasant voice.

"Not bad, hey? Home brew. The Master spends all his time distilling it. There's crushed petals and drops of sap from each flower and root in this hothouse. It takes years and years to mature. Come, I'll show you where it's prepared. The vat is in a very special place, not everyone's allowed in, and you can't just help yourself."

Daniel smiled and followed the shimmering robe. Everything was so bright and flowing! What luck he had spotted the mottled pink hand

8

beckoning at the hothouse door! Then he stiffened. There was a sharp pricking and hardening feeling in his temples. He wanted to lie down. He tried to find a bench. He collapsed onto the floor. He lay groaning, groping around. His head was buckling. A final tearing sensation, then touching his forehead, he fell back in horror.

The Hare Krishna raised Daniel's head; put a hairy arm round him.

"Yes, my friend. The Master teaches us all a lesson. He calls it 'corrective action'. Believe me, once you've been selected, things are never the same."

Daniel lay panting. Cautiously, incredulously, he felt the long, bony extension that had shot out of his forehead. The Hare Krishna propped him up against a pillar.

"I was living at the Temple on Goldreich Street. One afternoon, it was hot like today, I was lying down on the grass right near where you were. I was randy as hell. The Master opened the door and waved to me. I followed him in, and I can't say I'm sorry." He touched the horn on his own forehead. "You'll get used to it. It's only when you lean forward that it's a problem. Otherwise everything is so much lighter." He smiled. "There are such sweet girls in the neighbourhood. They'll do anything for a movie and popcorn." Then he laughed and poked Daniel in the stomach. "You won't want to leave! All we have to do is sweep and weed flowerbeds. And that's only for two hours a day. Afterwards we're free. There's all the time in the world to perfect yourself." He smiled sweetly. "You know the secret? Every morning at five o'clock we're allowed a goblet. That's it, just once a day, all of us linking hands round this pond, passing it from hand to mouth until everyone's had his share. Then we do meditation and levitation, nothing too strenuous but enough to keep us on our toes. There are also sessions on General Cosmology. Those are a bit heavy for my small brain, but I tell you, they're more interesting than dancing down Claim Street. I was getting tired of the gongs." He opened his arms. "Such sweet, clean, cuddly girls!" The hands waved and two watery eyes blinked. "You don't know how long I've waited for someone like yourself - someone who'll understand."

Daniel stepped back. No, that was sick! How could a grown man get hard for a kid? He ran his fingers along the base of his knotted horn as the Hare Krishna faded from sight. No, he wasn't a fool. But then he thought of the Boer in the flat next door, the post office worker who'd been retrenched and spent his time boozing cheap wine. One day he'd found him sprawled on the floor, half dead, a bitter, sad expression on his face. After helping him to his feet, and suffering a blast of foul breath, Daniel had given the man a handful of uppers for nothing, and that was dumb because you never know when you'll need the extra bucks. Especially when Claudia was always on to him for this and that - food, rent, electricity, medicine, clothes for the kid. . . ja, the kid, always something for the kid, some kind of scene with the kid . . .

Like the time the brat was sleeping in his room and they were on the stoep, Claudia was wearing the white, clinging dress that accentuated her fullness, he was telling a joke, leaning against the stoep wall, his head upturned, eyes shining with amusement while she tickled his stomach. Then he was kissing her, caressing her arms, and they slowly entwined their tongues, she stirring, smoothing his hair but the child woke up and started crying; they kissing, the crying growing louder till the brat coughed with rage, and he, Daniel standing over the small bed, lifted the boy and ran back with him to the stoep, then dangled him over the railing. Bastard laaitie! Always disturbing them as soon as they got down to business! That time Claudia had grabbed his arms, a powerful clamping of his arms so unforeseen that she had almost caused him to drop the hysterical boy.

"Yo, we shouldn't laugh while there are prisons and labour camps and execution chambers." The Hare Krishna came back into view, clapping his hands. "We shouldn't . . . but we have to. You see, my brother. You see?" He took Daniel's hand, kissed it and held it in a caress, not unlike the albino's but clammier. "We torture each other with burning cigarettes. We force each other into sealed rooms and pipe in gas. Hey, do you remember the neutron bomb?"

Daniel wrinkled up his nose. "Neutron bomb? What was that?"

The orange robe glowed, white light emanating from its folds and along its edges.

"It tears human flesh apart while buildings and other objects are left intact."

The incandescence intensified. The Hare Krishna seemed elastic. His body began to slowly dissipate. Daniel had to shield his eyes, the aura was too bright.

"What else is going on in the Gemors? Tell me, boeta. I lived in it for long enough. I remember every little trick and scam. So, what's new?"

Daniel could only see the rim of his sandals. He wanted to make it stop. Enough is enough. This was enough. The brightness and heat were overpowering. He was in the hothouse but the orange robe, the twisting kernel of horn, the sandals, the flask with shining liquid, had all disappeared. In their place was the Master.

"Isn't this better than roaming around out there? Don't you feel calmer?"

This time he wore a gown of hyacinths, and on his head, in place of the diadem, was a plain blue band.

"You think there's nothing worse than sexual frustration." The Master looked down at Daniel's soiled pants. "You can't sleep until someone's made it spurt." Then he looked away. "Why is it you ignore us? We've tried everything possible to show you the way." He bowed his head. "We've tried so hard to help . . ."

Daniel felt a tumultuous thrashing of air that almost knocked him off his feet.

A yellow-brown eagle, beak poised, talons unfurled, hovered above him. As the sky darkened, he was lifted up, twisted and spun into the haze like a screw - again the lekker blouetjie casting him into ether, sweet zero between heaven and earth till there was only a black hole expanding through his stomach.

The whirling sensation stopped.

He was lying on the lawn, the green frame of the hothouse silhouetted against the park rails, sprinklers shooting spray that made his T-shirt damp. His head was clear. He breathed coolness, transpiration of trees, evening soft and fluid with dim shapes.

He sat up, elated.

*

Claudia was still with Isabel at *The Three Sisters*. They had long switched to brandies and were feeling loose and mellow. She was doubly relaxed - Isabel had agreed to lend her half the rent money and store her things while the summonses were pending. In the meanwhile Claudia would stay with her mother in PE and wait a few months before returning to Jo'burg. Now they sat waiting for the waiter to bring a last round. As Claudia kissed Isabel in gratitude, down the hill in the park, Daniel looked up at the post office clock.

"Six o' clock!"

He'd go back to the flat. This time he'd catch her. He'd talk her into opening up. But if she still wasn't there or wasn't prepared to let him in, he would make another plan for the night. He would try Enoch, a long time connection, although Enoch rarely spent time in his cramped room squeezed on a rooftop. Another option was Professor. But at this hour Professor would be hustling for beer money. Lastly, there was Lucky down in Bok Street;

lekker little pozzie there by the pawnbrokers. The only problem was that Lucky always had a women with him and he didn't like to be disturbed.

The afternoon had drained away. Trees formed a full green arcade, leaves shimmering as the day's last light washed through. Daniel walked towards Wanderers Street. Light-headed, he moved with confidence towards the flat.

His better half?

Most nights it was just the two of them, except for the boy whining; just the two of them lying in bed, watching TV, then switching off the TV and putting on music, something slow and moody. Those were the nights he wasn't out dealing, when he wasn't at the clubs trying to make bucks; moving in the clubs with his hands spread over his jacket pockets, grinning with chipped teeth.

"Easy does it, Danny boy! She's just had three nips with Isabel. They've paid the bill and they're standing up to leave. Every single man is staring at Claudia. You know how fine she is, all snappy in her red suit. She's walking out of there like Cinderella dumping her dirty blankets by stepmother's fireplace and heading at the speed of light for the prince's castle."

Daniel breathed in the familiar scent of freshness, of invigoration, but he could not see the Master.

"Yes, you're a lucky man! You've found a beauty who's good-hearted and, on top of it, clever. And she knows how to work."

Walking past the overflowing rubbish bins in the yard and up the stairs till he was in the passage leading to the flat, Daniel rang the bell. There was no reply. He banged the door. There was still no reply. Then, almost as soon as he had stopped kicking the door, he was back on Wanderers Street, leaning against the concrete pillars of Hawarden Court.

"Damn bitch! I'll make her pay for this!"

A group of men with tired, mechanical faces brushed past him: a thick-necked white man in a safari suit with four black men in stained khaki overalls dragging their feet behind him. Parked at the kerb was a furniture removal van.

"What, Danny boy! Still thinking those stale, stupid thoughts?" The Master was massaging his back. "I thought we'd covered that nonsense." Daniel felt the strong, sinewy fingers withdraw. "You're a hard-headed one." The fingers returned. "Such a pity . . ."

*

As Daniel opened his eyes, Claudia and Isabel hugged each other goodbye.

"I'll book a bakkie tomorrow."

"Thank you, my darling."

Claudia waved as she strolled down Klein Street past the Hillbrow Meat Market. It was good to have someone to rely on, someone who stood firm on her own two feet. Not a spoilt somebody who's only there for you to clean his arse. She was in high spirits. But as she crossed the driveway of the Lutheran Church with the Hansel and Gretel garden, an orange robe brushed against her and a curved, grey horn almost poked into her side.

She turned to meet burning eyes.

"I met Daniel this afternoon. He asked me to tell you how much he needs you. He speaks of you, only of you, in a most moving way, superlatives, one after the other. He really has seen the light." The Hare Krishna took her hand. "He's turning over a new leaf. He'll get a job, you'll have kids." He glanced at her stomach. "You'll have three of them."

She was in the church garden and the horned man in an orange robe was pressed right up against her.

"Claudia, think again! He's a good boy. None of us can help disappointing from time to time." The man moved away, uncovered a tray which lay on a low table. A crystal decanter scintillated. "Here, have a sip, it's unbelievably refreshing." He began pouring. "My dear girl, to your health and good judgement!"

She blinked as her nose was squashed.

"Hey, lady! What you doing? You walk right into people! You drunk or something?"

She was flat on her back in the street. The middle-aged Chinese man helping her to her feet was more sneering than sympathetic.

"You alright? Nothing hurt? You go home now and sleep." He picked up her bag. Then slyly, "You want some business? I give you nice present."

Claudia pushed him away. She rubbed her eyes. The Chinese man moved off towards the bars in Banket Street. Had the brandies gone too far and messed up her head? What had he said? Let Daniel come back? After draining her money, almost killing her child, trying to sleep with Isabel and her other friends, demanding she cook for him, clean the flat, serve him? Just as well he'd gone out by lunchtime so she could get back to the flat and change the locks.

She crossed the park on her way home to Wanderers Street, passing the giant chessboard painted on concrete near the hothouse and the rows of banana trees. Clusters of men sat on benches watching a very dark black man play a gaunt white alcoholic. The white man was grimly defending his last castle while Daniel leaned against the cold stone of the columns fronting the flats. A thin peel of sun hung above Park Station, that giant mass of horizontal squatness. The city was suffused with the calm of a summer's day subsiding into velvet depths. Yet how agitated he felt! He longed for the moisture under her arms, the perfumed line above her lips.

"Claudia! Where the hell are you?"

Across the road he saw the Master, this time wearing a white blouse and skirt. On his back, in splotchy black letters, was written: WINKY'S WORS. The Master held a plastic plate on which wobbled a thick, juicy sausage flanked by a mound of pap. Daniel watched him dip the sausage into a puddle of tomato and onion sauce, then lick his fingers.

"You think this is meat?" On the pavement was a sizzling braai stand. "You think I'm preparing rubbish? You think these are all off-cuts that I found on the floor? No, boykie, these are made of soya, high protein stuff. They're sauteeing in a mushroom and leek batter. You know, you eat too much cheap fried food. That's why you have black-outs and you fart."

*

Claudia walked into the Chatham Cafe on the corner of Bok and King George's Street. She bent over the ice-cream fridge, checked the flavours and chose a Chocolate Delight.

WOMAN FREEZES TO DEATH LICKING ICE LOLLY

Give him another chance?

The Master dipped his fingers into the red plastic bowl, scooping and rolling balls of pap while taxi touts called out the names of towns in Mpumalanga and Swaziland. A Jehovah's Witness walked up and down, neat and slick in suit and tie, arms full of tracts.

MAN DROWNING IN MONEY SAVED BY JESUS

Claudia queued to pay for the ice-cream. Someone pushed against her. She moved forward, was again knocked from behind. It was the Chinaman from the Lutheran Church. He winked as she slapped him.

"You bastard!"

He stood smirking in a jacket that had too long sleeves and stained cuffs, a tub of margarine in one hand.

"Touch me again and I'll skop you where it hurts!"

He continued smiling. "Very stupid, miss. Very stupid. Do you know who's waiting for you?"

She stood to one side. The line was long and people stared at her.

"Hey, stop fucking around. Pay, man!"

There was one other woman in the queue. She wore a doek over her beehive of plastic curlers.

"Leave her alone, you doos!"

Claudia rejoined the line. The man clutched at her hand. His breath, rancid with alcohol, pouring over her.

"Listen, miss. You got a boyfriend. I bet your boyfriend don't give a damn about you. He wants a slave. He wants someone to make him feel good. But that's not what I want. Come home with me. I'll give you a beautiful present, I'll give you a nice big, hard one all night."

As he pinched her bum she lurched forward onto the shop floor and Daniel, watching the Master lick the remnants of sauce from his fingers, splotches of brown and yellow stain showing on the white uniform, felt a wrenching in his guts.

"Claudia!"

She staggered out of the cafe, her dress all rumpled, handbag dangling wide open, a knot of men screaming abuse at her and the woman with the doek. The Chinaman dropped his pants, flashing, and a cashier waved a pistol. Then the mob abruptly broke up, dissolving in all directions.

She ran hysterically towards Wanderers Street.

"Daniel! Daniel!"

He stepped forward.

"Daniel!"

*

He was holding her, she was clutching at him and sobbing, the scent of her sweat, her clinging arms all over him. He stroked her so tenderly.

"Don't worry, sweetie, it's OK. You know, I'm moerse glad to see you." He pulled her towards him. "What's up? I've been waiting."

She was flushed, taut nipples pressing through her blouse.

"Hey, you're really looking smart!"

He kissed her but she broke free and said coldly, "Find my letter?"

"What letter?"

"Don't start your . . ."

"You know I can't read."

"Very funny."

"Ja, it is funny."

"Have you taken all your stuff?"

"What are you talking about?"

"Why haven't you done what I asked you to?"

"Listen, Claudia, I was worried about you. I've been waiting..."

"I've got nothing more for you."

"Nothing?"

"Ja, nothing. You know, nothing."

"I've given you everything."

"Don't get funny, man."

"Claudia, listen ... "

Daniel took her hand. She was staring up at the neon springbok that lit up the west. He felt his pulse hammering.

"I don't want to talk. I just want to do this." He caressed her lips. "I don't want to talk." He opened her mouth with his fingers. "You know what's between us." He leaned forward. "I'm serious."

She shook her head.

"Don't fight me now." He withdrew his fingers and clasped her to him. The street was dark and empty. "It wasn't right what I've been doing. I've been an arsehole."

He stroked her; long, slow movements up and down her back. He felt her relax. She hesitated then nuzzled against him.

"I'll sort myself out."

An elderly man wearing a Zionist badge, carrying a large metal trunk, moved past them towards the Pretoria taxi rank.

"You'll see. I'll get something going." Daniel felt a wetness slide from her eyes. "Hey, baby, don't . . . come on, honey, it's going to be all right."

He wiped her cheeks and pressed her against his neck and shoulder. She clung to him, closed then opened her eyes.

Over his shoulder, she saw her blankets spread out on the pavement. Clothes strewn over pots, plants, records and magazines; the child's toys scattered about, although most still seemed to be in his special blue box. She couldn't see the gas stove or the fridge, and it seemed that all the furniture was gone, but jammed over a bottle of tomato sauce was the hat she sometimes wore to parties and half torn in the gutter lay the photograph Daniel had taken on their first afternoon together - that warm, lazy Sunday in the park near the fountain when he had sat down on the bench next to her, stopped an ice-cream seller, taken a cone and rammed it up against his forehead. And she had moved forward to lick the ice-cream running down his cheeks, her face wide with laughter, Daniel's hand raised towards the fountain, spume surging up, the half smashed cone tilted to the sky.

"Ag, don't worry, sweetheart, you'll see. We're going to get out of this gemors."

17

ATONEMENT

"The sense of solidarity which sustains, and, in fact, makes human communities possible, is easily eroded by the drive to achieve personal power, or alternatively, by the defence mechanism that pushes each of us to resist danger. Solidarity gives way to the submission, sometimes even to the destruction, of others. Thus the dominating Ego celebrates its victory over those who obstruct or are required for its gratification. But it is an illusory victory, tainted from the start, and doomed to end in the downfall of both the victim and the overlord."

Matthew Goldberg: Vanity Fair Magazine - film review of The Picture of Dorian Gray

Matthew would never forget his arrival at Dachau railway station; the dank, grey skies even though it was summer, the short muddy walk with a group of other visitors to the concentration camp gates, his sombre, awe-struck foreboding as he walked into the first cluster of barracks that are now used as a reception area and bookshop. And there, in the bookshop, in a corner reserved for general literature about the Holocaust, he had seen a young, dark-haired, slender woman who projected a state of deep quietness and solemnity. He was completely disarmed by her presence: the brown, oval face, the slightly slanted black eyes, the long tapering legs clothed in blue jeans, the simple white jersey that swelled over her breasts. Unnoticed, he had observed her carefully while she leafed through various books. And after she had taken a map of the Camp and walked out of the bookshop, he had followed her into the exhibition area, discreetly standing a few steps back while she examined each document and photograph.

It was almost an hour before he had gathered enough courage to make an approach. She was studying a photograph that showed a section of a bare concrete, bridge-like structure bisected in the foreground by a vertically laid hump of grass. The typed caption stated that it was the SS rifle range at Hebertshausen near Dachau. Thousands of Soviet prisoners-of-war had been executed there, shot down because they were too weak to slave for the Nazi war machine. There were two large openings in the bridge-like structure; into these, the corpses had fallen.

"There are some people who would say that this photograph is a lie. All it shows is concrete. Where are the emaciated, naked, bullet-ridden bodies of the murdered men? Where are the amused, well-fed, uniformed bodies of the executioners? And where is the smoke rising up from the crematoria behind them?"

Matthew had spoken and the dark-haired woman had turned to him attentively. But she had looked at him searchingly, and remained silent for some time, before responding.

"Are we not standing in a concentration camp that is no longer a concentration camp? Surely, this is sufficient proof of goodness? Nothing can endure forever, not even the most stupefying evil. Everything transforms."

They had stood together in front of the photograph without speaking further but, without understanding why, they had remained together, moving through the barrack hall exhibition and then along the path leading to the site of the human ovens. And, while they did not touch nor talk, he had been achingly aware of her seriousness and delicacy, her finely cut face, her soft eyes and rounded lips, her curving body that moved so lithely. Miraculously, in that single moment, a bond had been formed that made it enough for them to simply be in each other's presence.

At midday they had eaten a light lunch in the cafeteria, still together but apart, thinking private thoughts but thoughts that intersected. So it was only in the late afternoon, after the camp had closed and they were waiting on the railway platform ready to return to Munich, and he was about to invite her to have dinner with him, that Matthew had asked her name, and where she was from, and about her work and her family.

She had told him that her name was Gabriella, and that she was Argentinian. She worked for a publisher and was in Germany for a trade fair. Her mother had died when she was a child but her father was alive. He was a general in the military, and she was proud that he was a member of the Ruling Junta, proud that he was defending her country against the Communist workers and their student allies. The Communists were unscrupulous and deceitful, committed to destroying Argentina's national independence. Her only regret was that the Army was compelled to counter their force with force. But a war of self-defence is a just war. What the Army was doing was necessary, unavoidable - the alternative was to capitulate. And, of course, there could be no comparison between the Nazi bloodletting and the justifiable action taken against the leftist revolutionaries by Argentinian patriots.

*

It is sundown on the Day of Atonement. Matthew has spent the afternoon reading the book he bought in the information centre at Dachau. He has not fasted - he has not fasted since he was fifteen years old. The book is open. The page shows the photograph of the SS rifle range at Hebertshausen. He reads what he wrote in the margin almost ten years ago in a bug-ridden guesthouse after eating alone in one of the sausage bars in Munich's main railway station: *What is that force which creates the destiny of each individual human being? Why have we become so unbearably perverted? Is it inevitable that we will destroy ourselves and this planet?*

He looks up from the book as he sits in the half-light, reliving his self-disgust. How could he have spent much of his brief pilgrimage to Dachau fantasizing the seduction of the daughter of a fascist? How could he have walked beside her through that exhibition of suffering and madness and not been able to prevent himself from being infatuated by her beauty?

He closes the book. It is seven o'clock. He has fifteen minutes to eat supper before the Executive meeting. The committee members will soon arrive and the living room is still covered with newspapers. He also has to run himself a bath.

*

Marie looks at her face in the mirror. She massages a lotion into her cheeks and across her forehead, below her eyes and into her neck. The lines are deepening, turning into trenches, scraping, moiling into her flesh. But her long hair is still brown and full and falls down over her shoulders. And her breasts are still firm despite feeding three babies. And her waist, though not as perfect as it once was, is slim and proportioned. Yet even as she looks at herself in the mirror, she again asks these questions: "When will I know joy again? Can I hope to ever meet a man who will ignite me with his passion, concern and tenderness?"

Sunday in the Village has passed in a whirl of phone calls, meals and family squabbles. She is tired but a hot bubble bath has revived her. She is wearing her favourite kaftan, one bought many years ago at a Rock Festival in Hout Bay. The children are playing, pulling at the dog, tugging its tail and jumping on its back. The animal yelps as the older boy twists one of its legs. Barry slouches in front of the television. He looks so weighed down and bloated that it fills her with fear. Although the marriage counselors have spoken optimistically, she has seen their 'contracts' all broken, as time after time he gives in to his compulsion and treats her with a nauseating violence.

She hears him shout at the children. He wants them to undress for bed but they continue tumbling on the carpet. He shouts more crudely. To keep the peace, she will have to step in and take charge. But she will have to hurry. It is already seven and she needs to fix them something to eat before going out to the meeting. Tonight she must be on time. She has something serious to tell the Executive. She has finally made up her mind.

*

Nita, Matthew's wife, walks past him into the living room. Earlier, she had tried to engage him but he had rebuffed her, totally absorbed as he was in the book. The same ritual has taken place every Day of Atonement; from early morning he pores through the book, ignoring her, making notes, drinking cup after cup of black coffee. And this year she has been further shut out by his preoccupation with Oscar Wilde, and his novel, 'The Picture of Dorian Gray'.

Matthew has been commissioned to write an article for a women's magazine. It is to be a popular analysis of the sensation that followed the new film version. The role of Dorian Gray has been played by one of the current generation of Hollywood stars and the film has been a great success. All over the world the media are reinterpreting the story of the rich and artistic young man who preserves his outward beauty by transmuting all evidence of spiritual and physical decay onto the canvas of a portrait.

The article is consuming him. Nita has rarely seen him so involved in an assignment. It is as if Dorian Gray sits next to him in the car, stroking his thin elegant fingers as morning traffic jams the roads on their way to an eight o'clock tutorial. And there he is leaning across the table, shaking his head, while a faculty meeting drags on. Then, at night, Dorian's limpid yet cloudy eyes look over his shoulder at the newspaper headlines.

*

Marie is the first to arrive. The others are already forty-five minutes late. It is this inconsistent attendance that has paralyzed the Executive; as a result the Development Project hangs in the balance.

From the start, everyone in the village has had a chance to be involved. There have been numerous workshops to shape the proposal, which over a year ago was written up by a supportive NGO. The first step is for the residents to buy the village from the owner, Royal Mines; the second is to build another similar village on adjacent land. This extension will house the black miners who work at a nearby processing plant. But Royal Mines has, from the outset, claimed the expense will be prohibitive, that too many houses will be required. The White workers in the past who had qualified for the few existing houses had always been a minority. To extend their privileges to all workers will be impossible. As such they claimed that past practice could not be used as a basis for the future - it would be too costly. And that this was the economic reality everyone had to accept. And so, after months of talks, Royal Mines has persisted in refusing to sell the existing village, and refused to sell other land in the area at a price both the residents and the black miners can afford.

Matthew is speaking; he sees the incredulity on Marie's face, the struggle to make sense, for he knows she is incapable of moving beyond a fragmentary understanding. Confronted with what she does not want to hear, she immediately brings her defences into play, her automatic "thought police".

"You think you can just resign? That you're not a committee person but everyone else enjoys spending hours trying to make others see reason! You can't carry on but we must keep up the `good work'!"

He watches her flush, then turn away. Marie is stunned by his outburst; her clean face and round eyes, stiff with anger, her body heaving under the embroidered kaftan she always wears to parties. He hears his voice rise. It surprises him, but even as he registers that it is his own, and is shocked by its grating, he feels a curious lightness - at last he has penetrated the mask of good cheer she habitually wears.

"I'm so pleased to hear from you that Pauline and Linda support the plan. It's such a pity they've already got too many other commitments but it goes without saying that the rest of us will carry on . . . because we don't have anything better to do. Yes, we should welcome this chance to fill our aimless, boring lives, we should be grateful to those who have other priorities for giving us this chance. I've certainly got no other way to spend my time . . ."

Nita watches his hands as they jerk in the air. Everyone is in agreement that the Project stands at a crossroads. The meeting must take certain critical decisions. Now, while waiting for the others to arrive, what had started as a light conversation with Marie has taken an altogether unforeseen direction. As she stands in the doorway behind him, Nita realizes that in the five years they have lived together, she has never seen Matthew so outraged. His anger and passion make her anxious; his usually calm, controlled but energetic self has been completely pushed aside.

"We like the quiet, big old houses, the open lawns, the low rent. It's such a pity Paulina and Linda have other priorities. But mine must be Royal Village, mine and a few other idiots. We can arrange and attend meetings, write letters, follow up contacts. We need all these activities to test our endurance levels. Let the meeting types get on with the meetings and do all the work that has to be done. But they must report back, they must first get our mandate. They must convene meetings we are too busy to attend, and then they must wait for our OK. I mean, these radicals don't know how to handle Royal Mines - they fight for the sake of fighting. They need to be controlled. And when they go ahead and make progress, take a decision and implement it, then we'll stop them. How can they hold a meeting without us! They have the nerve to coordinate meetings and when we don't attend them because we've got better things to do, they think they've got the right to take decisions. Bloody Stalinists!"

Marie sits bolt upright, eyes fixed on the mantelpiece, on the row of masks that shine with red and black lustre. There is a gross obstruction swelling in her throat, denying her the chance to respond, to cut him off.

"I know you don't like the two of us. You made that very clear the way you rushed out last time when Nita and I put forward a view that everyone else supported. And you feel you don't have much in common with the miners. They're just ignorant blacks, aren't they? Christ, Marie, don't you realize how sick we are of hearing your stupid views about Royal Mines just needing a few polite words . . . As if you don't know their history. Ja, perhaps that's the point - you're scared to confront them, you're too scared of their power."

Nita sees the film of sweat spread across Matthew's forehead. He will soon start coughing. But he will not allow her to try and mother him. Should she intervene, he will ignore her and she will look foolish. Of course, everything he has said is justified, but Marie is such an easy target, poor Marie with her three kids and useless, dependent husband.

"I mean, we all make commitments which we break and we can't hold anything against each other because we're all equally guilty. In any case, you don't know that Papi and Jacob Lourens phoned Royal Mines about our occupation of Lindsay's old house. They told Oberholzer it wasn't a mandated action, just a few extremists with Nita as their leader. They actually phoned Oberholzer and told him this. Then, at the residents' meeting he specially calls, our drunken Papi announces in a loud voice how sorry he is that Sipho and I forced him to sell us to the Company. He's sorry he had to undermine us to Oberholzer. After all, if we hadn't been stupid enough to occupy the house, he wouldn't have had to take steps to save the situation."

*

Matthew is amazed at his furious concentration while revising the article. Pouring over it for days, struggling to achieve the right tone, there is the challenge of taking the average reader (who will be familiar only with the film, not with the novel) directly into the symbolism and the logic of the moral action; all this via the clash of characters and ideas, the interweaving of images and themes. And as he sits at his computer, he is proudly aware that he is becoming expert at stripping down the complex without sacrificing subtlety, and has over the past year begun to receive recognition for these popularizations; indeed, the mainstream media are giving him regular work and the commissions are bringing in useful, tax-free money.

His first draft began: *Oscar Wilde was acutely aware of the hypocrisy, stupidity, greed and absurd pretentiousness of the Victorian ruling class, even as he recognized the blind, ignorant, stubborn traditions of the ruled masses. And as an artist dedicated to creating 'Beauty and Truth', in the same way that the creator of crocodiles created crocodile teeth and crocodile appetites, shaped the power and inevitability of a tidal wave or a volcano or an earthquake, he knew that Pain and Decay are as intrinsic to human life as are Pleasure and Beauty.*

*

Matthew's fury reaches a crescendo.

"You didn't know that, did you? Jacob Lourens and Papi messed up our chance of ever buying the village! You can be sure that every time one of us leaves, Royal Mines will fill that house with one of their security guards. And you know how these guards lick their arses. Then, before we know it, we won't be a majority, and they'll kick out whoever is left. And that will be the end of the project. Dammit, Marie! You know this yet you defend Lindsay, you defend how she handled leaving the village. You think she was right to give Royal Mines the keys. She signed a lease, didn't she? Yes, she did. And leases are holy, aren't they? Especially when they're rigged in favour of the landlords. You defend her betrayal. The bloody bitch."

Nita does not like his use of the word 'bitch' but he is justified in saying

25

that Lindsay has behaved badly - she boycotted the village meetings and refused to explain her absence. Even Jean, another long-standing resident, who was sour and short-tempered, felt it necessary to send apologies. In addition, Lindsay worked in a trade union and was seen to be active in the Democratic Movement.

"You think it was her right to ignore us. So what if she lives here, she's entitled to do as she likes. If she wants to undermine us, let her. After all, that's democracy. If a person doesn't want to join in, they shouldn't be forced to. No one should have to leave the Village because they don't support the Development Project. We don't want people staying here to all be like-minded and serious. And we aren't in the middle of a major battle with a giant corporation that tramples all over us. This isn't a fight - this isn't a question of two fundamentally opposing principles battling it out. Is it?"

There is a tight dryness in his nasal passages, but his mind feels crystal sharp and despite the hollowness in his stomach, he floats with the words, anger working through him, becoming objectified. At other times, caught up in confrontation, he has experienced painful and disturbing emotions. But at this moment, his feeling is one of unrestrained enjoyment: he is telling her exactly what he thinks without any concern for diplomacy, allowing the frustration which has been building up over months to roll out in a breathless, unstoppable torrent.

"We're in the middle of a war. And if it wasn't for the mineworkers, we would have been kicked out by now. The bit of press coverage we did get made an impact but if Royal Mines had gone ahead with the eviction, what else could the newspapers have done? There are so many other stories about homelessness. They'd have written one more article about us then moved on to the next squatter crisis involving hundreds, perhaps thousands of people. For God's sake, can't you see that we managed to stop Royal Mines because the mine workers objected to our eviction?"

Marie stands up. When she and Barry had first moved into the Village, she was attracted to Matthew. However, the complicated, unrealistic proposals he continually brought to the residents' meetings and his overbearing hostility to those he called "the bosses", soon repelled her; he seemed so inflexible, so intolerant.

She stands up and faces him.

"I don't know why you're shouting! You always put people down. You're so negative. Why can't you be human for once?"

Nita, standing at the doorway, is aware that Matthew knows full well that Marie has no training in, nor gift, for analysis; neither has she any

26

organizational experience. Why then is he raving as if it is the first time he has become aware of her limitations? It is depressing to watch him demean himself by capitulating to his frustration.

"You're right. I am always finding fault, looking for bad points in people, harping on their weaknesses and mistakes when all they're doing is being 'human' . . ."

He stops, Marie is relieved. They face each other. Then, before she can respond, he continues, but very quietly.

"I was ten years old the first time my grandmother showed me photographs of mass graves and gas chambers filled with naked, herded bodies, pits crammed with starved, diseased skeletons. Have you seen them, Marie? Have you seen them? What else do you have to say about being human?"

Marie runs out of the living room, shouting, "How dare you treat me like this!" She rushes through the open door leading onto the stoep. "I'll never come here again."

*

She is on the lawn that runs the length of the houses. She looks up at the night sky. Stars are faint pin pricks, the horns of a half moon stick out over the factories beyond the fence that forms the village's northern boundary. Why did she sit for so long listening to his tirade? Why did she allow him to preach and humiliate her in front of Nita? Was she so weak and masochistic? How awful! His face had started to sweat, veins all blue and swollen. What right did he have to talk to her as if she is a fool who understands nothing of the situation's complexities? As for his accusation that she is a racist . . .

Marie walks aimlessly. There is no point in going home. Barry will laugh at her. He is in one of his moods and is waiting for Basil, his best friend. She sits down in the shadow of a tree, branches layering their way to the sky, and looks up. Clouds have snuffed out the rind of moon, blotted out the stars. Then she folds her legs in a lotus position; waits till her breath steadies and she is calm.

Alone with Nita in their living room, still waiting for the other committee members, Matthew thinks: "Pathetic hippy relic with notions of informality and opposition to structure and responsibility. She wants everyone to be friendly and helpful but doesn't know how to deal with those who aren't - and refuse to be."

27

*

The book stirs him deeply. The breathless beauty of the language, despite the torrents of prose that sometimes gush a little long-windedly, allows him to read and reread. However, its supreme achievement is that the force of the central metaphor is never overdone nor made too obvious. As a result, the climax, Dorian Gray's suicide, is utterly convincing. Weighed down by his past, he seeks to cleanse himself, but even when he decides not to seduce and ruin a young woman, he acknowledges that he has not genuinely and fundamentally repented. And having seen through his motives, he admits that if the act of contrition is mere play-acting, then there can be no true transcendence of despair - only death can bring an end to suffering.

Earlier in the month, Matthew had scribbled in his notebook: *Why, of all the book's characters, must it be Hallward, the artist, who confronts Dorian with his corruption? And having done so, why must he pay for this with his life?*

*

It is eleven o'clock that same night. Having flopped down on their bed, Matthew is calm. He feels Nita's breasts press against him. After intense debate with her, he has decided to write to Marie and apologize. He has acted too emotionally. He should have stated his views quietly, with dignity. Whatever her behaviour, no matter how stupid and duplicitous, it was unworthy of him to have surrendered to rage; she was a guest in their house and he owed her that basic and ancient respect. There is no alternative: in order to mend their relationship, he must explain why he acted as he did, and offer an apology for being aggressive.

Matthew also considers the following possibility: that Marie will reject reconciliation and instead agitate for his and Nita's removal from the Village. Furthermore, it is possible that when they refuse to leave (he would not be intimidated and would fight back), there could be violence. And even if such violence was initially confined to a few broken windows and punctured car tires, such acts would be enough to inflame everyone till the whole issue escalated and someone was hurt. On the other hand, hopefully before such a stage would be reached, a delegation would approach their gate. Vincent would be included to show how seriously people viewed the crisis - Vincent the veteran activist, on the brink of burn-out, exhausted after too many internal struggles, too many cliques, schisms and tendencies locked in rivalries; Vincent the Peacemaker who always tried to pacify and smooth over differences.

As a final measure, Matthew decides to call a special meeting of the Residents' Association. He will report on the clash with Marie in a formal, structured way, and raise what he believes are the real issues, those of commitment and accountability. Furthermore, he will address both the ethical and organizational aspects, giving, as far as he is able, the full range of arguments as well as commenting on the difficulty of harmonizing conflicting temperaments. He will focus on Marie's inability to handle confrontation and her naivete, factors which make her unable to properly evaluate the world. By discussing the incident in a calm and measured way, his outburst and her response will become part of the Village's social development, an opportunity for reflection and political growth, rather than being reduced (and confined) to the level of a personal squabble.

He sits up. Nita is already asleep. Shocked by the jarring confrontation, they had gone to bed much earlier than usual. He looks at her face laid on the pillow and caresses her lightly, smoothing back her hair, tracing the curves of her mouth. She does not stir. Then he slips out of bed and removes a small white bag from a wooden box inlaid with geometric patterns made of mother of pearl. Inside the bag are several neatly rolled dagga sticks.

"I must give Marie the book about Dachau. Then I'll show her a photograph of Serbian soldiers executing Bosnian women and children."

*

When Marie arrives home she finds Barry and Basil in the living room. Basil runs an outlet for a computer company. The two men are watching a music video featuring a rap singer called Ice Brown. The song, "Bring Me the Calabash", celebrates the black woman's sensuality and willingness to serve. An American cop holding a gun dances through the courtyard of a broken down ghetto tenement building while a woman dressed in a white jumpsuit and copper African bangles gyrates at Ice Brown's feet.

Marie puts on the kettle and, despite her distaste, casually watches the video. There is no point trying to speak to the two men; they are both a little drunk and she knows Barry will become threatening and abusive. She picks up the jigsaw pieces the children have left scattered on the carpet. Marie is tired of running after them but Barry takes their side, saying they are too young to be blamed for not tidying up. He switches channels. The sitcom characters lurch from one romantic and financial crisis to another, every infatuation and betrayal that can run rampant in a white, upper middle-class Californian suburb is on view.

She looks at the pile of unpaid bills stacked on the table; Barry's mess-ups, his schemes that always fail. Who will still lend him anything? Yesterday her brother, Vic, the one she could in the past always turn to when things were bad, also refused them a loan. Now, for the first time, she is absolutely on her own.

*

Matthew slips on his dressing gown, switches on the computer and enters a file name. Watching the text flash in front of him, he meditates then suddenly begins typing: *For Lord Henry, he was a rare phenomenon - one of the few people who could still stimulate and divert him. For the artist, Hallward, he was the epitome of male beauty and delicacy - a muse. But the lovely and gifted young man, blinded by their admiration, began to find pleasure only in the subjection and domination of others.*

He sits back, reads what he has written and yawns; he cannot see Marie, bursting with agitation, prepare a cup of coffee, her eyes still slightly swollen as Barry and Basil sit smoking in front of the television, intently following the soap's stilted dialogue. Matthew glances at the circles on the back of his right hand. The dark blue circles were tatooed in Cairo ten years ago during his six-year exile from South Africa; they lie drawn between his thumb and index finger.

Having boarded a ferry in Crete for Alexandria, but being oddly disappointed by the legendary city, it seemed faded and dull, he had taken a mini-bus taxi to Cairo. During a refreshment stop in a small and dusty town, the driver had invited him to the backroom of a restaurant and offered him a pipe of hashish. The room was hot and stuffy and the dark, fresh Turkish hash had almost knocked him off his feet. Only by a supreme effort of will had he managed to reboard the taxi, and on reaching his seat, found a young man dressed in a faded jalabiah sitting in place of the old woman who had sat there before. Soon after, they had left the town and were passing green, well-watered rice fields and plots of okra and beans, and the tanned, brown-eyed man had placed a hand on his knee and begun to caress him. That night they had wandered through Cairo, through the deserted alleys of the market quarter of the Khan el Khalili. Intoxicated with the hooded city, its crescent moon tipping over the minarets, but repulsed by the sour smell of blood coming from mounds of chicken heads stacked under the hotel balcony, Matthew had seen the dotted sign of a tatooist in a long,

30

rectangular booth. He had selected a trio of circles. Inside the biggest was a smaller one and, inside this second circle, a third.

*

Barry coughs. Basil has just left but the night is thick and heavy with their shared fatigue and the room smells stale despite the open window that Marie has insisted on. There are pains in his chest, the usual contractions. He coughs once more while she prepares herself another cup of coffee and props a magazine against a cushion.

"He's publishing an article next month."

"Who?"

"That bastard Matthew. He's publishing an article on this Dorian Gray movie."

"Oh, good for him. I've seen the trailer. It looks pretty heavy. I must say he did a great job on those Jane Austen movies."

"He's selfish and rude and he doesn't know what he's talking about."

"I wouldn't say that. He may be an extremist but he usually makes sense."

"He insulted me. He screamed at me when I said I was resigning from their bloody committee."

"So you're finally giving it up? About time! How can you work with that fucking Zweli? He's a fraud."

"You don't care that Matthew insulted me? He shouted me down, dammit!"

"Maybe he had a good reason."

"He called me a bitch and a racist!"

"Come on, doll. . ."

"Don't you believe me? You think I must just keep quiet. Jesus, Barry!"

"How do I know?"

"What do you mean, 'how do I know?'"

"I don't say I don't believe you, but Matthew's not likely to have said that."

"You're saying I made this up? Are you mad? You haven't been to a single meeting for months."

"Darling, if we both go, who will look after the kids?"

"You leave everything to me and I can't handle it any more." Marie throws the magazine down on the carpet.

"Hey, take it easy!"

"I can't handle your bloody passive way of living. You want to live here, don't you? Then why don't you get involved?"

"Because I don't want to work with arseholes! Why you making a fuss again?"

"We need this house, Barry. Where else can we live so cheaply?"

"This place is falling apart."

"At least we can afford it."

"The Executive is just stuffing around. Actually, Matthew's the only one who knows what he's doing." Barry kicks the magazine which lies next to his sneaker. "I wonder why he's taken to writing for bored fucking women like you."

*

On reading what he has written, Matthew is struck by the stiffness of language, its forced quality, difficult vocabulary and academic tone. The article is for a magazine that is trendy and accessible. Its readers will find this style heavy and opaque, and the editor will reject it. Why then is he persisting, day by day, in writing this way?

He throws the draft to one side and picks up a leather-bound copy of Oscar Wilde's 'Collected Works'. The pages are covered with yellow stickers, each flagging a point. He rereads a sentence. It is from the chapter in which Hallward, the artist, confronts Dorian with his debauchery, and is afterwards murdered. The words meander, then rush on like a river in spate. The writing is elegant, assured, charged with emotion and ideas. Matthew wonders how long Wilde worked on the novel. Did he repeatedly revise it? Although the feel is spontaneous, the sense of flow may have only come with much sifting and correction.

Matthew imagines Wilde, still living with his wife and children, sitting hour after hour in a study, writing furiously as different desires and compulsions burst and burnt within him. Then his mind abruptly shifts to an image from the book on Dachau: lines of prisoners at roll call, endless lines of broken, humiliated human beings in striped pyjamas and caps, hollow eyes that are simultaneously blank and agonized.

*

Nita is at the stove, warming up a packet of pre-cooked chicken breasts. She has already prepared rice and mushroom sauce and laid the table. She

does not mind making Matthew these post-midnight snacks. He is often unable to sleep. She has woken, stirred by his absence, and found him busy at his desk. Once she finishes preparing a light meal, they sit in the kitchen and he tells her what is troubling him.

After Marie had run from the house, she and Matthew had sat down and discussed his extraordinary tirade. Then they had lain down in the bedroom and kissed. It was a long, fierce kiss which aroused her but he did not want to make love. Instead, he had held her and said how happy he was to have finally released the anger that would otherwise have remained bottled up in him, unresolved and festering, and which sooner or later, gathering force, would have led him to take it out on those who are close to him, those he loves, instead of casting it out like boiling oil onto those who had caused it. Yes, he was pleased that at least one of the guilty was suffering instead of the innocent.

*

Marie looks at herself in an unframed mirror. She sees her long but full face, her greenish eyes, the slight curve of her nose. Yes, she is beautiful. But will a man come to her and caress her so that she can smile and settle on him her riches?

Barry lounges on the settee eating a ham sandwich. The kids are asleep and she can hear their regular breathing through the open door. Matthew's voice continues to ram against her ears. But this time she does not have an impulse to cry. This time she swears.

*

It is around seven o'clock the next morning. Nita is still asleep, head propped against the big green pillow they shared. Matthew is beside her, feeling her thigh press against him.

It is difficult to accept that no trumpets blast judgement, that judgement is in fact a little mouse chewing, day by day, at the remnants of conscience while an army of Israelites lays waste Jericho, killing every man, woman and child even as they slaughter the sheep and goats, and dig salt into the fields to ensure extermination and erasure. Bearing this in mind, is it worth convening a meeting of the Village to discuss what has happened with Marie? Will such a discussion be fruitful? Will a meeting not lead to further confrontation and back-biting, sharpening the fault lines and terminally sinking the Development Project under a weight of recrimination and accusation? At this stage, silence and inaction may be the most appropriate responses. Even if Marie tried to whip up a reaction against him, in a few weeks the whole incident would sink away and be forgotten; and if not wholly forgotten, at least be dimmed, pushed into memory to become a remnant in the private store concerning this chapter of his life: so do nothing and let dust obscure the features of that roaring which had seized him so violently when she had said she was resigning.

He eases off the bed, giving Nita a light kiss on her exposed shoulders. When he sits down to work at his desk he can see smoke rise up from the braziers standing in front of the ramshackle tin shacks packed on a small strip of land near the Village. The shacks are where the miners live. All through the morning, while he rewrites the article, the plumes of smoke spiral up.

THE BASEMENT

"And peace, too, with your neighbour's devil. Otherwise he will haunt you at night . . ."
Nietzsche

The wind dropped, then came up again. The street was a dim tunnel along which dead leaves were swept into corpse-like plastic rubbish bags. Mukoni's hands were wet in his gloves, his face shadowed by a tangle of branches under the trees that faced the old woman's window. He hunched up his shoulders in the cold. He was used to waiting under the bare trees dotting the pavement outside this crumbling block of flats in Berea, impatient for the old white prostitute to join the darkness that was smothering the city, so that even Ponte, the stained concrete cylinder-shaped building dominating the skyline, was swallowed up. The wind cut his neck and made his eyes itch. Every night the wind came up from the south over the mine dumps and filled the city, Across the street in the dimly lit foyer, a nightwatchman sprawled in a tattered armchair. The watchman had holes the size of eggs cut into his ear lobes. He dozed on, a kierie tucked under his arm. There was a small electric heater at his feet. Mukoni liked these old Zulus. They were talkative and friendly and if you showed them respect, they were trusting.

The light in the window evaporated; a pale white dog ran up, sniffed him and began barking. He threw a stone. The dog shied away. He took a swig of brandy from the bottle in his pocket and crossed the street, moving quietly alongside the flowerbeds past the wooden tubs with green plants. He reached the metal gate; it hung uselessly. Ahead of him mirrors flanked the two lifts. He saw his coat and scarf, purple pants with turn-ups and, over his left shoulder, the black bag with the American flag stitched under the zip. He clenched his fists; always this electric current rippling through him when he entered their buildings, this hot pounding running along his arms and legs, emptying the centre of his stomach before dumping down into his groin; this deep bass thudding all over him. Stepping past the dozing watchman, he ran up the stairway. It was time to deal with the witch.

Mukoni stood in front of her door. It was very quiet. He took a rope strung with keys from his jacket pocket. The fifth key turned the top lock; the next one, the bottom lock. The door opened but only far enough for a finger to slip through. He felt for the steel chain and took a wire cutter from the black bag. He snapped the chain, entered a dark, narrow entrance hall that smelt of cigarettes and beer. He moved slowly along the wall till his outstretched hand knocked against a curtain. He pushed it aside. Brittle light from a street lamp showed a sour yellow. He saw a wooden side table and lounge suite draped in plastic covers. On the far side was an open door. He walked towards it.

The old prostitute's head twisted across two pillows. The gruff trickle of her snore floated over her massive, slack breasts. Silver hair spread out beside her face, she had puffy arms, her body was barrel-like, grossly soft and yielding but her hands were slender. He was next to the bed. He could see the whiteness under her arms where the straps of her nightgown fell away. He stood over her, rasping. He had a knife in his hand and he was very hard and his mouth was dry, even dryer than during the hours when he had tracked her, sometimes all night.

She had gone out and returned to the escort agency several times. And each time she drove away in a taxi on new business, he had left his place under the awning of a clothes shop, and crossed the street to watch the other whores sitting about smoking in the front room. They were a group of four whites and a coloured woman. But there was only one who really interested him - a boeremeisie with very pale skin and red lips and a black feather boa that curled round her neck and arms. She was like one of those bitches spread open at the centre page of the magazines. One day she would cry for him, she would shiver with pleasure. He knew a man from Zone 5 in Meadowlands who had fucked her. But why spend money when he could get what he wanted for nothing?

It was almost a year since the first one. Dressed in a see-through blouse and a mini-skirt, long brown hair covering her eyes, he had seen her through the window of a bar laughing to herself while she drank. Then she had danced, a slow, whirling movement, pushing her bum into the air. Afterwards, when she bought dagga in Banket Street, he had followed her. And when she reached a block of flats in Troyeville and opened the security gate, he had held a blade to her back and forced her up the stairs. She had promised to do anything he liked, pleaded with him to use a condom. When he hit her she screamed but he slammed his hand over her mouth and made her shut up. He had come too quickly but still it was good.

That was the first time.

*

The streetlight fused.

He placed his knife on the carpet and seized the old woman. He squeezed the wrinkled, thick neck, both hands tight as two screws fixing a latch. She gasped, making crackling sounds, and tore at his face. One finger jammed under his ear. He squeezed harder. She tried to scratch at his face but the balaclava was too thick. She fell limp. He throttled her a little longer. He was very hard but before he could move she pissed all over the bed and his coat was wet.

He rolled her off the bed, ripped open her nightgown so her breasts rose up in front of him. Cupping his hand, he collected a mouthful of spit and smoothed her cunt. Then, pulling down his pants with one hand, he fucked her on the floor of her room. She was warm and he pumped in her, and when he came, he closed his eyes. But as he felt the semen drain, the room began to choke him with its staleness - the smells of talcum powder, left-over canned food and beer. He slid out. As he got to his feet, she began to scream.

The knife was in his hand again and he pressed it into her neck. She slumped forward. A gush of blood flowed down her chest. She moaned. He heard nothing but his own heartbeat, stood watching the spreading stain on the carpet. Then he began to work.

He cut what he needed, placed the body parts in a towel which he folded into the black bag. Afterwards he opened the drawers of the bedside table. There were panties with slits in the middle, suspender belts, stockings and big, bowl-like bras with pink bows. Then he opened the cupboard that stood against the opposite wall and searching under a pile of jerseys found a First National Bank moneybag packed with bundles of R100 notes. As he put the moneybag into a coat pocket, there were loud knocks at the front door.

Mukoni ran onto the balcony that led off the bedroom and climbed round to the next flat. He slithered from balcony to balcony till he was at the rear of the building. From there he ran down the fire escape till he reached the back alley.

*

He was in Abel Road. The street was deserted. He walked briskly.

First he would make a phone call. Then he would go to his room and lie down and breathe in slowly until his chest stopped pounding. He would drink more brandy and feel it burn through him, and take out the money in the bag and count it. Then he would slip the moneybag under the lino in the corner by the door and hide the black bag that hung on his shoulder under the bed, and deliver it in the afternoon.

He felt for the pack of cigarettes and matches in his pocket. Where were his matches? He checked the other pocket. They weren't there. He walked into the all-night spaza shop in Camelot and went to the pay phones.

"Ja. . ."

"Is that Mister Hans?"

"Ja."

"Mister Hans, the job is finished."

"Good, the boss will be pleased."

"It went smooth."

"I hope you didn't make a big mess."

"Of course not, Mister Hans. You'll see." Mukoni laughed. "I was a good boy."

*

When he arrived at his yard, only Mudau's light was on. He could hear the old man's slowly chanted hallelujahs filter through the door on which was painted a white staff. He moved across the yard to his own room. The outside lock was gone. He bit his lip. What was going on? He put his ear to the door. All was quiet. He turned the handle.

Inside he saw Vusi sprawled on the bed, snoring, his expensive leather shoes smearing the blanket with mud. Bladdy baboon! Couldn't he hang his feet over the side! This was only one of the reasons why their partnership hadn't worked. Vusi was too slow, easily frightened. And he often spent or got rid of the goods before there was a chance to think what to do with the stuff. Vusi who had big, heavy feet that stank and broke things in the dark. The only good thing about him was his new connection, Steenkamp. Steenkamp was said to pay good money and pay on the spot. They would drive the cars to a garage in Alberton. But first they would have to change the number plates and repaint them. Steenkamp was a Boer but he was genuine. They could start straight away. Of course, if they couldn't sort out the alarms and immobilisers, the other way to get cars was to take them with the drivers inside. They could find bigger guns. Vusi knew someone in Randburg. Yes, it made sense to do a few jobs and then, once and for all, send Vusi back to Ixopo, back home in a new car with red arm rests, to watch his brothers' sons bring in the cattle at sunset.

Mukoni stood at the foot of his bed. The bed was raised up, each leg resting on a layer of bricks. Jammed next to it was a small rickety table on which were piled a kettle, a stack of enamel plates, cutlery, a glass with a toothbrush and a roll of coarse toilet paper. Next to the table was a metal cupboard. Colour photographs of naked white women were stuck to the side that faced the bed.

He looked down at his pants. There was a dark smear along the purple hem. It was past three o'clock when he had followed the old whore up Twist Street to the flats. Now he had her bank bag and his sweat was drying and he was slowly coming out of the fever that overtook him when he walked into their rooms and stood over them. He watched Vusi turn, and suddenly smelt the too sweet smell of the oily cheek of the old woman rising from his own skin. He was hard again. He rubbed himself, smoothing the tip of his cock. Then he came so quickly he had no time to grab toilet paper. The room disappeared, his eyes and his whole body drowning in a hot wave. Semen spread stickily along the inside of his pants. He shivered, and opened the suitcase that lay under the bed. Taking out a clean overall, he shoved his pants into a bucket. Then he switched on the light and shook Vusi.

"What you doing here? I don't like it when people break my lock."

Vusi buried his face in the pillow. Mukoni picked up the bottle of brandy that was lying under his arm.

"Up, man! I need the room for myself. I'm expecting a woman."

Vusi yawned. "I'm tired, mfo. I was drinking by Mkhize. I was too tired to go home."

Mukoni shook his head. "You must go now."

Vusi yawned again. "Is she nice?"

"Where's the lock? I paid a lot for it! Why did you break it?"

"You're the one breaking things!" Vusi leaned forward. "The light's killing me."

"Where's the lock?"

"Take it easy, man. Look on the table. I don't have to break locks."

Mukoni switched off the light. The harshness crashed out. A subdued wintry dawn began to seep through the thin curtains. He took another shot of brandy. Vusi sat up, dangling his feet over the side of the bed.

"What about Steenkamp?"

"I'll tell you tomorrow."

Vusi smiled. "Like last week?" He put on a leather hat that barely covered the crown of his head. "You know what? I'll leave you to this woman." He yawned again, showing the gap where several teeth were missing. "See you tomorrow. We'll do the first job."

Then he barrelled his way past Mukoni and out of the room, and Mukoni locked the door and lay down, covering himself with two coarse, smoky blankets.

*

He was awake. The branches of the tree in the yard scraped against the window. He had slept deeply, and dreamt.

He and his mother were walking in the hills near their village when they came across a python lying in their path. He had shuddered with fear and wanted to turn back, but his old mother boldly picked up the snake and slung it across her shoulders - his tiny mother swivelled the snake's giant head like a corkscrew and forced a hole for it in the black earth while he, a grown man, was paralyzed and unable to act. His mother, all bent over and weary, seized the python, twisted its head and deftly covered it up. Yes, he had trembled with fear, but afterwards, though his heart filled with relief knowing that the glistening snake was securely buried and could not make its way back to the surface, he had felt a sense of loss and dislocation, of amputation.

He was washing in the basin, boiling the kettle for coffee, when Tsidi, the cleaning supervisor, knocked at the door.

"Tshivanda! What are you still doing here? It's past ten o'clock. Master is looking for you. There's a blocked pipe in number 9, at Chatham Court. He wants you to go and fix it straight away."

Mukoni dried his face. Flat 9. How many times had he unblocked the kitchen sink? The pipes were old and narrow and easily jammed. As soon as he cleared them, they gummed up again.

"Tell him I'm sick. I'll go this afternoon."

The brandy was next to the mug with his toothbrush. There was still a shot left. Flat 9 - that was the mechanic with red streaks in dull blue eyes. He had a living room crammed with pictures of trains. Each train was painted in national colours. South African trains with the old blue, orange and white were shown winding through mountain passes or swallowed up in the brown distances of the Karoo. The man was known to be a racist but a few months back he had taken in a young Sotho girl. She was from Bloemfontein. The rumour was that her family had thrown her out for messing with boys.

Mukoni bent down. Under the bed, his pants (the hems smeared with blood) lay soaking in washing powder. The bank bag was under the lino, the heavy wooden cupboard pushed over it. He had counted the notes and they were a tight, thick wad that made him smile. The old woman had been scoring those last few nights. He would send his mother a few hundred, and maybe even his sister. It was a long time since he had sent them anything. Now he would take a walk with the toolbox; but before fixing the sink he would go and make a check of another kind.

*

Mukoni stopped under the streetlight that had fused during the night. There was a guard in the foyer, a young man whom he recognized but whose name he did not know. Next to him was Ma Vilakazi, one of the cleaners. She balanced a mop in a bucket of soapy water. The young watchman waved his arms. Mukoni walked up to the security gate. They were talking about the murder.

The killer had chopped her up, her fingers and breasts as well as her hair and nails and the lips of her private thing had been removed. No one had been allowed into the flat except for Buthelezi, the nightwatch, who had found her. The police were still with him, measuring and taking fingerprints. Buthelezi swore he was wide-awake all the time. It was impossible for someone to have come through the foyer. Maybe he did go to the toilet - but only once the whole night. The reason the security gate wasn't locked was because Mister Stavrou refused to spend more money calling the locksmith. It was the tenth time this year that it had been broken by the tenants themselves or their drunken friends, who shouting and swearing, regularly kicked in the gate during their fights. No, he hadn't been long, he was very quick, so quick he had almost pissed in his pants - he was always so worried to leave the gate unattended.

While Mukoni stood at the gate listening, two young black men in blue uniforms and combat boots came down the stairs. One was carrying a briefcase. Mukoni did not know that inside the briefcase, wrapped in plastic, was the box of matches that had dropped out of his jacket while he was jumping from the old woman's flat. (Under the lion's tail was Steenkamp's telephone number.) The two men walked out of the foyer and drove off in a red patrol car. As they did so, Mukoni entered the foyer and the security guard and Ma Vilakazi turned to greet him.

"Hey, Tshivanda! You heard what happened? The makgosha in Number 33, she's dead!" Ma Vilakazi smiled. "That one! You know how the boss is going to miss her! Hau! That one was bad. . . ."

The old black woman sniggered, speaking of the caretaker and the white woman, even fatter than herself. Then she described how Buthelezi had

43

heard screams, it was past four o'clock in the morning. He had broken into the flat together with one of the neighbours, that amakulu from Newcastle. The makgosha was naked on the floor. When they examined her, they found everything missing. There was a lot of blood -they could not believe how much blood. The carpet in the bedroom was so stained Agnes didn't think she could clean it. Now she was waiting for Mister Stavrou to tell her what to do. Only an hour ago the police had carried the grey plastic body bag out of the foyer and driven off in a red bakkie with a siren on top. You should have seen how they struggled!

Mukoni laughed with them. He knew the workers in this block. They sometimes played cards and drank beer together. Occasionally he slept with one of the women, Buthelezi's niece, Gladys, whom the old man had brought out from Eshowe. Then, suddenly, Stavrou was next to them in the foyer, the old Greek with his whitened gums, reeking of the sour presence of his bed-ridden wife. Stavrou nudged him, spreading gnarled fingers over his overall.

"Why you here? Didn't the girl find you? Go to Chatham Court, you know De Kock doesn't like waiting!"

The shrivelled, sharp-tongued old man stood next to the lift doors leaning on his whorled walking stick with the ivory elephant head, and beside him, brushing a sandy moustache, was an enormous white man in a white suit. The white man had a shaven head, massive hands and the muscle-bound, pepped up body and swagger of a bouncer. Mukoni had heard about pills that made you fris and snappy, sometimes so snappy, you snapped. But the man in the white suit was relaxed, almost playful, with a satisfied smile.

And now he was standing in front of them, blotting out prying eyes with a pair of curved, reflecting sunglasses and talking to the cleaning woman and the young guard.

"I'll give you a lot of money if you know something."

The guard shook his head.

"And you?"

"Madam was very quiet," responded the old woman, "she always came home early."

"And last night? When did she come back? Who was with her?"

The cleaning woman cocked her head. "Is master her family?" She was a cheeky somebody, old Vilakazi.

"Ja, I'm her cousin, I've come from Graaff Reinet."

Mukoni saw the whore's face, all screwed up and pasty, as she stumbled from a taxi. How could he have desired the shrunken witch after she had done so much business! Her face was a monkey mask in the yellow light. But why lie to himself? He had agonized for her massive, scented breasts, the feel of melting as he pressed her to him and licked the insides of her ears.

"She never hurt nobody. Why they do this? Animals! No one deserve to die like that." Stavrou dabbed at his watery, squinting eyes. "Horrible! Horrible how everything was sliced off!"

The young guard looked round in disgust. Everyone knew what the white woman was doing. He turned away from Stavrou. What did these whites know of the world of the spirits? They had long forgotten the powers of sacrifice. They knew nothing about healing and pleasing the forces who live beyond the finger tips. Then he thought of the old woman and her rough voice. Sometimes he would do jobs for her, clean the sand basket she kept for her cats, or repair cupboard doors that fell off their hinges. But once she had called him a dirty kaffir who mustn't look at her like that. Now she would never say another word. Without knowing it, all chopped up, mixed with herbs and earth and special powders, she would make rich and powerful black men even richer and more powerful.

As Stavrou shook his head in shock, Ma Vilakazi touched his arm.

"Don't worry, master, I'm sure she'll go to heaven."

Mukoni turned towards the gate but the man in the white suit was saying that no one should leave till he was finished with his questions.

"It looks like nobody's seen anything." He folded his arms. "This is a bad thing. The person who did this must pay. I'll see to that." He stabbed the air with a finger. "Ja, that someone must pay." He touched the ends of his moustache. "This is the fourth this month."

Stavrou turned an even duller yellow, Ma Vilakazi propped him up. Mukoni remembered the soft sac of skin under the old whore's arms.

"You hear anything, you tell the boss. Tell him everything, it doesn't matter how stupid it sounds. He'll get hold of me. There's a nice present for somebody who remembers. Tell the boss anything you hear from the others." He shook Stavrou's hand. "I'll be in touch. We've got extra patrol cars for this area."

"Thank you so much, Captain. The man is crazy, no one is safe."

"Don't you worry, meneer." Two massive fists bumped together. "We won't let this sick bastard carry on killing our people."

As he said 'our people', the big white man looked at Mukoni, nodded and walked out of the foyer. Waiting for him at the door of a red car with a siren attached to the roof was a young man with an equally smooth shaven skull, massive hands and pumped up torso.

Stavrou gripped Mukoni's arm. "Go to Mister de Kock now. After fix toilet in Number 17. Then come to office. I got special job for you, something you like."

The old caretaker was trembling. He had a bad heart and he was washed out looking after his wife. Years ago, he'd given up everything. He had stopped going to Doornfontein, to Alec's, to play cards. He had stopped going to Natie's to play chess. Gone also were the Saturday afternoon's at Cafe Wien with the Greek newspapers and the Portuguese magazines, the London Financial Times and the Frankfurter Gazette. Hillbrow wasn't Hillbrow. For years he had sat by her side in the bedroom with the curtains drawn on her bent, wasting body. He had sat reading to her or listening to the radio while trying to manage the flats. And that was a job. The blacks were always stealing and drinking and fighting in the yards. There were so many of them. Yes, the conditions were bad but they made no effort to look after what there was, and Lipshitz, the landlord, was sick and tired of paying for repairs.

Stavrou put his arm on Mukoni's shoulder. "I got easy job for you, Abraham. And there'll be a bonus."

Mukoni looked at the weak red eyes. How much longer could Stavrou carry on like this? Every week the old man asked him to spy on the cleaning women's trade union meetings, and every week Mukoni made an excuse. Stavrou also wanted him to find out who had been taking coal from the cellar; at least six bags had disappeared.

"Come about five o'clock." A row of stained teeth remained exposed as he shuffled out.

Mukoni was still in the foyer, Ma Vilakazi holding his arm. The young guard had disappeared into the backyard. It was the lull of late morning. The air soft and light, blue sky soaked up the spaces between buildings and trees. Ma Vilakazi started mopping the foyer.

"What's with the big umlungu? He came here to fetch the body. There was a funny red van with him." She mopped round Mukoni, isolating him on a small dry patch. "How can we be sure he's police? These days you can't tell them from the tsotsis."

For a second time she circled the island on which he stood.

"Why should we worry, Ma, so long as the umlungus are the ones to die."

The old woman shrugged. "I suppose so, my son." Then she added, "She never gave me a Christmas box."

*

46

Outside the Caroline Street post office, Vusi made a call from a sidewalk vendor.

"I'm ready boss, but we must talk. When can I come round?"

"Anytime you like. Just phone when you outside."

The Boer was friendly; he promised a bonus if they brought BM's and Corollas.

Vusi hung up. This business could go well. He massaged his head. God, what a babalas! And to add to it, there'd been the fight with Mukoni. Where had that one been the whole night? Must have been out on a job he had done on his own - or with someone else. Mukoni was too quiet, always keeping secrets. You never knew what he wanted. All he seemed to do was look at the photographs of the white whores stuck to his cupboard; all he talked about was how women tricked men by falling pregnant and then demanding money.

As Vusi walked away from the phone vendor, the man in the white suit and the young bouncer drove up Claim Street in the red car with the siren clamped to the roof. They pulled up alongside the pavement and the man in the white suit grabbed Vusi and threw him onto the back seat. Then he jammed a damp cloth over Vusi's face, forcing him to inhale a sharp, bitter lemon vapour. Vusi felt his eyes cloud over, he fell back. The man in the white suit covered him with a blanket and the young bouncer accelerated into the traffic.

*

Mukoni knocked on the door. The runaway schoolgirl stood at the kitchen window looking at him.

"Lekgai, sisi. I've come with my tools."

She opened the door. The rumour in the yards was that she was only fourteen although her body was full and her light brown eyes showed the confidence of an older woman.

He looked into the entrance hall was standing in the cramped dark kitchen looking at the sink gummed up with a grayish, fatty mass. There was the cloying stench of hot oily mutton.

"You've been cooking sheep's brains again! You stupid! How many times must I tell you to throw the leftovers into the rubbish and not into the sink!" He opened the window. "This is bad, my girl." But as he said this, he smiled and touched her chin. "Don't worry. I'll fix you up." She looked away. "I'll unblock you all the way this time."

He unscrewed the connecting pipe and cleaned it with a steel rod and brush. Then he emptied a bottle of ammonia into the sink. Once the ammonia had started to hiss and froth, he took out a rubber pipe, fitted it into the sink hole and screwed it round till he felt it break through the stiff cake of oil and animal matter. Then he switched on the hot water tap and let it run as hard as it could. Once the water was running down freely, he washed his hands.

"So, what you been doing this morning? You finished your work? Want another job, my darling?"

He touched her blouse and pulled her towards him so that she was scooped up in his arms and held firmly all along her body. Then he guided her out of the kitchen past the small side tables and display cabinets in which the model trains stood. The radio was on. The song was a mellow, off-beat groove. Mukoni tapped out the rhythm on the girl's arm. She swayed. She held him now and was truly in his arms and they were kissing so tenderly it was sore, they were dragging into each other, making sweeps of each other's lips and gasping. He held her to him and cradled her head in his hands, he buried himself in her neck and she shivered. Then his hands circled her, clenching her buttocks that were so perfectly rounded and firm. They were dancing and the room glowed with sunshine, joining the rhythm of palms and reeds. He kissed her over and over, and she caressed him and sighed.

*

Vusi was spread across the backseat, arms and legs tightly bound with handcuffs and cord, the cloth with the sickening odour stuck tight with tape round his mouth, a blanket pulled over his head so that he could not see and struggled to breathe. He heard the muffled drone of cars punctuated by hooters and motor bikes. There was also a stream of words from the seats up front - the two white men were talking and he strained to make out what they were saying. He wriggled his head, stretching the blanket, trying to work it loose.

"Drop me near the Carlton. Unless I phone, don't worry about fetching me. I'll be back by eight." It was a deep, growling Boer voice that spat out each word. "They want more and more. This month we're going to make a killing."

"That's good, boss." The second voice was lighter and less accented but seemed forced, slightly hysterical.

"Ja, it's good for all of us."

Vusi wriggled harder. The blanket fell away from his eyes. He could see the man in the white suit glance at his watch. It was a small black watch with steel hands. In the centre was a luminous skull. Vusi looked on as he took a piece of paper from an inside pocket.

"Is there anything else I must order, Hans? I've got the extra syringes. Do we need more formaldehyde?" The young bouncer shook his head. "Jesus, you must tell that Venda boy not to cut what he likes. He made a bladdy mess of that prossie, a real butcher's job. He's got no skills, man. Actually, we can't afford him anymore. He's sloppy. I found him hanging round the flat, looking like a real doos, his eyes all blood-shot with booze, tongue hanging out. Also he left a match box in the flat. There was a phone number on it. Imagine if the Flying Squad got there first. There'd be kak, man. Imagine if the telephone number on the back of the box was ours? You know what, Hans, I think you'd better just sort him out."

They were cruising down Claim Street. Vusi shivered. Who was this 'boy' they had it in for? And if they were going to get rid of him so casually, what would they do with him, Vusi? And why, in the first place, had they grabbed him? What had he done to cause this? His stomach tightened until it was impossible not to release the wrenching that screwed through him.

The car filled with the odour of his shit.

"Vokken kaffir!"

The man in the white suit leaned over and, ramming the blanket over his head, thrust his face down hard into the seat.

"You big bladdy baboon!" He held his nose. "Jesus, Hans! I don't think I can take this. What's in this bastard? Drive to City Deep. We can dump him there."

"He stinks worse than the basement."

Vusi felt the moist mass slithering on his arse. Moustaches curled as the stench saturated the car and the bouncer accelerated through a red traffic light.

*

Mukoni and the Sotho girl fused together in the heat of their kiss. A band of light filled the bedroom where they danced to the music on the radio. Pushing up her dress, he was in an agony of marvelling at the roll of her high, full breasts, the delicate lines of her body. Then they were rocking, she murmuring low, drawling sounds as he sucked her nipples and licked the moist warmth of her armpits.

They moved to the bed.

Afterwards the sun warmed their naked bodies and they were full with a deep contentment. The girl snuggled close, caressing him, again arousing him; her sweet, young breath pouring over him, making him crazy till he stroked her in return and they entwined, riding a great wave of pleasure.

Then Mukoni fell into a deep sleep and had this dream:

He saw a big brick house. Nearby was a kraal; he could hear the lowing of many cows. There was also a neatly wired chicken run. And beyond these buildings stretched fields of fat, ripe mielies. To the east of the house stood a small koppie, its sharply angled slopes dotted with round black boulders, shrubs and stunted thorn trees. On top of this koppie was a small dam made of corrugated iron sheeting around which grew clumps of bull rushes that rose higher than his head. Mukoni was on top of the koppie. In the green water of the dam he could see the silvery tail of a mermaid. She had long braided hair; her smile was pure and golden, expressing both joy and sadness. But as he stretched out his hand to touch her tresses, he heard a wind move through the house, a violent wind that rattled the windows and doors. He looked down the slopes of the koppie. There in front of the brick house stood the white man in the white suit. He was waving, shouting that Mukoni should come down. He signalled the shortest, easiest path to take. Then a shadow began to engulf the man in the white suit and Mukoni strained his eyes. He was filled with a sense of great danger: the gesturing hands were slowly disappearing under the dark shroud. With a start he realized that the shadow breaking across the stoep, black bag slung from his shoulder, was the humped figure of Vusi. And that Vusi was in chains. But before he could raise up his arms in triumph and celebrate Vusi's humiliation, and before he could dive into the dam and grab the mermaid and hold her to himself and make her his for ever more, a sudden wind lifted him into the air, carried him over the boulders down the koppie and dropped him on his knees next to the house. And as he landed, he saw the man in the white suit walking towards him. In one swollen hand was a thick rope.

*

They rolled down all the car windows. The bouncer switched on the air conditioning. The man in the white suit looked at his watch.

"Dammit! There's no time for a detour. Forget City Deep. Just take him to the station and have him prepared." The bouncer hooted madly as a hawker pushed a trolley loaded with sacks of potatoes into the street. "Hell, these Zambians are tough! They want the best but they try every trick they can think of not to cough up." The man in the white suit blew his nose.

"Take me straight to the Carlton."

Vusi heard a match flare.

"Thanks, Hans."

"And the prossie? What do you reckon, Boss? Should I take her with the coolie or do you want to show her straight away?"

"Fix both of them as fast as you can and do this boy at the same time. Maybe they'll want ordinary parts as well."

They drove down town, crossing Commissioner Street. Vusi heard the taped muezzin calls blare from the loudspeakers strapped to the minaret of the mosque on Nugget Street. Then he heard the man in the white suit say goodbye to the bouncer and slam the car door closed. But, of course, he could not see him walk into the Carlton Hotel and meet three shiny black men in Room 333 who gave him a money bag filled with fifty thousand rand, as well as a cake tin packed with white powder. He could not even see the shiny red car he was stretched out in arrive at the bottom end of Kruis Street and turn into the yard of the squat fire station that took up the whole block. And he could not see the embossed fire station sign painted in flame-licking colours; the four brick turrets placed at its corners corresponding to the exact positions of the heavenly bodies of the Crab, the Rat, the Pig and the Dragon: four turrets signaling the four points of an altar.

As Hans pulled up in front of a glass reception booth, he truncheoned Vusi.

"Stay quiet, hey, or I'll moer you!"

Vusi cowered under the prickly strands of the blanket. The blow made his neck sting but the fact was, he was still alive and not a shapeless lump abandoned at City Deep - that area of mine dumps which stretches for several kilometres in a tawny bareness along the East-West highway: dumping ground for the defiled victims of rapists and serial killers. Yes, his survival was a victory, even if it was only a temporary reprieve.

He felt himself being lifted.

"Big one this, Hans. Where'd you find him?"

The stretcher sloped as he was carried down stairs and along a corridor that smelt of floor polish. A door opened and was slammed. He felt himself being lowered: an odour of rot and medical spirits rose up like a fist smashing his nose.

"Shift him over to the others."

"Isn't it a bit early?" Vusi heard a new voice.

"No, the boss said we must start straight away. Hose him down and do the other preparations. We must be finished by the time he gets back."

"I've got a fresh set of needles."

"Bertus, bring me the sheets. Then clean the trays. We need more ice." This other man spoke with a sharp, defined manner,

"What about the others? Should I feed them now?"

"OK, but don't be too generous."

"Don't worry. There isn't much left."

"Just be sure to have them ready by eight o'clock. It's almost dark outside." The man clicked his tongue. "That old woman, you should see her. Come over here, she's lying in the corner."

Vusi's blindfolds were pealed away. He blinked and tried to focus. The light was dim and sparse. The bouncer called Hans was looking down at him.

"What about this fucking shit?"

"Leave him for now. We'll do him last."

Vusi turned his head slowly. He could see, but did not know, that he was lying in a corner of a low, concrete basement which ran under the sleeping quarters where the fire fighters lived; under the administration offices, store-rooms and workshops; under the garages where the fire trucks stood ready to put out blazes, infernos and all other categories of incendiary catastrophe - bold red fire trucks and cars with hoses and ladders ready at any time for ascent or descent into smoke and flame, searing dust or exploding mortar, glass, even molten steel. And as far as he could see, a dirty black tarpaulin stretched taut across the length of the basement. But the tarpaulin was not flat and straight; it bulged, crinkled and punctured by awkward, lumpy objects that pushed up, creating irregular angles and indentations. Now in a daze, too fogged to think clearly, he watched as a thin, shriveled man wearing the regalia of an inyanga walked to the corner nearest the main door and lifted the edge of the tarpaulin. The inyanga rolled back the tarpaulin and Vusi caught sight of a bloated, off-white body (that of the old prostitute), stretched rigid on its side. Next to it was a small, brownish body whose ears had been scalpeled away. (This was the corpse of a clothing trader from Fordsburg who had been attacked while counting the day's takings in a backroom office.) On both faces was an expression of terror and yet of expectation, as if what they witnessed at the moment of death was something for which they had been prepared, had long fantasized and foreseen.

The inyanga took a metal prod and bent down over the two prostrate bodies. He touched certain pressure points. Then, while Vusi lay bound and gagged, shivering with fear, the zombies slowly began kicking into motion.

*

The girl woke up with a start. There was a sound at the front door. The clock on the mantelpiece showed five o'clock. The mechanic came back every day at this time from the workshop on Smit Street; he came home for an early supper and a bit of TV before going out to drink. What was she to do? Mukoni must dress and collect his tools before the key was fully turned and the mechanic tramped in with his greasy, black-nailed hands. Yes, it was better with Mukoni, much better than with the white man, but she needed this job.

"Quick! The umlungu! He's here!"

She glanced in panic at her dress and panties that lay on the carpet where Mukoni had thrown them.

The mechanic walked in.

She shrieked and covered her eyes. The two men stared at each other. Then the mechanic rushed forward and jumped on Mukoni. They wrestled furiously on the bed till they rolled off onto the carpet. But just as the mechanic seemed to be gaining the advantage, Mukoni grabbed a thick glass ashtray and smashed it down on the white man's head - the heavy, pointed object gashing his skull open. Then Mukoni battered him, raining down blow after blow till he was twitching, frothing blood. In a matter of moments the mechanic lay immobile on the carpet. Half buried under a blanket, the girl shivered in terror.

"Get up, you stupid! Find a cloth! Don't just lie there! Fetch me a cloth!" Mukoni stood over her. "You listen to me now or you're in big trouble. You hear me!"

He slapped her hard across the face. Then he went to the toilet. As he began urinating, he felt the girl, warm against him. Sobbing uncontrollably, she held his chest in a vice-like grip.

"Let go of me! Are you mad?"

She gripped him tighter, tears flooding onto him. He dragged her back into the bedroom where the mechanic lay crumpled, his face already ashen. The girl pressed against him, desperate to be held and protected. And while she held him close, and her tears were on his face filling his own eyes with their salt, Mukoni was stirred by her warmth and her nakedness; she was so elastic, soft and enveloping. His fingers caressed her spine till her heaving began to subside. Then he smoothed her thighs and parted them, probing, massaging, till she began to moan. And while the last rays of sunshine filtered through the window, he joined with her, burrowing deeper and deeper into her as she received and enfolded him.

They lay trembling. Day was becoming night, the zone of each star being invaded and blurred, each crossing into the other, leaving no definition. The mechanic's arrival had been unexpected, but then, every moment of living has its secret meaning. All Mukoni knew was that, at last, he had found something sweet. It was dusk, peacefulness settled on the city; in the dying light everything was hushed, less harsh.

He picked up the telephone. The girl nuzzled against him.

"Hello, Mister Hans, I've got another one for you. I'm not joking. Can you come and fetch him? I'm at Bok Street. I don't have a car. How am I going to do that? Please, Mister Hans, make a plan! See what you can do, I'll phone you back just now."

He replaced the receiver and gesturing to the blood-soaked body said to the girl, "He was a nothing. He didn't deserve you." Mukoni stroked her. "You know, you make me happy." He cupped one of her breasts but she pushed his hand away and picked up a doek which she tied round her head.

"What are you going to do with him?" she asked in a small voice.

"Just do what I tell you, hey. I'm your lucky one! You'll see."

She tightened the doek.

"You must get him out of here. There's another umlungu who sometimes comes at half past eight. They go up to Hillbrow, to the bars."

Mukoni tried to embrace her but she remained stiff and turned away.

"Come, my sweetheart, what's wrong? I'll sort this out."

He grabbed her but she stopped him, and sat with folded arms. At that moment he knew he would have to make sure that she would never be able to speak to anyone about what had happened.

*

Limbs disjointed and creaking, the old woman and the trader got to their feet. She growled; the trader was silent, revolving his half-face from side to side.

"Come here, you moegoes!"

It was the one called Bertus. The zombies staggered towards him. He carried two metal bowls which he thrust towards them. They lunged and manically rammed their mouths over the steaming rims, giving out little grunts and snorts as they slurped.

"Easy! There'll be more later! Get back to your places!"

He prodded them with a little black truncheon. Mouths red with entrails, they slunk back into the dimness. The basement hummed. A team of men in overalls ran to one side and hoisted up the corners of the tarpaulin. As they rolled it into a thick black sausage, Vusi saw a numberless mass, a sea of mottled, decaying bodies, spread out on their backs or sides, many of whom had been hacked and were missing limbs or had holes gouged out where organs had been removed. The basement was like an underground chicken run with its wash of weak light and the erratic buzz of blind, senseless creatures. But, in this instance, the sacrificial victims were being herded by a group of beaded, otherwise naked inyangas, who, dancing between them, jabbing and butting with whips, produced in the resurrected, enslaved beings groans and howls that grew louder and more savage as row after row of the zombies were brought to their feet.

Bertus was walking towards Vusi dressed in a white coat. Behind him, Hans wheeled a tray on which were spread a range of surgical implements. Vusi prayed that the amulet he had purchased under the highway arches at the bottom of Eloff Street would continue to protect him. The amulet had been blessed by a well-known sangoma from Witbank, and though he was still bound hand and foot, and his mouth was stuffed with a rag smelling of hospitals, its power had, so far, kept him away from the deserted, wind-swept dongas and culverts of City Deep.

The band of men in overalls stripped down to their waists; they stood behind carved drums that reached to their navels. They wore scarves round their foreheads. An inyanga raised his hand and called out. The drummers began to beat a slow rhythm, and while the zombies slavered for entrails, muttering to themselves, two men stood over Vusi and rolled up his shirt-sleeve. As the needle pierced the surface of his naked arm, a new eruption of shit filled his pants.

*

The mechanic was neatly rolled up in the bloody carpet, the bed was freshly made, and where the carpet had covered the floor, the wood was polished till it shone. The ashtray lay drying on the kitchen table; it had been scoured with detergent. Mukoni stood outside on the balcony looking at the crowds milling round the taxi ranks. He needed something to steady himself.

"Did he keep brandy?"

The girl took a bottle out of a cupboard. Mukoni poured for himself. She walked away to the kitchen, leaving him alone on the balcony. She sat on a stool. The stink of mutton fat had receded. It was the tart, stabbing odour of ammonia that overwhelmed her, and the slightly acrid smell of Mukoni's body. It was true he had acted to defend himself. But she would never forget his frenzy while he clubbed the white man with the ashtray's sharp ridges; the twisted, stiff look on his face as he smashed down and blood spattered over the carpet. She had only opened the door so he could fix the sink; she had opened the door for him because his eyes glowed with a fire that made her do as he told her - yes, she had blazed up. Was this her punishment? Everyone in the block knew she lived with the white man. And why should she hide that? Let the black men in the flats call her a whore and a shame to the African nation. What could they give her? All they would do would be to make her have a child to prove she was a 'real woman'. So she had defied them. But now she was facing serious trouble. How was she going to explain that the mechanic was gone? She must leave before the police came looking, go back to Bloemfontein before the umlungu with the cowboy hat was at the door wanting to go up to Hillbrow.

While she was sitting bolt upright on a stool in the kitchen, tightening her doek, Mukoni was on the phone again, smoking and flicking ash onto the carpet rolled in front of him.

"OK, I'll bring him in a taxi, but I don't have money, Mister Hans. You must be there to pay the taxi. Times are hard! I don't even have one rand!"

Mukoni laughed. He took a long draw on the cigarette. Why cry? The penis and testicles of the white man would fetch a high price. But first he had to sort out the girl. When he had told her to tidy up the flat, she had only obeyed after he had slapped her. Only then had she started washing and scrubbing till the flat looked clean and neat as before. In the meantime, he would take her with him. She could help carry the carpet. He would sort her out afterwards.

"I'm going to get a taxi. Stay here and keep the door locked. Don't open to anyone. I'll be back before you know it."

He ran down the stairs, and reached the street. But before he pushed his way into the crowds, he stopped. What if the girl panicked while he was away organizing things? What if she locked the flat and went to the police? Or called a friend for help? There was only one answer: once the body was dropped off, he would take her back to his room for the night. As he ran to the rank, he was all pumped up, and, at the same time, exhausted.

A taxi was secured. He jumped in and directed the driver; but when he ran up and called her, there was only silence. He turned to leave - he would have to go to his room and fetch the rope with the skeleton keys; afterwards, once the carpet was dropped off, he would visit Steenkamp about a job. Then he thought of Vusi. Where was he? Drinking the first of many beers in a shebeen?

Suddenly the girl came up behind him.

"Where were you?"

"I went to the shop for a cooldrink."

"I told you to stay here! You want to get into trouble? Now open the door, there's no time to waste."

She unlocked the door and Mukoni picked up the toolbox. Then they lifted the tightly rolled carpet whose ends he had plugged with newspaper, and carried it down to the taxi. They wedged the carpet under the back seats. But as the driver pulled into the traffic, the girl jumped out and ran off, disappearing into the crowds, and Mukoni was left in the taxi, wondering why he hadn't taken care of her while they were still upstairs, and why he had trusted her when she was a stupid and a child whom he had allowed to get under his skin for a few hours.

As the driver cruised down Wanderers St, he swore to himself that once he had dropped off the body, he would go back to the flat and sort out the little bitch.

*

At the first shuffle of the drums, the needle punctured Vusi's skin and a shimmering quietness flooded over him. Through half closed eyes he saw the zombies on the floor jerk their arms and legs into the air, and kicking, begin to move in imitation of a herd of galloping wildebeest; or was it particles of sand lifting off dunes, swirling and rippling through reeds and branches? They danced in jagged, winding circles, clapping while the drummers splashed sweat over them and the concrete walls reverberated and boomed with the talking cowskin and the stamping of feet.

Vusi sank into a deep trance where none but the ancestors could reach him. There, on a distant horizon, he was running freely: there was no baas ready to shoot, no madam to strut and order him about. There was no longer the stale dryness of Hans's armpits directly above him - nor the stink from his own pants.

*

The taxi pulled up inside the fire station. The red brick courtyard shone with order and attention to detail, all its components polished and shining. Here smoke and flames came together, while day and night the firemen went out to douse and capture conflagration.

Mudau, the preacher, had warned about those who eat fire. Mudau advised visits to places of water so as to subdue the fire within. He knew Mukoni, had watched him wake in the early hours of the morning and stumble barefoot out of his room as if the compression of that tiny space drove his turmoil - rather than the need for the smooth, soft flesh of women: the need to possess them, to exercize his will absolutely and tie their breath to his, all the while marvelling at their power to excite and inflame. Mudau comforted him during those nights when he would stagger to where the light always shone, to the prophet's sacred chamber from which rang out songs of prayer and repentance. There, Mukoni would sit on the floor, and Mudau would break out into wild crying. White foam surging from his almost toothless mouth, the old man would begin to prophesy: The Son of the Beast was stalking the land, peering into the houses of both rich and poor, the righteous and the foul-living. And when he opened their doors and windows, he burnt everyone up - young and old, respected and despised alike. One by one, the Son of the Beast devoured them. But even as he destroyed whole towns and villages, the fury in him became denser, and he stood to be swallowed up by it; indeed, the day was soon to come when it would burn him to ashes.

Now Mukoni was far from the old man's sanctuary. He was in the courtyard of the kingdom of fire surrounded by its four corners, and the taxi driver was shouting at him, demanding that he offload the carpet and pay the fare.

A security guard handed him a telephone. A clipped, guttural voice said, "Hello." In the background Mukoni heard thudding, booming sounds. He could not identify the voice but before he could say anything the line went dead and Hans was at the door.

"You brought the parcel?"

Hans paid the driver and the taxi reversed out of the yard. They carried the carpet through the office and along a corridor that led past the store rooms and down a steep flight of stairs till they reached a dull green door on which a black skull and cross bones were painted. The words "DANGER, GEVAAR, INGOZI" stood out in red letters.

As the door opened, a smell of rotting flesh, formaldehyde and chicken entrails swept out. The door closed. Inside, apart from the assault of this stench, the basement was saturated with a rising cloud of blood, the heavy sweat of dancing zombies. Yet all these sensations were nothing compared with the crashing buzz, the mad, throbbing pulse of the drums.

Squeezed together on a raised platform, the drummers uncoiled their fluid, vibrating muscles, rhythms pulsating along the shafts of a spotlight

that spun round and cut through the air in arcs, shooting up and down the concrete expanse. The zombies howled, readying themselves for the night's tasks. After midnight, the fire trucks would drop them all over the city. Some would go to Zoo Lake; they would tap on the windows of luxury cars and while terrified men (corporate executives, tow-truck drivers and other miscellaneous professionals) looked up from the stale and lumpy bodies of whores, the zombies would empty their wallets and mangle their penises. Others would be dropped off in townships to ransack the mattresses of pensioners and devout women of the church. A few would scour the mine dumps for special herbs that were needed to soak body parts; an exclusive handful were sent to the abattoirs where they would rummage through bins, selecting the most deformed organs of cows and sheep. All would do their work. Then, an hour or so before daybreak, they would be collected and their booty heaped in piles on the basement floor.

Mukoni dropped the carpet; Hans continued dragging his end towards the nearest support pillar. The mechanic's head, tightly bound in a transparent plastic bag, trailed out. Hans released the carpet, unrolled it and unwound the sheets that bound him. Then he pulled off the mechanic's overall. The wounds on his head had clotted; a mottled film covered his otherwise floury features. Raising him onto a trolley, Hans swabbed the body with a light blue liquid then sprinkled him with a coarse brown powder that smelled of wet earth. Once the mechanic was completely covered with a layer of powder, they injected him with a number of different solutions.

The zombies continued their dance. The basement whirled with the horde of shambling, agitated, gray bodies, each bearing scars and mutilations and the pallor of infusions that kept them from the final peace of death. In the middle of the throng, despite the vapours that stung his eyes, and despite the sameness of the lumbering forms, Mukoni recognized the old white prostitute and the Indian trader. They were shuffling and stumbling over each other, bumping into the steel trolleys stationed at the edge of the tumult. And there, on one of these trolleys, his mouth all twisted and slack, he saw Vusi.

*

Hans screwed up his nose, "He's shat himself again. The little bastard!"

"What a bangbroek! Worse than a bladdy woman or a Pedi," barked the lead inyanga, showing a row of snuff-stained teeth. Then he danced about feverishly, sweat running off his arms, leaving little pools on Vusi and the mechanic's chests. A drummer left the podium and made his way to the trolleys. He placed the drumskin near Vusi's ear and began beating it. As the beats entered his being, Vusi saw his father's house in Ixopo.

There was a large, striped tent in the yard, and there were many people crowded inside it. Giant pots steamed with pap and gravy while two cows were braaing on grates of wire suspended over a bed of white hot coals. The line of people waiting for food stretched all the way down the hill. It was a big funeral, the most lavish the area had seen for many years. His family was assembled in the living room; his mother and sisters in black dresses, their heads covered with black doeks. His mother, bent as she was with arthritis, sat quietly wrapped in herself; a stroke had shrouded her in silence, but all the other women were crying out their grief. The older village women took over when his aunts and sisters flagged. He watched as his father and brothers greeted each person. The line from the gate kept growing; in addition to many neighbours he recognized the young men he had schooled with. They filed into the living room. And there on the floor, laid out in a polished wooden coffin with bright handles on which were engraved five flying pink angels, was his corpse.

Dressed in a white shirt with a tie, a red flower had been placed on his chest. But despite his joy at seeing the tie (it belonged to his eldest brother and was one he had long coveted), he was shocked: his face was puffy and ashen, there were black burn marks on each temple and his scratched hands were rigidly folded on his stomach as if asking, "Are we forever condemned to poke our fingers into our own eyes?"

Outside in the yard, mourners made their way to the braai stands where steaks and entrails sizzled. Only the food held their attention until a sangoma walked into the living room. A leopard skin covered his chest, his forehead shimmered with cascades of beads, a leather band snaked round his head; one wiry hand gripped a long, pleated sjambok, the other swung an incense burner. Vusi watched as his aunts and sisters began to ululate. The air in the close, stuffy room vibrated. The sangoma circled the coffin, hopping about with quick monkey-like movements, then, swooping down, lifted the lid of the coffin and threw it open. The ululation grew more frenzied. The sangoma rolled the corpse out of the coffin and poured a potion over the eyelids. Vusi recognized the smell – it was the same as the smell that came from the handkerchief used by the white man in the white suit to drug him outside the post office.

His body rolled over, then sprawled awkwardly on the floor. The sangoma called out to the ancestors to purge the demon forces. Stepping back, he raised the sjambok and cracked it down. The tip flicked across Vusi's body. His body jerked up like a doll. The crowd in the living room shrieked and moaned as the whip flashed and his body shuddered and the tip curled round and ripped at his flesh, then disengaged to be raised again and flicked so that each time it slipped round another limb which was also jerked up into the air. Over and over, the sjambok lashed his corpse from side to side. The gathering shouted out in awe while the sangoma's high-pitched incantations did battle with the spell that had turned him into a zombie. Suddenly a sheet of light flashed from the side of his body. Vusi saw, and did not see, a small white dog appear, and then disappear, through the wall. Women and small children fainted as the dog and his corpse both evaporated, leaving a wisp of smoke and the smell of burnt flesh.

Then he was on his feet, standing in front of the house, the gate was open and he was at the back of the great crowd that was crying out in excitement, pressing in at the windows all around the stoep. He could see his father inside leaning rigidly against his eldest brother. A few moments later, as if in a trance, the old man turned to face the front door. When Vusi walked towards him and crossed the threshold, he collapsed and men and women, screaming in fear and celebration, embraced each other.

*

"He's gone, dammit! He's disappeared!"

Hans flexed his fists, gesturing stupidly at the empty metal trolley on which only seconds before Vusi's slumped body had been laid out. The metal frame with a torn, brownish sheet partially covering it showed only a stained outline.

"What the fuck! Did he roll off? Check around, man! See if he slid off somewhere. Hey, help us, you bladdy fool!"

Mukoni, nauseated by the stench, and agitated by the pounding drums, staggered towards the trolley. Hans grabbed him by the wrist, and picking a syringe off the tray, rammed it into his arm.

"We'll take you instead, you good for nothing!"

Mukoni opened his mouth to scream but his tongue had become a dead fish and he could only listen as Hans said to the inyanga, "What's the odds? Either of them will be OK. They aren't worth much but every buck counts."

Hans pulled out the syringe. As Mukoni slumped to the floor he saw the Sotho girl, the well-toned flesh of her buttocks and the sheen of her brownness. But before he could embrace her and burrow into her moist tunnel, he saw the old prostitute leave the chanting crowd and stagger towards him. And behind her was the Indian trader with his head half cut off. And behind him was the woman he had strangled in the bushes near

62

Houghton golf course. And behind her was the runaway boy he had cut up in the parking lot next to the Protea Gardens Hotel. And behind him was the girl with pink bangles he had raped and dismembered in the toilets at Hillbrow hospital. And behind her was the very dark woman he had chopped up in the veld midway between Eldorado Park and Lenasia.

They bore down on him, the colony of zombies, shrieking and swearing, their hideous wounds gaping as the drumbeats smashed into his brain and his jaw went slack and his muscles were blown away by a cold, dry wind.

Someone ripped off his overall. It was the white man in the white suit. In his hand was a butcher's knife. The blade flashed down. The carpet from the mechanic's flat, now spread out on the basement floor, spattered with his blood. Then the old white whore peered down at him, gently smoothing the stumps of her lopped off breasts as the drums merged with her arms and she began stuffing Mukoni, deeper and deeper, into a bottomless black bag.

FELLOW TRAVELLERS

Hendrik had finished the jobs he had been instructed to do in Pongola and along the Mocambique border. Now he was driving down the Kwazulu north coast, in heavy rain, on his way back to Villiers, though first he had to stop over in Durban to collect a parcel. He had been away for almost a week and was more than ready to be driving home.

It was late afternoon. Fields of sugarcane rippled and waved in the low hard wind and the pelting rain. He was thinking about Marita who lived next door. Over the past months he had found himself constantly thinking about her - this tall fattish woman with sensual lips and an inner fire that simmered without flaming up or being extinguished so that he was battered by conflicting emotions. The brick wall separating their houses seemed to have collapsed, but at the same time, a new obstruction was raising itself higher; and as much as this collapse promised union, so it threatened to block out the rest of his world.

Marita was alone with her three girls; her husband had left her to live with another man. Since the divorce, Hendrik had helped her with household repairs - fixing her washing machine and her toaster, changing lawnmower blades and mending the roof; all this in return for coffee and cake. Once, while he was straightening a gutter, she had brought him a tray with some treats and he had kissed her hand but she had instantly recoiled. The next day he had brought her flowers and chocolate. She had smiled graciously, placed the flowers in a vase, and given the chocolate to her chubby girls. But always, and this is what had brought him close to her, having finished each job, they would sit together in the living-room and talk, moving from subject to subject, then touch on each other's private lives, their deeper, seldom expressed states of mind. This was especially true of Hendrik. And so it was that he had begun to spend almost as much time with Marita as he did at his own home. And in the mornings, before leaving for work, avoiding his wife, Aletta, he would stand in the kitchen and watch Marita, despite the presence of the maid, hang out washing: her breasts rising as she lifted the sheets high and strung them out; her long, powerful arms raising up bundles of dresses and jeans and t-shirts and school clothes and underwear for her three daughters. Thereafter, during the rest of the day, he would daydream about her flawless thighs, their milky whiteness exposed as her dress rose.

The last few weeks had been especially intense. His emotional balance was being badly affected. And yet, this frequent contact and growing intimacy seemed not to alarm Aletta, and for that Hendrik was thankful. What could he say? He was aware of Aletta's belief that Marita continued to suffer terribly because of her husband's switch, and was in a state of deep recoil from all men. Aletta had repeated to him what Marita had told her: that her husband's action had been completely unexpected, unforeseen, undreamt of; he had never seemed remote or indifferent to her; and yet, a cataclysm had broken down their home and deprived their children of the fundamental security of two parents living together. With regard to her own sense of self and beauty, how could she now trust another man to be truthful with her - and desire her? For all these reasons, Aletta did not believe that Marita might be overcoming her anger at men and thought that Hendrik was simply showing his most sympathetic side in helping her maintain her house.

That Hendrik did not understand his infatuation was also true. His marriage with Aletta was good; he did not feel particularly dissatisfied or restless. He had not been in a state of search. And yet now, driving down the winding coast, he was again thinking of Marita, squinting at the curtain of rain and gradually feeling his eyes tire with strain. Then, just before double-vision or a black out resulted from fatigue, a signboard for Ballito came up, and he decided to leave the main road and rest in the small town that lay at the bottom of the hillside by the ocean.

Near the beach he found a burger joint at a small shopping centre. After eating, he drove back up the hill towards the Durban road, but took a wrong turn and was soon lost in the steep hilly side roads. It was still raining heavily, the sun was setting and visibility was bad. The windscreen kept misting up despite the defrost working at full strength. Suddenly he saw the outline of a man walking ahead in the rain, and, hoping that he would know the area and direct him back to the main road, Hendrik pulled over.

The man greeted him courteously and began giving directions, then having done so, asked Hendrik if he was going to Durban, and if he was, if he could have a lift. As far as Hendrik could see in the half light, the man was not carrying a bag nor did he seem in any way prepared for a trip. Hendrik felt apprehensive - over the past years it had become dangerous to offer help to strangers, and many attacks by hitchhikers were reported in the press. Then, without wavering, without conveying desperation or hope, the man looked at him through the half open window, his hair falling down over his forehead, dripping water, and smiled, acknowledging Hendrik's ambivalence.

66

"Hey, my friend, I'm not a bad fellow. I wouldn't dream of doing you any harm."

Hendrik stared back and became conscious of his safe and comfortable position in the warmth of the car while the man stood sopping wet in the road. And despite his justifiable caution, he felt ashamed. Why was he hesitating? Was this reluctance not unreasonable, even a little paranoid? Is it not unhealthy to live in fear of attack from others? The man had thus far been helpful and polite, was well-spoken though with a trace of a foreign accent; dressed casually in jeans and a denim jacket, his appearance was not unkempt, dirty, nor in any other way alarming.

Impulsively Hendrik opened the passenger door. Without another word the man jumped in then directed him out of the town. In a few minutes, they reached the main road and were on their way to Durban.

*

Rain continued to fall, blanketing the road, and Hendrik battled to see the white lines. The traveller mentioned that in such weather many accidents take place, in particular, when cars try to overtake slow-moving trucks. Hendrik mumbled agreement. He thought of Marita again - she was slowing him down, and, at the same time, speeding him up.

A last ray of sunset broke through the clouds. Hendrik commented to the man about his foreign accent.

"Are you Dutch?" he asked.

"No, you'll never guess - I'm from Venezuala. My name is Pedro."

Indeed, Hendrik was surprised; the man did not seem Latino, he had light almost bleached hair, and fair if suntanned skin. They continued making small talk. Pedro told him he had been brought up by nuns in a boarding school. But he had left the school at the age of sixteen to work on oil rigs. With this experience, he had found a job in Texas and thereafter lived near Aspen, Colorado, on a farm which bred rodeo horses. Then he had come to South Africa on contract, worked on the Mossgas project in the Southern Cape, and once it had expired, bought a house in Ballito near the beach. In general, he loved South Africa's climate and the fact that he could fish and surf almost all year round.

Hendrik was impressed by Pedro's fluency and easy manner. He was clearly a master at befriending and putting people at ease - a quality that Hendrik lacked. Indeed, meeting new people was a source of difficulty and tension for him. As a result, more often than not, he became a means for the satisfaction of other people's well-being rather than an agent for his own welfare and happiness.

The two men sat comfortably in the warm car while daylight ebbed and the highway was covered in darkness but for the intermittent beams of oncoming traffic. Suddenly, ahead of them, there was a loud screech of tires and a tremendous bang.

Pedro let out a shout, and pointed.

"A car . . .! Did you see it? It's left the road! A car's just driven off the road! There! Look!"

Hendrik followed his gesticulating finger: within seconds they came abreast of the red tail lights of a car which protruded from a clump of thick bushes off the roadside.

"Pull over!" said Pedro. "Let's see what's happened! They'll need help. That was a hell of a speed they were doing!"

Pedro was decisive, yet without seeming to be giving orders or acting in an overarching way. He had witnessed the accident and reacted with just the right measure of urgency and clarity so that Hendrik instinctively felt directed by him, not imposed upon. He was happy to have Pedro take command, and immediately pulled over.

"Lock the car," Pedro said.

They ran back along the shoulder of the road and crossed to the other side. An expensive landcruiser's tail jutted up into the air; the front end was buried in a thick mass of foliage. As they approached the vehicle, a young man staggered out of the undergrowth and collapsed on the tarmac in front of them.

"We're coming!" Pedro called out.

The man lay on his back breathing heavily, then began shouting hysterically, "Where's my cell phone, for God's sake find my cell phone, I must phone Lenny. Dammit, get me my cell phone!"

He thrashed about on the side of the highway, heaving like a demented creature. But there were no signs of bodily injury - no blood on his face, no stains on his clothes. It was extraordinary; the man seemed physically untouched, unharmed by the accident which might so easily have killed him.

"Are you sore anywhere? Pedro asked.

"Jesus, just get me my phone! It's in the cabin, in the cubbyhole. Just get it, man! I've got to speak to Lenny! He's not going to believe it. The bladdy car's just come out of the panel beater!"

"I'll find the cell phone," Pedro tried to reassure him. Then he turned to Hendrik, "Wait with him. There may be someone else in the car." Without another word, he broke a way into the undergrowth leaving Hendrik to manage the moaning young man who was so amazingly alive.

The vehicle was stuck fast in the bush, covered and held by branches and overhanging vines. The driver's door was twisted open, the windscreen smashed, the bonnet totally concertinaed. There was no one else in the car.

The driver lay sobbing by the roadside.

"What can I tell Lenny? He'll kill me! And I'll fucking well kill Bruce! Did you see him? Did you see what the bastard did? I've got to phone him, where's my cell phone? Find my cell phone!"

Car after car passed them, looming out of the rain, headlights shining brightly but none stopping. Hendrik dared not walk about for fear of being run over. Then a car travelling from the opposite side, pulled over. A woman and her daughter walked up to them. The woman ran to the prostrate young man.

"Are you alright? What a terrible thing! I'm so sorry I didn't stop straight away. I saw what happened. I turned round to come back. Are you alright?" Then she shouted, "He must have been crazy the way he cut you off! Why were you both going so fast? How could he do this to you?"

The driver and another young man had been racing each other on a short section of the road which had four lanes. And as the lanes narrowed, ready to join and become one lane for each direction, they had driven even faster, each determined to win by forcing the other to back off. Then the other young man, the most desperate, or the drunkest, had used the most dangerous tactic of all: he had cut across the driver of the land cruiser and caused him to crash.

Pedro came back out of the foliage. In his hand was a cell phone.

"I found it in the cubbyhole."

"Thank God, you found it!" yelled the young man. "Give it to me!" Then he frantically pressed several digits, moaning over and over again, "He's going to kill me, Jesus, what have I done . . . he's going to kill me!"

The woman and her daughter who had been driving behind the two speedsters, stood next to Hendrik, each repeating how lucky the young man was. Who had ever seen a car as squashed and as mangled? That he could walk out of such a collision and be completely unharmed was truly a miracle, except to say that modern technology was starting to even out the odds of surviving the most hazardous of threats. But for the airbags that had shot out and inflated at the instant of contact with the tree, the young man's skull would have been instantly fractured by the windscreen, his lungs and rib cage smashed by the steering wheel.

"We had better phone for an ambulance," said Pedro, "he looks OK but he might have brain damage. He'll need scans and x-rays. Some whiplash is inevitable."

The woman took out her phone, "What's the number? I can't remember it I'm so shaken."

Pedro gave her the number and she telephoned the emergency service.

"I don't think there's much more we can do," Pedro said to Hendrik.

The young man was still lying on the road waiting for the person he called Lenny to answer.

"We're going. Will you handle this?" Pedro asked the woman.

"Yes, we'll wait till they arrive."

Hendrik and Pedro jogged back to Hendrik's car. Their conversation during the remainder of the trip to Durban was mainly about the accident and the stupidity of boys who take such outrageous risks. When Hendrik dropped Pedro off in town, at the bottom of West Street, they said goodbye with a feeling of warm friendship, almost of gratitude that they had shared the experience of the accident, and that death had not forced a brutal and violent way into their ride.

*

The next day, checking out of his hotel room, Hendrik left Durban and began the trip home to Villiers. In contrast to the previous day it was warm and clear, almost cloudless, and he unbuttoned his shirt. At ten o'clock, as he left the toll station beginning the ascent to Pietermaritzburg, the radio carried cricket captain Hansie Cronje's initial statement, his false confession, to the King Commission's enquiry into match fixing.

Cronje's unmasking was a tragic drama, or so it seemed, that made Hendrik shiver because of the magnitude of the man's disease, and the degree of his deception. Cronje, a rich, boereseun who had succeeded in the English sport, trapped himself in a web of deceit and corruption which was even more fascinating than the machinations of former Boer politicians who were now advising the Volk to cooperate with the Blacks and give up their own identity.

Nothing could have prepared Hendrik for the story that Cronje told: his expectation that the bookies and match fixers who gave him (not paid him!) substantial amounts would tolerate his taking their money but not delivering results. Hendrik smiled to himself. Who did this idiot think he was dealing with? Stupid coolies from Sasolburg who didn't know how to conceal their greedy smiles when setting out a petty, measely deal? No, these were experienced con artists from India itself, sophisticated dealmakers from the big cities that stink with human excrement and where the rich live in palaces and seduce white women.

Hendrik glided along the highway flanked by green hills while Hansie Cronje swore that he had never thrown a game and had always played his heart out for South Africa. Hendrik felt a lump in his throat. Hansie showed great remorse for what he had done, apologizing to those he had harmed for bringing disgrace on himself, and on them. Yes, what he had done was worse than stupid, but still, here he was big enough, brave enough, to face the world and admit his responsibility. After all, no one had proven that he had actually thrown a match - he had just strung the bookmakers along, pretended to have discussed fixing matches with other players but in reality doing nothing of the kind. (Days later, Hendrik will hear Cronje confess that he had manipulated payments to other players, cheating his friends and playmates, so as to secure a further cut for himself. Days later, more details of Cronje's actions will be revealed by other witnesses - the bookmaker, Marlen Aronstam, the sweet seller, Hamid "Banjo" Cassiem, and other personalities of the gambling nether-world).

He passed Pietermaritzburg. The concrete two lane highway rolled up and down hills; traffic was sparse. The radio suddenly crackled and blurred into fuzziness. Hendrik strained to pick up the broadcast, switching from station to station while the highway snaked along, following contours. Eventually, after several fruitless attempts to reconnect, he was forced to accept this loss of history to physical obstruction, to mountains created by geological time and its grand impediments to human intention.

Beginning again to reflect on Marita, he recalled her quick laugh and her delicate way of pouring tea; he visualized her long white legs as her dress crept up. Then, in his mind's eye, while he watched her stoop and stretch, he caught sight of the Ultra City petrol stop near Ladysmith. And as he flashed past the big yellow Shell sign that stamped the corporate world on the horizon, he saw a young black man hitching at the side of the highway.

The man was wearing blue jeans and a thick winter jersey; pulled down over his head, almost blocking his eyes was a woollen balaclava. Hendrik slowed down. He had never before stopped for a black man on the highway, particularly a young black man who was likely to be even more dangerous. But now he had stopped for this black man and was waiting for him to reach the car.

He watched the man running in his rearview mirror, legs crossing over each other as he stumbled towards the car. Then he was standing breathless at the car door, waiting for Hendrik to speak. Hendrik looked at him, startled. The young man had very dark liquid eyes that were almond in shape; his eyebrows were full but not bushy and beautifully arched; his skin was dark and smooth like rivers and Hendrik felt himself flush with a strange emotion. He opened the door. The young man slipped into the car and closed the door.

Hendrik examined him again.

"Where you going?"

The hitchhiker looked down at the dashboard and said, "Warden."

"You live there?"

The man offered no reply. Hendrik repeated the question but again the young man did not respond. He drove off. They sat silently in the car. Then, at length, after several kilometres, Hendrik said, "Can't you talk?" When he was again ignored, he switched to Afrikaans. "Waar bly jy? In die lokasie? Jy weet, ek ry na Villiers."

The smooth, finely contoured face of the passenger remained impassive though there was a hint of coyness in his eyes. It seemed nothing would make him answer. Hendrik stared at the young man's chest. Was there a certain swelling that could be a woman's . . . that could imply that the young man was not a . . . ?

The flow of traffic dropped. The sun had risen to the centre of the sky. Hendrik accelerated and opened a window. He inhaled deeply. The air was fresh with a tinge of smoke. The landscape flattened out between slight rises and the fields on either side were brown with dried mielie stalks. They had left the greenery and the hilly slopes of Kwazulu-Natal as well as the mountain pass that led up to the Free State. Beyond a handful of small towns lay Johannesburg.

Hendrik drove faster. A petrol tanker laboured ahead of him. He crossed over into the fast lane. Suddenly a car filled his rearview mirror; a luxury sedan was sitting right up against him, almost touching his bumper. The driver, who wore sunglasses and a cap, hooted furiously, but it was impossible for Hendrik to pull back into the slow lane behind the tanker, and oncoming traffic made it difficult for the car behind him to overtake. The driver with the sunglasses hooted without stop, maintaining his hair-raising proximity. Hendrik looked fearfully in the mirror. The driver made a rude sign with his fingers.

"Don't you worry, man" Hendrik said to the hiker, "I'll teach this bastard a lesson. "Fuck you, you doos," he shouted, and deliberately slowed down. The hiker looked at him nervously. Then he slowed even further so that he was alongside the tanker cabin while the oncoming traffic flashed past in a continuous stream of cars, kombis, pantechnikons and busses.

The driver with the sunglasses continued hooting savagely.

"Let's see what this doos does now," said Hendrik, and maintained his slow speed so that he rode in tandem with the tanker completely blocking the two lanes. He winked at the hiker who stared down at his hands. "Come on, cheer up. He'll back off now. Hey, you still haven't told me where you're going?'

"I go to Warden," the young man said, and pursed his lips.

"You're a girl," Hendrik cried out. "I could see it when you ran up. Jesus! You're a bloody girl, my friend, you're a bloody girl!"

The hiker smiled but kept his face averted. The car behind them sustained its harsh barrage. Hendrik and the tanker approached a low hill. As Hendrik said "Why are you doing this? You scared of men? Scared of what they'll do to you," the luxury sedan drew abreast of him and the driver of the car pointed a gun at him and fired. Hendrik vaguely registered the explosion but felt no impact and the bullet entered the panelling of the passenger's door. The enraged driver did not fire again and before he had time to do anything, the sedan had crested the ridge and disappeared.

"Fucking maniac! Can you believe it?" His hands were shaking. "Shit, he could have killed me!" He turned to the young man. "What do you say? He could have shot me and then the car would have left the road and you would have died as well! Both of us vrek!"

But there was still no response; the young man continued looking straight ahead, avoiding him. The pencil straight road droned on. Hendrik took the young man's hand in his and stroked the warm fingers; he stroked them and intertwined them with his.

"Haai, tell me why you're playing this game? Why you dressing like this?"

"My name is Musa," the young man said.

Hendrik studied his hands; the nails were quite deliberately manicured.

"Dammit, you're a girl, man!" said Hendrik.

The passenger withdrew his hand.

"Don't you like me to touch you?"

Hendrik felt his whole body quiver. The passenger folded his hands in his lap and Hendrik looked carefully at the longish, shaped nails and knew that more than anything else at that moment he wanted to again hold the warm hand with the tapering fingers, he wanted to do this very badly because there was the delicious sense of the male and the female all mixed up and he wanted to feel the two come together. So he placed the cupped palm of his left hand over the passenger's chest and felt a round, warm mound. Then he caressed the passenger's breast. But when he tried to twist his hand under the thick jersey, his hand was pushed away.

"Don't worry! I won't force you to do anything you don't want to do."

They drove on in silence. Fields of dried mielie stalks flashed by, small herds of rust-brown cows grazed. Hendrik became more and more frustrated - he wanted to caress the young man's breasts that were so round and firm. But instead he again took the warm hand that lay on the faded pants, and was shaken by a strange almost demonic force. Then, as he raised the hand to his lips, he was slapped.

"Hey, don't do that! I was only joking!" he said, and dropped the young man's hand. What was he to do? The impulse had been so rough, so determined. And now he was ashamed. Yes, he had overstepped the limits.

"Why you going to Warden?"

"I'm going to see my uncle . . . for shoes."

Hendrik looked down at the young man's feet; he wore expensive winter boots. He was obviously not telling the truth.

"Are you going to see your girlfriend?"

The young man smiled but said nothing. Hendrik saw a pair of crows hovering above the highway. The carcass of a small dog lay in the slow lane; the intestines smeared across the tar. Hendrik drove over the dead dog as the crows dived down. Then he pushed his hand against the man's breasts and rubbed them violently. The young black man sat without reacting. Hendrik tried to force his hand down the front of the thick jersey but his hand was immediately stopped.

"Jesus, I'm sorry," said Hendrik, "I shouldn't have done that. I . . . Tell me, what do you think of Hansie . . .?"

"Drop me there," said the young man, pointing to an oncoming road sign. Beyond the sign was a clump of farm worker houses.

"We aren't near Warden," said Hendrik.

"Drop me there," he said, almost shouting.

Hendrik slowed down and pulled off the highway. The young man got out of the car.

"I'm sorry, "said Hendrik.

"Thank you," said the young man, averting his eyes.

BUT, DAMMIT, HE WAS A WOMAN.

Hendrik drove off watching the young man walk through dry mielie stalks. He would be home in an hour. Perhaps Marita would be having lunch and he could help her clean out her cellar before Aletta came back from work.

THE DESK

Family Day, 1968

T he first flush of darkness thickens the pale blue of afternoon; the sky loses its curved vastness to a lush, enveloping, ever narrowing arm of violet. Reuben is in his bedroom. He looks up from a typewriter. In front of him on his desk, set in a heavy gilded frame, is a photograph of his grandparents taken in Kimberley after their engagement in 1882. Behind him, posters cover the wall: Che Guevara, Jimi Hendrix, Karl Marx, Franz Fanon, Eugene Marais and a girl with strong but fine features wearing a straw hat. Reuben has a string of Swazi beads around his neck. His thick brownish hair reaches his shoulders. On moon lit nights he goes down to the ocean with his friends. They drink white wine and walk on the shores of the cold Atlantic. He breathes in the fresh, sharp, salt air and knows that a few other moments in his life will be as self-contained.

In six months' time, on his twenty-first birthday, he will hold a party in a girl-friend's garage. He will wear tropical helmet and dance drunkenly after midnight when his parents have left and only party's hard core are still on their feet.

*

Abe and Maisie Levine face the camera .They do not touch. The only indication of intimacy is the way Abe leans towards her. And one immediately understands why. Despite the almost too earnest, intense expression on her face, Maisie seems very soft, sensuous. How sad that later, obsessed with money, when she failed to match her ambitions, those features hardened, set in disappointment and recrimination that only senility could mellow.

Abe's face has a blank, unformed look quite unlike his expression in later photographs. Those suggest a strong sense of self, despite his always having lived on the margins of power, never having made the fortune others of his family and friends did. In this engagement photograph he seems to float, predictably unaware of how the years ahead will make their demands. It will always be a struggle to satisfy Maisie's needs, there will be many confrontations.

Their son, Harry, Reuben's father, is an internationally recognized economist, an academic and former political activist. At this moment, Harry is massaging his son's temples and in response to Reuben's request, is retelling the story of Uncle Bennie, Maisie's young brother.

Years before, Bennie was a well- known doctor in Johannesburg. In October 1951, when still a relatively a young man, he died of pemphagus, a rare but fatal disease whose primary symptoms are sores in the mouth; such sores later break out all over the body. Pemphagus is caused by malfunctioning of two glands located on top of each kidney. It is a debilitating disease that breaks down the body's immune system and was at that time incurable.
Uncle Bennie made a difficult and unusual self-diagnosis but local doctors disagreed with him and he was reluctant to begin treating himself. But when his condition worsened, and it seemed he was dying, he flew to America to consult a Dr Sulzburger, at that time the world's leading researcher into the disease.

Sulzburger, who had reported great success in treating pemphagus with a new drug named cortisone, confirmed the diagnosis and Uncle Bennie remained at his clinic undergoing treatment for six months. He then returned to South Africa and was able to live a more or less full life for another five years. The ultimate trigger of his death was septicaemia, induced by pricking a finger on a rose bush in his garden.

*

Next to the photograph of Reuben's paternal grandparents is a photograph of himself. It was taken in Lesotho on the banks of the Caledon River during the time of his visit to Cecily Marshall.

Cecily was a volunteer teacher at a village school. Her boyfriend, Leon, who had gone to Europe on holiday, was one of Reuben's best friends. Reuben slept on a mattress next to her bed and listening to her breathing. Every night he dreamed that her hand was caressing his hair and neck , moving up and down until he could no longer bear it and he, in turn, began to kiss and stroke her hand; every night he would wake from the 'dream embrace' to find his arms empty.

As even Reuben acknowledges, the photograph seems contrived. It shows an intellectual student, bushy beard and visionary eyes. He is sitting on a black rock in the sunshine holding a pen and notebook. Unbeknown to Cecily, she had photographed him writing a letter. The letter was addressed to her and spoke of his attraction to her - as well as his sense of guilt about Leon. But after her surprising him on the rock, he had been unable to continue and it had remained unfinished, so that Cecily was never to have confirmation of his feelings, believing him affectionate but aloof.

*

The third photograph on the desk is of his father at Oxford dressed in black gown and mortar board on the day he received the John Maynard Keynes Award for Socially Responsible Economics. Harry had received the award for a series of articles on the contradiction inherent in the concept of a 'cooperative capitalism'.

Thereafter, for twenty years, he became an important figure in the trade union movement where he taught, wrote and organized with great dedication. This period of his life lasted until the socialist movements in South Africa were crushed in the early 1960s.

When the Party was banned and all activities forced underground, he withdrew from public life to concentrate on theoretical work.

*

Above the desk is an old wooden clock that strikes the hour. A gift from the University of Blantyre, the clock is made of soft but durable wood. In the words of the dean, Dr Khambuye, the wood's qualities are a metaphor for the nature of long-suffering Malawians who first bore British occupation and then the despotism of Hastings Banda, their own home-grown, Anglicized dictator.

On top of the typewriter is a letter that had mistakenly arrived at Harry's private post box. Attracted by the bright stamp of a central African bird, he had brought the letter home, shown it to Reuben and then forgotten about it. Consequently the letter is still unopened. It lies sandwiched between an old copy of the Cape Times and a coffee mug.

P O Box 40332
Kamengo
Lilongwe 4
Malawi

23 July, 1967

Dear Penpal,
*   I am very glad to write this letter to you and how are you by this occasion? But me I'm not so bad.*
*   I am a boy of 14 years old and I'm doing a business course in Lilongwe. And we are six children in our family, two boys, four girls, and among them I'm the first born. My hobbies are playing and watching football, watching films, exchanging gifts and traveling. I enclose my snap shot in this letter, and please reply in time and put your snap inside.*
*   Lastly pass greetings to all your friends, wherever they are, and don't forget your parents.*

Yours faithfully
Evans Alfred Mbewe

*

Every evening in summer, seven shades of blue manifest by degrees in the sky along the coast of the peninsula. This occurs as the reflection of light off the ocean deepens and sunset exhausts it reds and yellows, and the land soaks up this light.

Reuben has been writing a letter to Veronica Gomes, the daughter of his mother's cousin. Veronica is a ballerina. She had spent the previous year in Cape Town and danced the leading role in a production of *Sleeping Beauty*. Reuben is infatuated with her but the opening paragraphs of his letter are dry and awkward, lacking originality and feeling. This quality of emotional reticence is inherited from his mother, Silvia, who continually oscillates between sentimentality and iciness.

During the third week of Veronica's in their house, Reuben had crouched at the bathroom keyhole. His parents were out and the maid was in the kitchen making chicken and asparagus pies. With an awed but sinking heart, he had watched Veronica undress, then slide into a steaming bath that did not completely cover her. For months afterwards his masturbation was consumed by the image of her body rising out of the water, all fresh and glowing, porcelain white and supple.

Reuben will post his five page letter to Lisbon where Veronica has resumed living with her parents. He does not know that she has a boyfriend, Roberto, whose father is the Spanish ambassador to Portugal. Portugal is still in the grip of the decrepit Salazar regime; Salazar being one of Franco's last and most conspicuous allies. Occasionally she sends Reuben a postcard, but the truth is that she has never been attracted to him and is very much in love with Roberto.

The letter is an invitation to her to return and spend the coming year in Cape Town. Reuben continues to hope that he will kiss her again in his Beetle on Signal Hill. He covers the letter with his hand while his father speaks. At this point, he is on page three. He has yet to reach the paragraph in which he calls her, 'My darling dark one who inflames me'.

*

Harry picks up one of the books on the desk. It is a new copy Camus' *Outsider*. Harry has recommended Camus's work to his son. He is unaware that Reuben has stolen the book from the CNA branch in Rondebosch and that Reuben has started a shoplifting campaign. This decision, to 'liberate' books was taken after the shop manager had refused to order a rarely prescribed philosophy text book from England on the grounds that the company's profit margin would be too small. At this time one of CNA's senior directors is the chairman of the University of Cape Town's governing council. In Reuben's view it is not coincidental that the university does not have its own bookshop and students have no choice but to buy from the sole designated supplier, namely, CNA.

*

Both Maisie and Uncle Bennie were brilliant at school. Maisie's ambition was to be a teacher and Uncle Bennie's to be a mathematician, but the family was too poor to send both of them to university. And though she was older by three years and should have had the first opportunity to study further, she was a woman. So while Bennie went to study medicine in Britain, she had to leave Cape Town where she was finishing high school and travel up-country to work in the trading store her mother and father managed on behalf of a wealthy uncle. The store was a cramped, musty, whitewashed building with a corrugated iron roof. It stood in the middle of a clump of buildings next to a railway station surrounded by veld. Working from five in the morning till seven at night, working everyday of the year except the Day of Atonement, they saved enough money for Uncle Bennie to continue his studies.

Bennie matriculated at a well-known school in Bloemfontein at the age of fifteen. He passed the final exam with distinction. The next year he sailed to Scotland on a Union Castle Liner. At Aberdeen University he was the only Jew in the class. He won four gold medals in his first year and an average of three medals every year thereafter. During the second year his excellence in mathematics was such that the professor asked why he had chosen to study medicine. Uncle Bennie explained that it had been his mother's choice. After graduating cum laude he spent the next seven years working in Birmingham. At the age of twenty-nine he was offered a professorship. But at two o'clock on the day this offer was made, he received a telegram saying that his mother was dying in South Africa. He boarded the first available ship and sailed from Southampton to Cape Town, reaching Kimberly in time for the funeral.

*

Reuben is majoring in economics. His lecturer, a young Englishman named Andrew Kenny, is a die-hard monetarist and outspoken advocate of rolling back the influence of the state. Kenny is a decade ahead of his time. By the end of the 1970s, the international tide will start swinging away from the Soviet version of socialism as well as from social democracy. A new gospel of unbridled market driven individualism and pride in wealth accumulation will take hold – the egalitarian, collectivist dream, even as an abstract desire and vision, will sour.

Next to a Shorter Oxford dictionary is a textbook. The book is open at the following passage: *There is the further difficulty that in most countries anything from one-third to two-thirds of all highly qualified manpower is employed in the public sector at administered pay scales which gear earnings directly to paper qualifications within any effort to check whether more education means better job performance. If the private sector sets the rate of for the public sector, the fact that the marginal product of labour is difficult to define in the public sector raises special problems.*

The section has been highlighted. The yellow lines stand out sharply against the black print. Over the past week Reuben had been struggling to read the article. Tomorrow he must hand in an essay on the way in which Value is created by the State Sector. The article has been recommended by Kenny as an incisive example of formal argumentation – ideas are carefully set out and explored. Reuben has split coffee on this page more than once; the brown coffee stain mixes well with the yellow highlighter.

*

Under the letter is a book on whose cover is a painting of a tortured face. It is a collection of short stories by a new South African writer, Dieter Malcolm Coetzee. The title story, *The Trial of Job*, is set in the 1950s in a small town in the Little Karoo. It describes the breakdown of Job van Wyk, the local family doctor.

Job van Wyk cannot maintain his practice. He begins to see his patients as either ignorant, neurotic hypochondriacs who have all the necessary means for living healthy, satisfying lives but who, because of their pettiness and selfishness, fail to do so; or he sees them as pitiful victims who serve as cannon fodder, miserable slaves of the more powerful and ruthless. Over time, Van Wyk grows wealthy buying up houses and farms. But his sense of fulfillment is impaired: why strive for these things when the activities necessary to acquire and maintain them are so dull and vulgar, part of the predictable, tedious round of work and ritual, the mere counting of money? Finally, he questions the love of his wife and children. Why live with them when they are consumed by self-interest and small-mindedness? They humour and manipulate him, praying in secret for his death so that they can inherit the wealth he has spent his life creating.

As his world constricts and confines, Van Wyk's depression grows more and more immobilizing.

*

Reuben has often thought of writing a story about Uncle Bennie but the idea is still hazy, and though in twenty years time he will write a draft in Washington (where he will live for most of his adult life), nothing will ever be finalized. At this point he urges his father to divulge every aspect of his uncle's life so as to create a complete character. Harry obliges and adds this information:

83

After his mother died, Uncle Bennie had to decide whether to remain in Johannesburg, a provincial African backwater, and build a career, or return to the wider, richer world of the European metropolis. After months of weighing up his options, he decided to remain in South Africa and was appointed to a post at one of Johannesburg's premier hospitals. In four years he became superintendent of the hospital, his private practice grew meteorically and he started out on a very successful investment career on the stock exchange. At the age of thirty-five he could afford a large property in an exclusive suburb where he was grudgingly accepted by his English neighbours. Apart from his professional and financial success, Uncle Bennie was adept at tennis, golf and bowls. He was also an accomplished poker player.

Years later, both Maisie's children, Harry and Frieda, were sent to live with him so that they could attend good schools in Johannesburg. But all their lives, no matter what they achieved – and their achievements were considerable – neither ever received recognition or praise from her. Their mother's fixation remained on the brother for whom she had sacrificed so much.

*

The cover of Coetzee's book shows the head of a man with a red slash for a mouth, two black smudges for ears, and a downward dab for a nose. The atmosphere is of dread and foreboding in the manner and spirit of the Scandinavian religious mystics and existentialists. But the drawing is by a Capetonian of Khoisan descent. Reuben bought the book, fifth hand, from a junk shop in Salt River noted for its stock of thrillers, teenage romance magazines and a selection of old hats and shirts. He had been browsing through the shelves when the book, delicately balanced above him, fell onto his head.

In the Old Testament version it is assumed that Job's test of faith is not perverse, that systematically stripping a man everything he loves and values is the is true means of acceptance of God's absolute right to rule individual destiny. What shocks the reader is that the biblical Job passes this test. Utterly alone and destitute, afflicted with boils and other physical privations, and despite his agonized raging against these catastrophes, he is able to transcend the narrowness of human love and possessiveness. Then, in recognition of such faith in God's power, his acceptance of human impotence, Satan submits and God restores happiness to Job

A receipt from a kaffie on Main Road - for milk, eggs and a newspaper - acts as bookmark. It is now fitted at the last page (which Reuben wishes to copy out in his diary). Job van Wyk, having lost everything he loves and values, unable to rebuild his life, hangs himself from the branch of a tree in the courtyard of the local Dutch Reformed Church.

*

Reuben hopes to be an economist like his father. In this he will succeed but the consequences will be other than those he now anticipates. His first job will be in New York where he will be employed by a multinational oil company. He will marry a Swedish anthropologist named Inge Johanssen and be the father of two boys, Olaf and Samuel. Veronica Gomes will become a successful journalist specializing in environmental and health issues. He and Veronica will stop communicating in 1976, the year of the Soweto uprising, when he will leave South Africa and, instead of visiting her in Portugal, decide to cut all contact. At that point, Roberto will have divorced her and she will be living with a left-wing lawyer who adores her and gives her expensive presents. Veronica's involvement with Maoist organizations will soon peter out, but she will remain active in the democratic movement in Portugal. By that time, Reuben will be an executive director of the oil company and have long ceased any political involvement.

*

Reuben received a birthday gift of a Beetle on his eighteenth birthday. It is painted in psychedelic colors with green chameleon sloping across the roof. The car runs well and has taken him and his friends all the way to South West Africa where they drove through the Namib.
Two traffic fines lie on the desk, one of which reads: AS DRIVER OF THE VEHICLE CA 52476,YOU HAVE FAILED TO COMPLY WITH A DIRECTION CONVEYED BY A ROAD SIGN DISPLAYED IN THE PRESCRIBED MANNER: TO WIT, LOADING ZONE ONLY WHEREAS THE SAID THE VEHICLE WAS NOT DESGINED AND USED AS A GOODS VEHICLE, MOTOR CYCLE OR MOTOR TRICYCLE FOR THE LOADING OR UNLOADING OF GOODS, OR

WAS SUCH A VEHICLE, BUT WAS USED FOR A PERIOD
UNREASONABLE FOR THE LOADING OF GOODS.

*

At boarding school the head matron gave Harry the affection and attention
he needed. His sister Frieda, on the other hand, though poetic and
imaginative, was moody and antisocial, and the hostel teachers were
unsympathetic. After school, in the late 1940s, she lived in London and
Paris, and spent some time on a kibbutz near Jerusalem. On her return to
Johannesburg in 1954, she worked for a firm of technical publishers. For
many years she edited the work of others, then, unexpectedly, began writing
herself.

One of Frieda's poems (none of which were ever published) is typed out
and stuck on the wall next the wooden clock. The poem is written in
calligraphic fashion, in letters that arch up and down but without excessive
ornamentation; the script, in dark blue ink, is inscribed on tan coloured
paper.

> *I was walking*
> *saw a star*
> *falling*
> *as it hit the world*
> *its light went out*
> *nevertheless*
> *I picked it up and kept it for u*
> *(because it may shine*
> *again*

*

The second traffic fine reads as follows: OPERATED MOTOR VEHICLE
CA52476 WHICH WAS EQUIPPED WHITH A PNEUMATIC TYRE OF
WHICH THE RUBBER COVERING WAS SO WORN OR DAMAGED
THAT THE FABRIC OR CORD USED IN THE CONSTRUCTION OF
SUCH TYRE WAS EXPOSED.

*

Harry steps back and sits on Reuben's bed.

"You shouldn't neglect Clara. She looks forward to her outings with you. I know she can be difficult but have a heart, Rube, she's your sister! How are you ever going to love someone else if you can't find an hour a week for her? You're the only she feels relaxed with."

Clara is sixteen and neurotically introverted. Harry is right. She does love and feel at ease with Reuben; in fact, she loves and trusts him more than she does her mother and father. But Reuben finds her repulsive. An expression of Clara's depression is a refusal to wash. She gives off a smell of smell and vinegar, and her hair is always unkempt and greasy.

He has no desire to talk about her. It is her third year since her breakdown. The family tragedy is not one they have easily learnt to live with. Clara was a brilliant, confident child but adolescence unhinged her; this entry into larger world of people's expectations and demands, the world of the body with its strange, twisted dreams.

*

On his arm is a moth. It has been sitting suspended on a cushion of hair. The moth is grayish brown and has yellow markings across the triangles of its wings and centre section. The gold markings stand out brilliantly – the lower one in the shape of a broken boomerang, the upper a more defined curl in the middle of each wing creating the shape of a seagull. The tiny, delicate creature perched on his arm forms a perfect equilateral. Antennae raised, it is a picture of both calm and vigilance. Reuben feels that it has chosen him, and that this, without doubt, is a lucky omen.

*

Under the economics text book is a second page of Reuben's letter to Veronica Gomes. It conjures up the perfume of pine cones crushed into a wave of hair that cascades about an oval face whose twin centres are two coal black eyes, and whose equipoise is maintained by a perfect half-peach of a mouth whose lips come together and melt into scarlet .

"Yesterday I was in my room and a storm came up. In seconds, the tin roof was drumming so loudly I could barely hear the Schubert symphony I had been listening to on the record player. I thought back to that afternoon we spent at Grant's father's farm; the walk we took in a apple orchard and then by the lake, and how when a cloudburst took us by surprise, you unbuttoned my shirt and licked me under my arms, and then you ran away when I wanted to kiss you. I still do not understand why you pushed me away after you had shown me your desire."

On the fourth page of this same letter, Reuben will write in this manner of her departure at Cape Town airport:

I sat watching the aeroplanes on the run way. I saw the sun glint on their wing; a row of sleek, perfect machines ready to do the impossible. Nearby, a man and a woman sat talking and laughing with their children. The youngest, a girl, curled up on her father's lap. The older boy ran around the table asking questions about aeroplanes. And I wondered if you and I will be like them in twenty years time, with our own close, loving family; all familiar, secure and attentive. Then I wondered how you will react to this fantasy. Probably think me sentimental and respectable, not exciting enough. That may be true, but still, I don't think it will be a bad way to live."

*

Silvia Levine enters the room and places a cup of tea next to the typewriter.
"Reuben, don't forget to get milk from the kaffie before supper."
"I haven't forgotten, ma"
She turns to Harry." What are you nattering to him about? Let him finish his work. Exams are coming up in a week."
"Don't worry, Silvia. We're just having a chat."
"Chat after supper, the roast is almost ready. I told Doris to make rice, not potatoes. I couldn't face potatoes again. And peas. She's just opening a tin."
"Darling we're talking about Uncle Bennie."
"Leave off already! You and your obsession with Bennie! When I think of what your poor mother did for him and the shameless way he treated her afterwards. Really, it makes my blood boil!"
"Silvia, for God's sake! Did you expect him to leave his own family in Jo'burg and move to Kimberley? He had everything to lose. In any case, what difference would it have made? Mom and Dad were never going to make a success of it, they were too cautious. They didn't have the head for business."

*

In the small waste paper bin under the desk, there is space for just one more sheet of paper on which Reuben will write a postscript. This after-thought will not be included in the letter he currently agonizes over and will finally post two months later.

"The young Malay woman working at the bar washing glasses has closely cropped, very lush black hair whose curls roll out in sharp, abrupt waves. She picks up a broom, walks to the middle of the restaurant and begins sweeping round the tables. Once she has finished, and the fallen food gathered into a neat pile, an older woman with missing front teeth and bland, flat features passes a wet mop over the area. As I look up from the floor, you plane has already lifted off the ground and is climbing out over False Bay, the family at the nearby table has stood up to leave and I am seized with the knowledge that we will never kiss again."

*

His mother comes back in the room and tells him that supper is finally ready.

APPETITES

"November 7th is dedicated to the people who made the Russian revolution and pioneered the creation of socialism against enormous odds. Before telling the story of their achievements for the benefit of new generations of South African freedom fighters, we need to remind ourselves of the impact of the Revolution on our country and its people - both oppressors and oppressed - six thousand miles distant from the centre of the revolution and the rise of Progressive Power.

"On this day we celebrate the fact that there has never been a time when people did not rebel against the difficulties and miseries of everyday life. In every age of which we have a record, whether from history, literature and song, or from legend, men and women have dreamt of a new and better world; the record is filled with accounts of their longings, and sometimes too of their actions to bring that better world about. The greater the brutalities and oppressions of the world in which they lived, the more people turned to dreaming, fantasizing of a way of life which would redress their sufferings. Such dreams inspired religions, prophets and sects of many kinds who have visions of a new dawn, a new social order. Through the ages a common thread runs in those dreams and visions. In the new world - so the dream inevitably ran - there would be no more divisions, no more hostilities, between masters giving orders and servants carrying them out. There would be neither rich, powerful and privileged nor poor and weak. Instead there would be a community of equals."

Extracts from 'Seventy Years of Power'
A tribute to the Russian revolution by the South African Communist Party

ABOUT BERNARD

The first anxiety attack had taken place exactly a year before. Late afternoon on the M1, driving past a golf course on his way to a meeting in Woodmead, the BMW almost steering itself, the tape of Simon and Garfunkel's 'Greatest Hits' pouring out from the speakers, he had caught sight of a white ball soaring over the highway. And suddenly he was that white golf ball, leaving a faint vapour trail over the six lanes of cars and trucks, then slamming down into a clump of bushes on the far side under which a rusting beer can and two soggy condoms were half-covered by a plastic bag. And as he tore through the air, more terrifying than the inexplicable transference and the bullet-like trajectory was his knowledge that, thereafter, he would lie lost to the world, suffering an endless attrition of rain, lightning, hail, mist and heat-stroke, until finally, cracked and peeled, all scabrous and smeared, he was reduced to a tiny blackened core.

The attack almost overwhelmed him - the abrupt spinning that was the earth losing focus - but he managed to pull over to the side of the highway, and grope for his cell phone, and press the automatic dialling code for his office. However, when the switchboard operator answered, before he could tell her where he was and what was happening, he was gripped by paralysis, and blacked out. Half an hour later, he woke up in the car, drenched with sweat but reasonably coherent and able to drive again. Back at home in Northcliff, he concealed his shock and distress and told no one.

A month later he had another attack, this time late at night. He was alone in his office working on a fast food ad. Knocking a hamburger off his desk, in the same mysterious way that he had become the golf ball, he became the tomato-sauced meat-cake as it revolved madly then fell to the carpet. Once more the consuming fear was that he would remain grounded, immobile, forever unseen, rotting, suffocating in dust and cobwebs, to be gradually picked apart by cockroaches, ants and other minuscule scavengers.

And so it was that Bernard lived under this new shadow. The months went by, attacks recurring at odd intervals without warning, each bringing the same sensation. He strained to assert his self-control but in trying to, there was an additional aggravation: there was no obvious explanation for his instability.

He had slowly filled the vacuum after his separation from Lucille with a string of companions, and his resentment at the manner of his having been forced to leave politics, the bitterness and emptiness that for so long choked his vitality, had finally ebbed. A whole generation had changed, all his old comrades moved on to new positions. Now he was known for other things: contacts in advertising and the rights to stage American musicals, rehashes of old Broadway shows and song repertoires; these kept him busy, and made him rich. And being in the entertainment business guaranteed a relentless round of social activity during which he lubricated the wheels of connection with glass after glass of tequila and mango juice. Thus, though the attacks were serious, they were not fatal - the world did not lose its attractions, however precarious and expensive, however slight. And the creeping baldness that exposed the dome of his forehead made him look distinguished; and the paunch spilling against his soft leather belt, requiring the opening of a further notch each year, was proof of good appetite and sensual enjoyment.

At the same time, let it be said, Bernard had always aspired to be neither selfish nor spineless. He still wanted to believe that he was one of the rare ones who is able to unleash and satisfy the needs and desires of the ego whilst at the same time obeying the imperative to temper and rein them in.

BERNARD AND DUMA GO SHOPPING

They were in Pick 'n Pay, Duma pushing a trolley while Bernard loaded it with the delicacies he knew others loved and appreciated. The pile grew higher.

"Hey, easy! I'm going to get a hernia, man! In any case, it's not worth it. This cocktail party you've planned is a. . ."

The pile almost collapsed.

Duma, struggling to keep things from falling, realigned the trolley. Bernard winked and threw in another pate - it jammed between a bottle of gherkins and a tin of anchovies. Duma pushed back his dreadlocks. As Bernard berated him, "Keep pushing, jou bliksem!" they came in view of the bakery.

Duma hated supermarkets with their fake light and piled shelves of duplicated things. Though he had never travelled north of the Limpopo, he would speak eloquently about the markets of Africa and the Middle East - the dustiness and the freshness; the sounds of traders calling out, barking dogs, crying children, squawking chickens; the sheen of fabrics and fruit; the intermingling of too sweet perfumes and the gagging stench of shit. For Bernard, however, the one-stop Johannesburg shopping malls were the acme of modern freedom: hygienic, well-processed and packaged products stacked in impeccable order under bright neon, all offering immediate pleasure and gratification.

"We've already got rolls. Keep going. This has got to be it, I can't see over the top."

Duma bent down to push the trolley past the dairy section and swung it round to the pay points.

"Leave those cheeses! Hands off, you vark!"

The line was long. Bored, abstracted faces eyed the racks of chocolates and gossip magazines stacked at the pay points.

"And what's the idea of inviting all these people who have nothing in common?"

They were at the car. The trolley was finally empty, pushed back to the side of the parking lot, the boot crammed with waves of plastic bags. Duma sat holding the wine bottles while Bernard drove them out of the spiral shaped complex. On the dashboard was the bent manuscript of a play.

At a robot Bernard, ignoring a man selling *Homeless Talk*, launched into a diatribe. He described how frustrated he was by the play's excessive twists and turns; he had been confused by the digressions, supposedly elaborating emotions and ideas about emotion; and the plot itself jarred, the action sparking up, then dying entirely in accordance with the author's caprice.

Bernard talked all the way to the house. Then, while he locked the car in the garage and set the alarm, he identified further weaknesses in the script, noting the esoteric interchange of identities and relationships, the inadequate build-up of tension, the climax that meandered off into fantasy. But most of all, he was irritated by the obvious revelation that no one is clean, everyone tainted, compromised by a web of conflicting needs.

Duma walked into the kitchen carrying the grocery bags. He held three in each hand, the plastic handles looping, stretched to their limits. Duma asked Bernard what he intended doing with the play. Bernard stopped next to the fridge.

"You know what? I'm going to stage it if certain changes are made." Playing with his bunch of keys, he added, "Ja, despite all the problems, there are scenes of absolute brilliance." Bernard watched as Duma lifted the bags onto the stainless steel sideboard. "Despite all those very real limitations, I've rarely come across a script that's excited me so much with its extraordinarily varied yet unmistakable characterization. Each of the characters is completely individual, yet it's obvious they share the same overall culture." He opened the fridge and began arranging milk cartons in the open spaces. "They're unmistakably South Africans, but very different South Africans. They come from completely different ghettoes yet each one speaks a common, underlying language." He tickled the big grey Persian cat that arched against his leg. "Ah, it's one thing for me to talk, but you know what? She won't agree. She's arrogant and never takes advice, no matter how constructive and well-intended . . . one of those people who can't stand being corrected."

Duma began shoving tins onto the shelf above the sink, smashing them against each other. Bernard pushed him in the ribs.

"Hey! I'm joking! I'm not going to put it on. It's not as good as yours! You're a stronger writer. You know how to immediately define. She can't sustain things." Bernard patted Duma on the back. "You're in no danger, my friend, even though you're a failed playwright and a drunken poet. In fact, I need you to do a rewrite before I speak to her."

"Jesus, Bernard, stop your bloody games! It's almost three years since you agreed to direct 'Exiled at Home'. Do you realize that? Three years listening to your promises! And every time there's a chance to do it, something else takes its place. You always want to do something else as soon as my play is in line."

Bernard began unpacking the fruit cans.

"You can't put them there. I always keep fruit cans on the bottom shelf. If there's an earthquake, this stuff can fall on your head."

DUMA MAKES VARIOUS PLEAS AND IS REBUFFED

It was mid-afternoon. The house with its large windows overlooking the valley was cool with the shade of trees. They could hear the scurrying of birds across the lawns blend into the drone of cars.

Duma's eyes softened. "When can you do a production?"

The fridge hummed.

"Duma, we've been through this so many times! You know as well as I do, to invest is to use money to make more money. Where does that leave your work? Who will take a chance with a story that meanders on about meeting basic needs and the unemployment crisis? Money thinks before it splays itself across anyone's palms - your's and mine included." Bernard took down the last tin of guavas. "Esoteric visions of Love and Meaning in the middle of this Chaos." He began stacking the tins in the cupboard next to the vegetable rack. "Your work is too tortured, overwhelmed by problems. Lighten up, my bra. We're in a new world of equal opportunity."

Duma crumpled the Pick 'n Pay bags in his fist and compressed them into a tight ball. Then he threw the ball against the dustbin. Bernard watched the crushed plastic uncoil.

"Why be angry? Don't you recognize the objective forces? Who can believe your plot? Your obsession with revolution is crazy. How can there be radical change in this country? The ruling power bloc is too strong, their wealth, their technology and their ideological control are too powerful and sophisticated to be challenged. In any case, they buy off whoever stands in their way. For Christ's sake, wake up! Everyone else has." He placed an arm round Duma. "Come on, pour us something to drink. I'm thirsty after all that running down aisles. I'll open the macadamia nuts. I got them specially for you. Just don't sulk. For God's sake, don't sulk, that's all."

Bernard opened the fridge.

Duma shouted, "Face your self! Face where we are! Don't talk to me about fucking nuts!"

Bernard almost overturned a chair.

"I am facing myself! That's exactly what I'm doing. It's a pity you haven't gotten round to that. You know how difficult it was. You know what a long process it was to leave the Party, how agonizing a decision. Don't come and tell me I'm a sell-out! I fought the cabal. You know how they manipulate, how they play with people. Especially Nyati, your strategist, your organizational genius."

Bernard glared and Duma folded his arms. When the telephone rang a few moments later, neither moved. The telephone positioned on the oak counter opposite the fridge was a Victorian piece that Bernard had brought back from Paris, an elegant fixture which cost twice its original price to restore.

The phone rang and rang. Bernard stalked out of the kitchen to the bathroom. With a sudden lunge, Duma answered.

"Hi, I'm fine. He's busy at the moment. Should I call him?" There was a pause. "Lost your invitation? Don't worry, mfo. I'll give you a new one at the door. There's a whole pack coming - the usual sour faces and some English director who wants a co-production." There was another longer pause. "No, just savouries. He says he's too tired to make duck and dumplings. He's been whining the whole day that cooking is spoiling his waistline. Make it by seven, before the speeches start. Of course, it's a crass idea. Bad taste has no limits. I mean, defeat shouldn't lead to ridicule."

Bernard flushed the toilet.

Duma was still talking. "Good, see you in an hour. Sharp."

BERNARD ENTERS ANOTHER ZONE

He opened the bathroom door. Ahead of him, the big mirror reflected the shower and its curtain, the taps of the washbasin, the medicine chest nailed to the side of the mirror. And there, sleek and gleaming, covered with bubbles, leaning against the bath rim, smiling with all the whiteness of her teeth, was Nondumiso.

Bernard stopped.

"Oh, darling," he said. "I didn't know you'd arrived. If only I'd known."

He kicked the door closed and taking her face in his hands, kissed her forehead, licking her lashes with his tongue.

"When did you come?"

"About an hour ago. I was feeling all grubby so I thought I'd freshen up for you."

"For me?"

"Yes, for you, you silly man." She began stroking his pants and he felt himself begin to throb. "When's Taylor coming?"

"At eight."

"Have you given him my CV?"

"I faxed it last week."

"I want that part, Bernie. I want it."

"I know. I know, darling."

"Is he definitely coming?"

"He confirmed about an hour ago."

"I hope that little whore with the silver hair isn't around."

"He's with some German woman. Another independent."

"Oh, Bernie. Just imagine me going to London!"

"I'll miss you."

"I'll miss you too, darling. But you know what a chance this will be for me!"

She leaned back and he covered her with bubbles: the flat, firm, ebony expanse of waist; the high, slightly oblong breasts; the sharp, jutting shoulder blades.

"Why didn't you come last night? I stayed up till two o'clock."

"The rehearsals are coming together now. Things are getting really intense."

"You could have phoned."

"The public phone was broken."

"What about the phone in the office?"

"No one had the key."

"And Rick's cell phone?"

"He forgot to charge it." Nondumiso fondled his hand. "Stop getting uptight. You're the only one. You know that, don't be boring! Where could I find such a generous creature? Come closer. Let me give you some honey."

Her mouth wrapped round him; her warmth was overpowering. Then he felt her broad, strong tongue stroke him as her slender hands caressed his buttocks.

"Oh, my darling!"

He was floating in a world of warm lappings, cooings, sliding in and out, straining to be deeper, always deeper, past the tender, moist lips that were sucking him into the spiraling, dark shelter of total release. Now he was pressing her to his groin, naming her his loved one. In their absolute ability to please each other, they reached a simultaneous climax.

DUMA AND JAN DISCUSS A MUTUAL FRIEND

When the doorbell rang, Duma picked up the front gate keys and switched off the alarm system.

"Coming!" he called. "Shit, you've been quick."

"Ja, I've got to learn two scenes tonight but I couldn't resist your pitch. Hoe gaan dit, my skat?"

Duma opened the gate for Jan who stood next to the bougainvillea hedge, helmet squeezed against his leather jacket, streaked blonde hair dangling over his face. The big silver motorbike stood in the carport. They shook hands then embraced. Duma tickled his chin.

"By the way, you never mentioned what you wanted with our Great Director."

"Want anything from him? Nee, wat!"

"It isn't just the chow, is it?"

They walked into the lounge past an unframed canvas of a naked, small-breasted woman resting on a rock at Clifton. In the background, a single cloud floated alongside Lion's Head. The woman was painted in strong pink and brown flesh tones. Her face showed total sun rapture. Bernard had bought the painting on the Parade during the Cape Town run of one of his farces. He'd hung it in his bedroom, but after meeting Nondumiso decided to move it.

Duma threw himself into an easy chair splotched with giant purple flowers. "This time I'm not joking. I'm not prepared to work with him any more. He's abusing our friendship." Jan placed his helmet on the carpet. "He's making demands beyond our professional relationship but he won't pay me extra. He expects weekend work for nothing. And tonight he wants me to rewrite a script. Some new play by a woman he's never heard of. Suddenly it's the most brilliant thing he's read in years but I've got to redo ninety percent of it. Can you believe it?" Duma spread his hands. "Can't you speak to him? I'm really upset."

Jan combed back his hair. "You know what the Chinese say: if you go to war, be prepared for war. Now make me some coffee - that Turkish stuff. Make it thick with two sugars." Duma switched on the kettle. "What's happening with your play? Is he going to do it now?"

Duma took out two mugs and a side plate.

"Are you crazy?"

"I thought he was casting."

"Jesus, Jan! He hasn't even read my rewrite of the second act, which is crucial. No, as usual, he's stalling. Haven't you heard about `objective forces'?" Duma measured out a heaped spoon of coffee. "This enough?"

"A bit more."

"You can't believe how reactionary he's become. He's concocted the most elaborate rationalizations, he's commercialised all the issues. And the worst thing is how he lies to himself and then pretends no one's the wiser. Then, on the other hand, he's always worried what others think. He's petrified of bad press. I mean, his leaving the Party and then going into business was noted by a lot of people." Duma poured the hot water.

Jan nodded. "Ja, he's still very pissed off about that leadership struggle. He hasn't adjusted. He liked being a big shot in the bigger picture."

The mugs were full. Duma placed them on a tray and carried them back into the living room.

"I'm sick of trying to justify his behaviour. First he's rude then he falls all over me. He changes his mind every two minutes. He can't take a decision and stick to it." Duma kicked Jan's boot. "But I can't afford to leave yet." He paused. "I've got to feed my appetites."

Then he picked up an exercise book that lay on a side table on which stood five wooden giraffes. Bernard had bought them from a young boy in a parking lot at one of the observation points overlooking the Blyde River canyon.

"Check what I wrote yesterday. I was alone here and the sky was split by lightning. It's a prose poem." Duma pushed the book into Jan's hands. "Read it, man. Read it and tell me what you think."

Jan held the book in his hands. "OK, I'll read it. But if it's kak I'm going to tell you."

"Feedback, man. That's all I want. Straight talk, nothing less."

Jan read two pages then moved to the window and looked out at the distant towers of the city's skyline. The room overlooked a lush green hive of expansive, walled, swimming-pooled houses and one of the flanks of the Melville Koppies.

"Sorry, old chap, it is kak." He took out a pipe and lit a match. "Stick to drama, man. That's your scene."

Jan began sucking and the room filled with a sweet aroma. "Why bother about him if things are so bad? Don't let him get away with it. He's not the only director in Jo'burg. You can get other jobs. You've got credibility."

"Credibility? Don't talk shit! I wasn't in jail and I wasn't in exile. I stayed put, year after year, trying to write People's Theatre. I wasn't out there in Lusaka trying to liberate Swedish millions." Duma kicked the tanned cowboy boot again. "Don't you know there's a purge going on? Those who want real change in this country are being marginalised."

"And what's wrong with that?"

Duma removed his shoe and threw it. "Don't give me your line about no change is real change." He shook his head. "If I don't have a job, how will I have time to write? I need a steady income. Otherwise I get so depressed hustling for bucks that all I do is drink."

"Pass me the coffee, man. I can smell it from here. Are there any biscuits?"

"It's depressing. I get fucking messed up." Duma smiled. "Only rusks and you can't soak rusks in Turkish coffee."

"I'll soak your head in it if I want to. Bring them." Jan stood up. "But first, my little piccanin, let me soothe your brow. I can see those back muscles are all stiff. Let me relax them."

NONDUMISO MEETS AN OLD FLAME AND IS REIGNITED

Bernard and Nondumiso walked into the lounge. Bernard opened his arms.

"What a wonderful surprise! I was worried you wouldn't make it."

"I thought I must show solidarity," Jan answered. Then he blushed as Nondumiso ran up and kissed him on the cheek.

"I'm so glad you've come." She looked at him with affection. "Still got your bike?" Jan nodded. "I loved those rides we took over the golf course."

Bernard took her hand.

"It's going to be an intimate little gathering, nothing pretentious, you know, in keeping with the occasion. Frankly, I need a little social variety. It becomes tedious to only engage with a certain incompetent dramatist."

Jan sipped his coffee; a crumb of rusk dangling from his moustache. Duma had placed four rusks on a porcelain plate that Bernard had bought in East London. He had spent some weeks there during the run of a West End drama about a man who is involved with both his personal assistants - one a man, the other a woman. The plate's surface was ringed with lambs chasing each other's tails round a spindly bush.

Duma looked at Nondumiso with distaste. "Sneaking in as usual."

She stuck out her tongue.

Jan remembered the golf course. He had offered her a lift home on the night of the first rehearsal of a two-hander they had done for the Grahamstown Festival. The play was about a Hillbrow prostitute who befriends a Nigerian drug dealer. The twist was that the Nigerian was white.

"This coffee is excellent."

"It is," said Duma. "Bernard gets it from some Saudi businessman who's in with M-Net. Do you want to know how many camels have contributed their dung to flavour it?"

Bernard picked up a rusk and dropped it into Jan's mug. "Go on, enjoy. I've always respected you. You play the rugged parts very well, especially the heroes, the ones who leave women behind. You abandon them stylishly, not like me."

He gestured to Nondumiso, and pulled her towards him, at first playfully, then with increasing force as she resisted and laughingly tried to twist free.

"Those soap commercials you did at Zoo Lake were a real highpoint, real Tarzan stuff, my darling."

Jan flicked a strand of blonde hair from his eyes. Bernard pulled Nondumiso onto his lap and buried his face in her back. Then he brought his hands out from behind her and waved.

"Why should she kill the one she loves when he's about to give her everything she dreams of? She just needs to wait a little longer." She pushed his hands down as he tried to hold her tighter. "Isn't that so, my love?"

Nondumiso smiled at Jan. "Has this old crock given you any work lately?"

"Of course he has!" Duma snapped, fishing out the remnants of the rusk in Jan's mug. "There's a special role earmarked for Jannie-boy in a musical. He's going to play a Broederbond law professor who leaves the university to devote himself to governing Die Volk and all the other natives, and in the process sets up that marvel of the civilised world, Bantu Education. Ja, our Jannie is getting lots of work. He's diligent because he's a Calvinist - even if he is a little short of hellfire."

Nondumiso stroked Bernard's knee. Jan sipped his mug.

"Can I have another one?"

"Of course, liefling," said Duma. Wedging open Jan's mouth, he shoved in a particularly large rusk. "There now, Onse Jan happy?"

"Are you going to give him the part, Bernard?"

Bernard pressed her hand.

"What's the big deal, Bernie? Tell us! Is he going to play Retief? If you suggest it, Taylor will agree. And then I can play Dingaan's queen, the first wife."

Bernard smoothed her hand.

"Let's get down to business," Duma snarled, as Jan cleaned the corners of his mouth.

101

BERNARD HAS ANOTHER ATTACK

He felt it start in his chest, a sharp thudding that made him feel he was being remorselessly sucked into the black void of LET ME DIE I'VE HAD ENOUGH. He was cold and liquid and tremulous: he had become the gob of spit that hovered on Duma's lips and would soon cascade down in a spidery arc to the parquet floor.

Then he collapsed, lay spread-eagled, a splattered, bubbling pool of saliva at the mercy of even the most ragged kitchen cloth. And Duma hovered over him, frayed lappie in hand dripping dirty sink water onto his face; Duma exuded a cat-like hissing. Next to him, wide-eyed with shock, stood Nondumiso and Jan; her sinewy arm resting lightly on Jan's leather jacket.

"Chickening out, Bernie? For Christ's sake face the fucking music. I insisted Jan join us so I'd have a witness. It's time we sorted something out. I've been your assistant for almost five years. That's right, five long years during which I've been getting a pittance, a few measly bucks for all my trouble. I've been sweating away down here on the ground while you've been climbing the ladder of success, darling of the festivals, here in our Beloved Country and there over the blue seas, all the way to New York and Dakar and Berlin, with different productions about the Struggle. Ja, Bernie, you've been getting all the pats on the back, and on the cheeks, and never on the arse, or just occasionally on the arse, while I've been sucking my pencils getting nowhere. And now you're sitting pretty in this lekker little pondokkie on Northcliff ridge with zebras and flamingos, and I'm still stuck in Dobsonville without running water. Jesus." Duma pulled at his dreadlocks. "I'm sick and tired of being fucked over." He pulled out a piece of paper and pushed it into Bernard's hand.

"Sign." He turned to Jan. "Sign next to him."

The document was a contract setting out a basic wage rate, an overtime rate, a Sunday work rate, a public holiday rate and conditions covering paid compassionate leave, sick leave, paternity leave, annual leave, study leave as well as provisions for a housing allowance and a transport allowance.

At the end of the contract, in large print, was a clause stipulating the following:

I, Bernard Halton Innes, resident at 99 Teak Drive, Northcliff, being of sound mind and body, enter into this undertaking of my own free will and volition. It is hereby recorded that the four act play, Exiled at Home, by Duma `The Spear' Mofokeng, shall be performed at the Barney Simon

Memorial Theatre at the Market Theatre, Newtown, Johannesburg, within six months of the date of the signing of this contract. However, should Exiled at Home, for whatever reason, by design or by accident, not be staged within this six month period, a penalty of R50,000 shall be payable to the playwright on the second day following the expiry of the six month period. This amount to be paid out in South African currency and not with bullshit or cow shit or horse shit or donkey shit or wildebeest shit or any other variety of kakstorie."

Bernard leaned back on the carpet and folded his arms behind his neck. The gob of spit had been wiped away; he was calm. How could Duma try to humiliate him? He had done so much for him, year after year, pulling him along, and now this.

"I'm not going to give anyone, and especially not you, whom I befriended and for whom I have created so many opportunities, the satisfaction of manufacturing a fight which can only end in your losing everything." He caressed Nondumiso's fingers. "But now that we're talking, perhaps you'll tell us how far you are with the script I gave you last January. Where is it? And where's that documentary you were supposed to be working on? And the collection of short stories you had almost wrapped up? Where, where, where? Have you finished any of them yet? Poor boy, he's all snowed under with projects."

Bernard sat up and poked Duma in the stomach.

"Listen, comrade, if you want more, you've got to do more. Productivity is the name of the game and you rank low in those stakes. As for Exiled at Home, if you really insist, let's try and raise some money through Winnie."

EVERYONE FINALLY GETS DOWN TO BUSINESS

The porcelain design with crumbs of rusk lay bare to their eyes as sunset washed through the windows. In the garden, a jacaranda showered purple explosions; the alarm wire strung along the hedge became a black snake sliding to protect them. On the side table carefully arranged on a white tablecloth, rested salads and loaves of onion bread, platters filled with pate, pies and cold meats, bowls brimming with assorted dips and other delicacies.

"So you want me to lick your arse forever? Is that the idea, Mr Director?"

Bernard got to his feet, faced the side table and uncorked a bottle of white wine. "No, my boy, that's not what I said or what I intended. I would simply like a little respect and acknowledgment for what I have done. And that is as much as anyone wants and has a right to. I have given you the breaks, now it's up to you to use them. Put yourself in the right frame of mind and get on with the job."

"I am getting on with the job, Bernard! Exiled at Home is ready. It's waiting to explode! Christ, when was the last time you looked at it? In fact, have you bothered to read the last act since I did that rewrite?"

Nondumiso massaged Bernard's shoulders as he began filling glasses.

"Have you, darling?" She asked sweetly, then ran a sharp nail down his back. "Come on, give him a break."

"Honey, there's no market for that type of theatre anymore! You know that, I know that, we all know that. What drew crowds yesterday is not what's packing them in today. Fact. End of story."

"Just a small production, Bernie, nothing elaborate. Test the waters, just a one week run at the 'Laboratory'. You know, a . . ."

"Dammit, Jan! Whose side are you on? I don't want some small time experiment with half trained actors. I want the real thing!"

Duma grabbed his arm but Jan only laughed.

"Boyo, you've got to start somewhere. And the Laboratory is where they all start."

"But those are kids! They've had two or three script writing classes and they crank out a play and think they've mastered the medium. Shit, I've got years in this game!"

"Duma, the fact is times are hard, theatre is a dying art form, everyone's talking screens - big ones, small ones."

"But there's a core who still want the real thing!"

"A small core? We all love Coca Cola, pal."

"Shit, Bernard, where's the last drop of your progressive consciousness?"

"Hey, Comrade, it's right here in my hand." He knocked back the last of his perfectly chilled white wine. "I don't think we should wait for the others. Let's start our little commemoration. It's late already and I can see you're all starving."

When the English director arrived almost two hours later, a fresh crate of wine was raised from the cellar, the platters with snacks were replenished and the looks of anger and self-pity on Duma's face gradually gave way to a forgiving contentment. At the same time Jan struck a deal with Bernard regarding the role of Retief, and Nondumiso was able to captivate the Englishman as his sidekick did not appear until nearly midnight when everyone raised their glasses to Bernard's toast.

"To the future of the global village, to the trafficking of ideas and products, to the spirit of adventure that quickens the blood, to the joys of sensual pleasure that are the rewards for risk taking, to the trickling down of these good things to the masses."

LIONESS

KEEP YOUR ENGINE RUNNING
KEEP YOUR WINDOWS HALF ROLLED
SHOULD THE LIONS BITE AT YOUR TYRES,
DRIVE SLOWLY FORWARD

The lion enclosure is surrounded by grassland; small herds of zebra and wildebeest roam the area which is bordered by an electrified perimeter fence and a ring of tarred roads. It is half past one in the afternoon and swelteringly hot. Miriam and I have just driven in. Across the way from us, a blonde man in a muddy white bakkie parked under a tree sits slouched at the wheel. In front of him, two drowsy lionesses paw at a carcass. The bakkie's windows are rolled down and the engine has been switched off. Miriam and are both dripping with sweat but, motionless behind the wheel, his cigarette creating a haze of smoke, the blonde man seems cool and distant.

On their haunches, gnawing bloody chunks of meat which are half covered with sand, the two big lionesses ignore us. Some distance away, sprawling in the sparse shade of a cluster of thorn trees and a eucalyptus, are the rest of the pride; about twenty lions panting and heaving, one on top of the other so that they seem to make up a single pulsing body whose most mobile feature is a multitude of mottled red tongues, all gasping for air, indifferent to the chunks of donkey flesh spread on the ant-covered earth.

The blonde man in the faded blue denim shirt doesn't lift his eyes.

"What's wrong with them, daddy?" Miriam points at the panting animals. "They look half dead." Then she points at the two lionesses ripping up the meat at their paws. "Only those two lions are strong. Look, daddy! Look at their teeth!"

"Not lions, darling. LIONESSES," I correct her. "See, they don't have all that hair round their heads like the daddy lions and they're smaller. But you know something, they're fiercer than the daddies and they're much better hunters."

Last night I had described this small game park near Jo'burg as a unique remnant of Africa in the times before the gun. I'd been a little drunk, it was after supper and I had indulged myself, presenting the park as a pristine environment, an example of what life was like before the human exercise of power over all other creatures. I had explained to Miriam what a revolution this has been - our dominating the planet and restricting, or wiping out, almost all other species. Now we only live with millions and millions of other human beings, plus our dogs and cats, birds and fishes, as well as the few other species we breed for our food, or for other practical uses. Yet our dreams are still so tied up with these defeated, trapped animals. Miriam is too young to understand what a symbol is. But by now she must see that the park is just a glorified zoo.

*

It's Sunday. The two of us are spending the last day of the year together. We're going to have a picnic lunch. This evening Miriam's rejoining her mother, Patricia, and flying down to Cape Town to spend the rest of the summer holidays. Miriam is five years old and is lively, affectionate and imaginative, although over the past three months I've picked up signs that her equilibrium's under pressure, may even be breaking on account of the strain of her mother's ongoing, relentless war against my girlfriend, Dominique. From the start, Patricia attacked and slandered Dominique claiming we had started an affair behind her back while she and I were still married. She speaks badly of her to Miriam, telling the child, over and over again, that Dominique was the cause of the break-up of our family. Patricia's refusal to accept my new relationship has forced us to suffer three years of stress and tension. She even knocked me out of the way with a chair once when I stopped her from taking Miriam out of my house. And last month she hinted that she may cut off my access to Miriam altogether. She knows this is the surest way to hurt me; and her bitterness is so great that poisoning all of our lives is preferable to allowing someone else the pleasure of my presence! To make matters worse, there's also the complication of Dominique's resentment and her own insecurities.

Yesterday Dominique attacked me for watching cricket on TV. At the time she was cooking supper and looking after Miriam. My position has always been: so what if I watch sport every now and again! I have enough pressure to deal with, I need to unwind and it's not as if I do no housework - she doesn't have to push me to fit a new rubber on the washing machine or repair the toaster. But lately she's been on edge, been on at me for 'lazing around' even though she knows I'm not a slob who spends the whole day switching channels. In fact, most of the time we do what she wants, which is to go out to an Italian or Chinese restaurant and then on to a movie. Although she hates TV sitcoms, Dominique will happily watch the big screen equivalent. But she ridicules my watching cricket despite the fact that I keep the volume down and fetch my own beers. What pisses her off is the camera's constant tracking of young girls in the stands. My point is that I watch the cricket, not the girls. And when I want to spend an evening without her, she accuses me of secretly desiring Patricia. I mean, really! All I do is occasionally go out to my friends, male friends, with whom I play bridge. That Dominique doesn't like their women isn't my problem. She thinks they're stupid, boisterous and cheap.

*

Miriam is dozing on the backseat. I'm also feeling wiped out. The car windows are half rolled down and the air inside feels compressed and heavy. I'm feeling doubly tired: apart from the heat, none of us had much sleep last night. There had been another argument with Dominique, who, once again, was upset by Miriam coming to our bed during the night. Dominique sees this as an invasion of our privacy and is determined to discipline her. I feel she's over-reacting - every adult should be sympathetic to the insecurity of a small child whose parents have separated. After all, the only reason Miriam wakes is because she has bad dreams. And she has bad dreams because of all the domestic conflict around her. So seeking comfort and reassurance, she comes to me, her father. Unfortunately this is between two and four o'clock almost every morning. What am I to do? Can I just order her back to her bed? Yes, it's a complicated situation. Particularly because there's another element: aside from my desire to comfort and reassure Miriam when she's had a nightmare, she and I have a very close physical bond. We're completely at ease with each other. We bath together, use the toilet in each other's presence and enjoy each other's nakedness. And because I know that this period of physical intimacy will end with her adolescence, I want to enjoy it fully while I can. After all, I know her more intimately that any other being on this planet and that is something I treasure. Every night, lying down together after reading a story, I sing her lullabies.

And yet, despite all these positive things, now with Dominique's insight, I see that in the past I made a bad mistake. Before Dominique and I began living together, I allowed Miriam to imagine she had replaced her mother and become 'the woman in my life'. This in turn led to her being jealous of Dominique who was supplanting her. The truth is that after my separation from Patricia I was very short of money and didn't have a clear idea of what I was going to do. The break-up had been very bitter and during that time I rented a flat that had only one bed. When Miriam came over on weekends we would sleep together in that bed, and as a result we built up a special contact. Yes, yes, you'll say, another daddy's girl! All these conflicting emotions!

On most issues Dominique is very understanding, but now her resentment has grown to the point where she's lost all perspective. She insists that our bed remain out of bounds to Miriam no matter the circumstances, and that should Miriam come to us, I must immediately take her back to her own bed. On this score she has become very adamant. But to be fair to Dominique, despite her vigorous position, a few weeks ago, during a particularly tense period with Patricia, she allowed Miriam to stay in bed with us. Snuggling up between us, Miriam dropped back to sleep. Without prompting, Dominique admitted that Miriam seemed genuinely scared. However, apart from the issue of bad dreams, she observed that Miriam was beginning to use other threats and doubts as justification for coming to us: rustling curtains, moving toys, strange shapes by the door. And this being the case, it was best for her to confront and overcome her fears on the battleground of their occurrence, namely, in her own bed. I agreed that Miriam should learn to be brave. I have always emphasized to her how important it is to stand up for yourself and for what you believe in. But I feel bad, knowing that her insecurities are on account of us, the adults in her life, and our messed up relationships. I've always tried to reason with Miriam, explaining exactly why and on what grounds I've taken a decision on her behalf, but on this issue I've had such mixed feelings that I probably failed to properly explain Dominique's position. So I'm feeling torn.

A week ago when we'd planned today's picnic, Dominique was lying snuggled up against me, it was late afternoon, the curtains were drawn, we were feeling tender and relaxed having spent the previous hour making love. The idea was that we'd go out, the three of us, together. But now she's at home and Miriam and I are taking strain on our own.

*

The bakkie is caked with mud. Freshly mown grass is scattered over the back section. Propped against a tyre is a hessian sack and a metal box. The blonde man slumps against the wheel. The two lionesses dawdle over the meat, their broad, red tongues, criss-crossed with marks, dripping saliva. I sense that the man has been sitting alone in the bakkie's cabin for a long

time. He seems oblivious to everything around him even though he must have seen and heard us.

*

For years I've tried to be even-handed. In particular, I try not to overcompensate by giving Miriam more attention than I give Dominique. "How can I?" I ask Dominique. "I love you both. Besides, you're an adult woman and Miriam is my child. How can I treat you in the same way?" Sadly, Dominique's insecurity relates not just to Miriam - it covers all other possible rivals. And here I'm talking about all other women. She refuses to believe that I'm absolutely faithful to her and that I'm to be believed when I say there's no one else with whom I could have a better relationship. As such she constantly seeks assurances that I'm not having affairs and though I embrace her with both my arms and my words, she continues to agonize over my supposed infidelities. Sometimes she laughs and says it's just who she is, not to be taken too seriously, it's not as if she's falling apart, she's just expressing herself, letting out her emotions; she's just being 'Italian'. On the other hand, when it comes to fear, Miriam dreams that I'm being cut up by small pieces of glass. Every night she replays my piecemeal destruction.

Let me put this in context. Patricia refers to Dominique as 'the rat' and tells Miriam bedtime stories based on gossip about Dominique's first marriage. She completely distorts Dominique's character, tries to make her out as weak and dependent. The truth is that Dominique, despite her hypersensitivity, is as determined and focused as Patricia. When I first met Patricia she was ambitious but easy going, relaxed, unpretentious. Now she's full of hype about fashions and networking and obsessed with making money. My greatest fear is that once I'm finally chopped down in the cross-fire, Miriam will be left fatherless. It's not difficult to imagine what personality distortions are likely to set in once she's in the sole hands of her mother. The other problem is that my own stress levels have reached danger point. I haven't been sleeping well so I'm on edge and start snapping - which I can't afford. I try to cool down then act as if the whole thing is already under control, even if it's spinning in a direction I'm not at all sure I can handle. This is my greatest challenge: keeping everything together in the face of our conflicting needs. It is this anxiety that I believe Miriam is picking up.

Another thing to bear in mind, which strikes me again and again, is that if it wasn't for Miriam, I wouldn't have any contact with Patricia. She'd be out of my life. She'd have made a total exit, apart from the odd flash of memory. When a relationship is over it's better to sever all contact. I don't believe in false intimacy. Otherwise people tend to develop false faces. On one side there is often still pain, longing and anger; on the other, either indifference or revulsion. I certainly don't love Patricia anymore though I once did and have never denied that, neither to her nor to Dominique. But to cut all ties would mean losing Miriam - something that is out of the question.

*

Another car, the latest, most expensive Mercedes, drives into the paddock. The driver is a thick-set, fleshy man in his sixties who looks like an old lock forward and rich mielie farmer. Next to him is a woman in her late fifties. The two of them ignore Miriam and look straight at me as if to say, "Why the hell as a responsible adult aren't you stopping this hysterical child from screaming at the lions?" I suppose they have a point. In trying to get the lions to move, Miriam has been making an unbelievable racket but the lions have been totally uncooperative, barely managing to lift their tails to swish away the hordes of flies buzzing round their nostrils.

"Shut up already!" I shout, but she carries on.

The mielie farmers sail by along the dirt track, passing between us and the bakkie. The blonde man doesn't seem to register their presence any more than he did ours.

Miriam stops screaming.

"Let's move on, love."

I'm about to reverse back onto the track when the Mercedes re-appears. The mielie farmer rolls down his window and barks, "Hey, do you know where the kaffie is?" I stare back. What a rude ugly man! I shake my head.

Miriam suddenly shouts, "It's by the gate! Down there over the hill."

"Are you sure that's the way?"

"Don't answer, Miriam!"

The farmer glares at me. They drive off. The blonde man lights another cigarette.

*

Dominique says that Miriam is instructed to spy on us, that every detail of our lives is relayed back to Patricia. Of course, such information is often distorted because of Miriam's unreliable five-year-old memory. What makes things worse is that Miriam sometimes tries to please Patricia by making up stories about Dominique's wickedness and stupidity, and by exaggerating the frequency and intensity of the conflicts between us. It goes without saying that the most popular theme is the 'Wicked Stepmother'. According to this ongoing story, Dominique doesn't give her proper attention, either by not serving her enough food at mealtimes or, if she does dish out generous enough portions, the food's rotten. Then, if the weather's cold, she refuses to provide Miriam with enough blankets at night. And if Miriam can't think of anything else, there's always the one in which Dominique forces her to wear dirty clothes or, at the very least, torn ones, or ones that are too small and too tight.

The other major irritation is that as soon as Dominique answers the phone, Patricia slams it down. And when Miriam is with us, she phones every day, often several times a day, so that this aggression is enormously disruptive. Quite apart from this tactic, Patricia talks endlessly to Miriam but I can't limit her calls because they're sometimes genuinely necessary. For instance, to make arrangements to pick Miriam up or to discuss nursery school matters. In most cases she phones to check on the child, to find out what she's doing and who she's with. She tries to disrupt the flow of her time and to also persuade Miriam to cut short her stay with us before the weekend is over. She tries to tempt her, proposes special parties and outings. Fortunately Miriam has begun to see through these tactics. The other day she said to me after one of these incidents, "Mommy is really being silly. She knows I'm not going back to her till Monday".

*

There's a thick, grubby lion smell mingling with the scent of eucalyptus leaves and the stench of meat. The blonde man's eyes still seem to be locked on the lionesses. Miriam tells me she can see his sunglasses on the roof of the bakkie. She's right. Towards the back of the roof, overturned next to a woman's handbag are a pair of silver-rimmed glasses. The outer surfaces catch the sun, sending a small concentrated ray towards us. The handbag is open; I see a cheque book and a small purse, partially hidden by the bag and a long, blue hairbrush.

The blonde man lights a match, lets it flare up along the side of the box. The box catches fire, bursts into flames. He throws the box out the window.

Miriam shouts, "Look what he's doing, daddy!"

114

The matchbox falls onto the sand and continues burning; underneath it blades of grass start to smoke.

Miriam claps her hands, "There's a fire, daddy!"

*

Apart from the hostility prompted by the night visits to our bed, Dominique shows Miriam affection and consideration and tries to incorporate her as much as possible into our life so that despite the tensions she should feel that we make up a family - even though we're a different kind of family. On her side, Miriam, despite occasional shows of anger, displays a great deal of affection towards Dominique. So much so, it crossed my mind that perhaps this is also disturbing Patricia: having already lost me to Dominique, she now sees her as another kind of rival, threatening her place as Miriam's mother. And who can tell if this fear isn't justified? When she's older, Miriam may yet incline towards Dominique. And because Patricia knows and fears this, she becomes angry and vindictive, trying at every opportunity to blacken and discredit Dominique in Miriam's eyes. Of course, I understand that in a situation of divorce, no parent easily accepts that their ex-spouse's new partner may be genuinely loved by their child. At the moment Miriam bitterly resents being banned from our bed, but in the not too distant future she may develop a far closer bond with an affectionate and lively Dominique than with her ranting and embittered mother.

*

Miriam hasn't been very enthusiastic about the park. She was only excited when a man in a Landrover stampeded a herd of wildebeest - the whirring of his video camera panicked the herd and we had the chance to watch the thirty odd animals scatter over the veld.

My mind swings back to last night. What a disaster!

Miriam's nightmare was the same one I've mentioned: I'm being pierced by extremely sharp, minute glass spears; I'm being lacerated and she is helpless. She loves her father and she can't stop the icy tips slashing him. I see myself stabbed, strength waning as each splinter lodges, penetrating my skin, puncturing and bloodying me. Somewhere round three o'clock in the morning Miriam woke up in fright and ran to our bedroom but Dominique told her to get back to her own bed. All I had wanted to do was sleep. Despite the holidays having already started, I felt depressed. Work this past year had been exhausting, nothing had gone right, just round after round of cajoling stupid buyers. Earlier on, we had spent the evening at Joe and Katrina's, our closest friends. And not for the first time I was forced to admit that they bored me. The evening had been tedious, all of us retelling the same stale anecdotes and jokes, the same rehashing of opinions. Coming home I'd fallen into a deep, almost drugged sleep. As a result, when Miriam came into our bedroom and pushed up against me, despite my previous agreement with Dominique not to allow this, I let her stay. Dominique woke up and shouted at Miriam to get back to her bed. When neither Miriam nor I reacted, Dominique threw off the blankets and ran to switch on the light.

*

The matchbox flares up, the grass and small twigs surrounding it catch fire but the blonde man, instead of jumping out of the bakkie and stamping on it, takes another matchbox out of the cubbyhole and lights the cigarette he's holding in his mouth.

The fire starts to spread.

"Hey! There's a fire!" I call out to him. "Under your window!"

He drags deeply, then slowly exhales. For a few seconds we can hardly see him because of the thick plumes of smoke that pour out of his mouth, tobacco smoke mixing with the smell of burning grass.

Miriam shouts, "Daddy, he's lighting his shirt!"

Leaning back in the bakkie's cabin, the blonde man has pulled up a corner of his shirt, and stretching it tight with one hand, holds match after match to the edge. Sweat pours off us. What craziness is this! But after a few more attempts, the blonde man drops the edge of his shirt. It has failed to catch alight.

"Look, Daddy! He's opening the door!"

Then Miriam says she wants to swim, she's had enough of the lions and this strange man who does funny things. I smile and pat her cheek. She's been very patient. Perhaps we should leave. The blonde man certainly seems over the top. Why should I allow him to frighten Miriam more than he has? As for the lions, what is to be said about their heaving, listless bodies, prone and motionless but for the odd flick or shake of a head or tail in order to dislodge clouds of flies?

116

*

Dominique was crying uncontrollably while Miriam huddled next to me. All I could think was that Dominique was being unreasonable: tonight was a valid exception - the child had been away for over three weeks because Patricia had kept her longer than agreed, and she was uncertain of her position, torn by the loyalties she had to each house. As a result her subconscious was throwing up a monster that only love and Daddy's warm bed could defeat. Though blinded by the shock of the bedroom light and feeling exhausted, I knew I had to act. I forced myself to my feet, and told Miriam to come with me to her room. Dominique was still shaking with rage. I lay next to Miriam in her bed. While I hummed a comforting song, she quickly fell asleep. Then I prepared blankets for myself on the settee in the living room.

I was seething, lashing out in my mind against the suffocating sense of being trapped - knowing that Patricia will never accept that I do not love her and that she will continue to attack Dominique. Caught between Dominique, the 'rat', and Patricia, the aggrieved wife and mother, there will always be negative swings in Miriam's feelings which I will have to deal with. In addition, I will also have to bear the brunt of the pressure on Dominique. Whether I stayed or left, I would always have to live with crisis and loss. Then, after what seemed an age, the question formulated itself: if you're mentally healthy, why consent to live in a locked room?

I lay awake, horribly tired, wondering what to do once I'd taken Miriam back to Patricia. Suddenly Dominique walked into the lounge, stood next to me and said she was going out. It was now after four o'clock – the darkest, loneliest time of night. I looked at her in astonishment. Then I thought, why not? Let her go. Let her go so I can also do what I like. I closed my eyes. A few moments later, I felt her hand on my cheek. She was dressed in her tightest, most revealing black dress - the one she knows causes waves. I thought to myself, "Alright, let the stupid woman go now and give me some peace." Then I analyzed my resentment, even as it gripped me. I was caught between too many needs. And if I tried to take the easy way out, I couldn't, because there was no easy way out. Whatever I did, I was damned. Of course, the most difficult thing in the world is the struggle to overcome one's own weaknesses; and in balking at the task, the stock response is to deny them.

I heard her leave by the side door. The house was quiet. There was only the inner hum of blood rushing through my ears. Yes, Dominique was right, but on this occasion, unjustified. She knew that Miriam was particularly unsettled; she should have taken that into account before exploding and causing a scene. My anger rose. Then I heard her car start and drive off, and I lay on the settee and thought how ironic it was that she was the one going out at four in the morning to blow off steam. But again I caught myself. I knew she was only trying to shock me into seeing how dangerous my attitude was and, in so doing, trying to force me to take steps to control it. And if she was right to do so, how could I blame her? I lay sick with the whole situation, the pattern of crisis after crisis. It was intolerable. Yet how many times had I reached this point of realization and remained paralyzed? After each blow-up with Dominique I swore to absolutely bar Miriam from our bed. And after each blow up with Patricia I swore to take legal action to enforce, once and for all, my rights of access.

*

The blonde man stands next to the bakkie staring at the blood-marked bones that lie scattered on the dust. It strikes me that, in addition to the bones, there are shreds of green cloth strewn on the ground in front of the lionesses. The man starts walking towards the lionesses. The animals look up at him. He moves forward. I shout to him, "Watch out!" barely believing what I'm seeing. He continues walking. I hear Miriam's high-pitched voice, "Isn't that dangerous, Daddy?"

One of the lionesses stands up and faces him. He is only three or four meters from her. She growls and trots forward. I press the hooter. It blares out. The lioness stops. I repeatedly blast the hooter. She turns round and runs toward the car. I carry on hooting. Suddenly all the lions are on their feet, grunting and snarling at us. Miriam starts crying. I keep blasting the hooter. A young lion jumps onto the bonnet. In panic, I accelerate. The lion falls off as the car lurches forward. Then, before I have time to change gears, the lions turn and amble away. Ignoring the blonde man, they lope off towards the first section of the enclosure where the ticket booth stands at the entrance.

The blonde man seems to sway on his feet; he looks completely dazed. I drive up to him. He won't face us. Miriam sits gasping. I imagine she still sees the young lion jumping onto the car, the bonnet buckling under his weight.

"Are you alright?" I call out to him. "How are you feeling?" There is no reaction. "That was pretty dangerous what you did there. Don't play around, they might seem knocked out by the heat but they'll kill you." I see

119

a flicker of movement in his eyes. Then he turns and walks back to the bakkie. "I'll drive out with you, if you like."

He slides into the bakkie's cabin and waves to us, pumping his hand up and down as if to say, "Go, go!" then he sits back and covers his eyes with his hands. I wonder if he's drunk or drugged but remember that it was only his stumbling when I blew the hooter that had made him seem confused.

"Come for a cup of tea at the restaurant."

Once again there is no response. The sweat is pouring off me, my whole body pumped up with adrenalin. It strikes me that the dirt track is the only way out of the lion enclosure and that it leads on to another bigger paddock and then to the park exit. The ticket collectors must have heard the hooter blaring. Why has no one come to investigate?

Miriam suddenly says, "Daddy, let's go. I don't like this." She's trembling.

"Don't worry, darling. We're going now. I just need to check that the man is alright."

She nods, accepting my explanation. I think to myself: she's a tough kid, reasonable too. "We'll get something to drink, darling. Would you like a chocolate milkshake?"

"Daddy, can I also have a hot dog and a packet of chips?"

I will get her whatever she likes. Giving the blonde man a last look, I drive out of the enclosure. Sitting stock-still, staring at the lions, he seems oblivious to us. The two lionesses have rejoined the rest of the pride. A handful of white birds with delicate legs take pecks at the carcass. I pull up next to the hut at the entrance. Where are the ticket collectors? I blow the hooter. No one comes out. Then it hits me: why bother about the man, Miriam deserves her refreshment, it's incredibly hot and it's not every day that you get charged by lions.

I drive off to the restaurant which is about two hundred metres from the fenced off area. We sit under a thatched umbrella by a swimming pool. Kids are splashing around. Miriam has a vanilla ice cream and a Coke. I begin to relax. I smear sunblock over her and then over myself. The children in the pool jump about, wetting our feet; I can see Miriam is dying to join them.

"Dive in, darling!"

She looks anguished, "But I don't have my water wings."

I tickle her tummy, "Don't worry, daddy's watching."

Giving me her most adorable smile, she takes a long suck of her Coke. Then, as she jumps in amongst the slithering brown bodies, we hear a loud roaring from the direction of the lion enclosure. The children in the pool stop playing. The roaring becomes even more ferocious. A few of the younger children start screaming. I listen for other sounds. There is nothing to give an indication of what is causing or bearing the brunt of this outburst. Then it strikes me that perhaps the enclosure gate has been left open and that the lions can now walk out and reach the restaurant as well as the main road.

"Stay here with the other kids!" I shout to Miriam, "I'm going to find out what's happening!"

I drive back. There is no one in the first section. But as I swing into the middle one, next to the bakkie's open door on the driver's side, I see the blonde man's head sticking out from under a furry mass. Only his shoes are visible, the rest of his body is completely obscured by a pile of lions. The blonde hair is streaked red and there are only empty sockets where his eyes have been sucked out. Crouching to the side, a lioness chews one of his legs. I turn away, my stomach tightening. Next to his body are the bloodstained remains of a green dress, a woman's sandal lies close beside it.

Suddenly a large male scrapes up against the car. He roars - a huge, echoing roar. Another lion trots up. A group of about three or four break away from the pride and run towards the car. One of the females jumps onto the bonnet. A second joins her, while a third manages to get onto the boot. I try to drive off but the engine stalls. A flurry of paws leave the windshield smeared with blood. I try to restart the car. Another male, the biggest of the lot, crashes against my side window. Then the engine abruptly catches, the car lurches off, the lion is knocked to the side and the other two topple off. The way is clear and I drive madly towards the gate.

A group of men on foot come into view, two of them carrying rifles, the others with sticks. I slow down. They run up shouting. I tell them what I've seen.

One of them answers, waving his hands wildly, "He told us to fok off and leave him alone and take the day off, he doesn't want to see our faces, we must fok off and go to our girlfriends and leave him to feed the lions. He and madam, they were screaming, saying bad things . . ."

*

On the way back to the city, Miriam and I are both unusually quiet and then, as we near home, unusually talkative. We find Dominique has prepared tea and scones - she's even bought youngberry jam, Miriam's favourite. When

I take Miriam back to Patricia in time for their flight to Cape Town, Patricia is relaxed and we swop stories about Miriam and talk pleasantly about the coming holiday. We plan to meet and have lunch on her return to discuss which primary school Miriam should go to. I don't tell either Dominique or Patricia what had happened.

TIME AFTER TIME

MONTHS AGO

Azur is back in the city. Having finished work, he sits down at a café, orders a beer. Depression does not rule him as absolutely as it had in the past. He has found a few jobs. He has met two interesting and attractive women, and is sleeping with one of them.

Mid-afternoon; sunglasses; brightly coloured, sloping umbrellas but the glare is still strong. Sipping slowly, surrounded by relaxed crowds, he leans back. Life is good again, the difficult period has eased; he can breathe and not feel that he is doomed to always fail. Then he thinks of Ayanda. Why has he not kept contact with her? Their walk in the desert of the city had seared itself into his memory. The trust in each others' imagination had been unique. Why then had he abandoned their beginning? He has had several months to build on the intimacy they had unexpectedly, but effortlessly, created. What is it he fears by avoiding her?

He orders another beer. Ayanda? Yes. But where to find her now? And who can help? Unsurprisingly he has an almost immediate answer - there is only one person. Magnets create circles, interlocking, they connect the sympathetic, the attuned. Ilana stands at the centre of many such circles; she will be the one to know about Ayanda. As he thinks of Ilana, he smiles to himself.

Azur leaves the cafe and begins walking. He crosses several avenues, turns down a side street over the hill from the city centre, reaches an old building, and climbs the stairs.

The woman who opens Ilana's door has cut her hair into a sleek, soft flowing of golden brown. Her tight fitting dress insinuates a slim, shapely body. A set of perfectly shaped, gleaming white teeth show when she speaks.

He bows.

"Oh!" she says. "You're back . . . you're back in the city."

"Yes." He is shaken by the transformation - her freshness, her beauty. "And how are you?"

The woman at the door looks at him coolly; she who had always made him welcome seems distant, disinterested.

"I would like to ask you in, but . . ." She stares past him. "A friend is picking me up."

"Can't I entertain you for just a minute?" He spreads his hands, clown-like. "Give me the pleasure, madam, I will not fail you."

She shakes her head. "It didn't work last time. Why should it now?"

Azur does not avoid her accusing look. Instead he tries to engage her eyes. Ilana stands her ground.

"Have you forgotten?"

The first and only time they had slept together, they had missed each other.

"A glass of water . . . please . . . it's been a long walk." In his desire to enter the flat, his instinct is to push her aside. "Gosh, you're looking well." She does not move; her eyes drift away to the skyline.

"I need your help."

"You're still lost."

"Lost? Yes, I suppose I am. But maybe this is the right path . . ."

As he says this, she opens the door and walks back into the flat.

He is overjoyed.

They step into the living room. (It is unchanged from his last visit, except for a large painting of a boat nearing a lighthouse that now dominates the main wall.) Overcome with light-headedness and a sense of invulnerability, he asks her to phone the person she is waiting for, and pretend she is sick. Then, amazing himself, he suggests they go out for dinner to the restaurant he had gone to with Ayanda.

With an amused smile Ilana slips on a jacket; Azur phones for a taxi. On the way they speak with the driver, an elderly man who needs to work because his government pension is too small to sustain him, and his children do not offer support.

At the restaurant they order wine. Sitting in a sheltered garden at a subtly lit table in a corner under giant ferns and other green monsters, it crosses Azur's mind (not for the first time) that there are always new sources of light to illuminate darkness - provided one forges the right attitude and temperament to see and feel them; and that if one fails, then the consequence is death. And that he has died many times.

"You seem so gay and carefree, so different. . . " Ilana turns the ring on her finger round. "Are you in love? Are you seeing someone?"

A breeze comes up, the tablecloth lifts. He can see the moon over her shoulder.

"Yes, I am in love. But that doesn't matter right now."

Is such an admission possibly true? Is he showing Ilana his shallowness or is he being honest and brave, truly able to live with this paradox?

"A recent conquest?"

"Why use that horrible word?"

"In honour of my sisters. Even the slaves. Aha! Is she another of the romantic ladies who makes you flower?"

Azur turns away, removes his glasses.

"She's wonderful, but why should that blot out the present." Then he feels uneasy. "I don't want to speak badly of her. It really is a very important relationship."

"What does she mean to you beyond sex?"

He does not reply. A waiter brings them the wine. As the rich red liquid is poured, a sense of frustration, almost despair, comes over him.

"Ilana, forgive me, I know this may be indelicate but I came to visit you hoping to find out about Ayanda . . . where she is. You see . . . but . . . now that's not the only reason."

The waiter serves their dishes.

"You haven't changed."

She makes the statement flatly but shows no sign of wanting to silence him or leave. And after his stammered explanation, and a second bottle of wine, she becomes quite radiant. Azur is profoundly grateful. They speak frankly and easily about many things. Once the restaurant closes, on the way back to her flat, in the taxi, he takes her hand; she caresses his in return.

Now, whenever they speak of his very first visit to her flat, she almost forgives him. In fact, she often refers back to that night because now she considers their relationship to have few if any illusions, and she is proud that they live so well together despite such a traumatic foundation.

YEARS BEFORE

A summer's evening; Azur is still in the city. Usually, after finishing work, he immediately returns to the village where he rents a house. But on the infrequent occasions he stays on, he always eats in a restaurant and goes to a play or a film. But today he has not followed his habit. He is restless; a sense of disquiet fills him.

He sits on a bench in a park. Between the trees, he watches the squirrels and pigeons – particularly the squirrels chasing their tails, chasing the shadows of pigeons. The afternoon moves slowly on. He watches light angle down through the leaves of trees; people walk by and the sounds of a band playing in a nearby section of the park dilute as he tries to clear his mind and allow loneliness to ebb out of him; that heavy sense of forced solitude, dull yet aching. His parents relentlessly urge him to remarry. They stubbornly attempt to pair him off with the daughters of their friends - but the memories of his first failed marriage intervene to cloud a fresh

127

beginning. He seeks another partner - a lover, a muse - but he lives, struggling to release the past, his loss, still overcome by rejection.

The evening is serene, composed but he cannot join its tranquillity. The park gradually empties. Soon he is alone on the bench and even the squirrels and pigeons disappear into the trees. And then he remembers an invitation: Ilana, whom he has just recently and briefly met, has asked him to stop by whenever he chooses. He strolls towards her flat - narrow, winding streets filled with trees and small gardens, bright flowers spilling out of pots, figs and jasmine, large bushes spilling over onto the pavement. He so much needs this sweetness.

Ilana is energetic, intelligent. He has been impressed by her. She has a degree in history, but is never just academic. And their mutual friends encourage them. Azur agrees with their opinion - barring one aspect: tall, bulky, with blotched skin and big teeth, he has never desired her. Ilana does not arouse him though he has sensed her desire.

*

He reaches the flat. The lights are on. Ilana opens the door and embraces him. He kisses her on the cheek, and steps into the small two-roomed flat. Another woman is seated in the living room. She rises, introduces herself as Justine. Ilana explains that they are childhood friends who lost contact through living in different places but Justine is now studying in the city and they have been able to resume their friendship. Ilana mentions that Justine is staying the night.

Azur greets Justine. She has a long angular face, a tapering body proportioned like a slender branch. Ilana makes coffee and they sit on cushions and tell each other stories, exchange dreams. They laugh a great deal. Azur is struck by the harmony between the two women. They complement each other without ostentation and critizize each other without showing competitiveness. He comments on how privileged he feels to be able to experience the warmth of their friendship.

Ilana touches Azur's hand, asks him to uncork a bottle of wine. But he and Justine are busy talking, engaging each other. He hesitates; a quietness falls upon them. When he does not respond to her touch, Ilana pulls a face at him. Then he smiles and follows her into the kitchen.

The kitchen is filled with utensils and pots, a large cupboard for storing provisions. Ilana leans against the counter, faces him. Then, before he can react, she embraces him; kisses him passionately on the mouth. Azur shakes his head and moves away. She blushes, ignores him, busies herself cutting up onions and cucumber, opens and closes jars of olives and sun dried tomatoes. He feels embarrassed but not overwhelmed.

She asks, "Why don't you come and live in the city?"

"I need to be away from this tumult, I need more solitariness than a city can provide, real stillness, not vacuums between people."

"You seem such a sociable type."

"Seems . . ."

Ilana cuts up a long loaf of crispy bread.

"Don't be so tentative, grab things. Don't just wait for them."

Azur opens the bottle of wine. He sees Justine through the doorway, lifting and dropping her hair.

"I'll leave you to your concoctions. I'm not much of a cook. . ."

He is about to return to the living room but Ilana comes to him again, more urgent than before. She tries to kiss him. He is alarmed, then feeling a sudden weariness, brushes her forehead with his lips and gently pushes her away.

*

They have dinner. The mood of companionship revives. Ilana spreads out comfortably on a mattress covered with a bright African cloth. Azur does likewise. Justine sits, legs suspended over the rim of an armchair. They talk about oceans and deserts, the lives and deaths of saintly people. Then they talk about their loves, past and present.

Justine and Azur are a little guarded in her revelations but Ilana is frank about the complexities that make up her relationships with friends and lovers, her parents, her sisters. Once again Azur appreciates her intelligence and honesty. They talk unmindful of time. But eventually, well past midnight, Ilana rises.

"And so . . ." she stretches her arms, faces Azur. "Where would you like to sleep? Here or in my room?"

He finds himself looking at Justine. He wants to touch her but he has the sense that Ilana, despite his delicate though unambiguous rejection, still expects to sleep with him. And even if this expectation should not place him under any obligation, whether as a mark of consideration for her hospitality, or as a mark of respect for her as a person, he faces a serious dilemma: how can he take up her invitation and visit, then sleep in a room with another woman, particularly a close friend?

He looks away, at a photograph on a wall. It is of a quiet, protected harbor filled with gleaming boats.

"In your room."

Ilana rises and kisses Justine on the cheek.

*

The bedroom is small and sparsely furnished. Ilana fetches the mattress from the living room, places it in a corner. Then she switches on a small bedside lamp and flicks off the main light. The room looks soft in the glow. Azur takes off his shoes and lies down on this mattress. She takes a large shirt from under her pillow and leaves the room. He closes his eyes, but cannot calm himself. He wants to please her, to acknowledge her, and still persuade her to accept his disinterest. But how can he dissuade her without being awkward, without being insulting?

A tap runs in the bathroom. The living room light is switched off. He examines the books stacked on a low shelf, selects one (the cover is well worn) - Milan Kundera's *Slowness*. He has read *Slowness* some months before. It made a strong and favourable impression. But now as he reads, he feels his concentration slip away.

The sound of running water continues from the bathroom. He stands up, crosses to the window that looks out onto the street. The palm trees and firs lining the pavements shift in a breeze. The city is silent, immobile. He imagines Justine in the living room, spreading a sheet on one of the settees. He imagines her wondering why he is not with her. At the same time, he knows she must appreciate his loyalty to Ilana, his refusal to undermine her self-esteem.

Ilana returns from the bathroom dressed only in the large, loose shirt. Azur draws the curtains. She is perfumed, a fresh and subtle scent surrounds her. The shirt is half unbuttoned. He glimpses her breasts. She passes by the mattress. He lifts the book and shows her the cover picture of a courtly eighteenth century European couple.

Ilana leans back on her bed. The shirt slides up her thighs. She has long, shapely legs. He has been mistaken. Despite her apparent ungainliness and blotched face, Ilana has an attractive well-proportioned body and a sensual mobility. He sits up. She switches off the bedside light and calls to him. He makes his way to her bed. They touch. He draws her close and begins to kiss her but their mouths do not fit, her tongue is wet and slides on his lips, and her hands on his body feel clumsy. He continues to kiss and caress her but suddenly wilts, and the more he tries to reignite his desire, the more he remains inert, unresponsive. Then, in his distress he visualises Justine. Surely her last lingering look at him as he left the living room implied that while he is joylessly touching Ilana, she is lying awake imagining them making passionate love. He sees Justine's eyes, her mouth, her supple body, while at the same time embracing Ilana, he tries to overcome, and control, the growing distance.

He turns away, but Ilana holds him. They remain in this position: Azur facing the wall, Ilana pressed against his back. Then, feeling ashamed of his revulsion, he forces himself to turn and again begin touching and kissing her. She instantly responds. It seems to him that she does not sense his reluctant compulsion. And, at length, caressing himself surreptitiously, achieving an erection, he manages to fuck her, and she seems satisfied. Afterwards, exhausted, without speaking, they fall asleep.

He wakes, oddly refreshed, on a deep, dreamless pillow. The morning traffic is at its height. Justine has already left. Ilana brings him a cup of coffee. He tries to be casual. They talk superficially about mutual friends and their problems. Then he kisses her goodbye.

A YEAR LATER

Azur is back in the city. The streets are filled with yellowing leaves but the trees are not completely bare and the city does not feel stripped and wintry. It is late afternoon. The sun is white and low in the sky. He must return to the village where he still lives though with increasing dissatisfaction. For some time he has found it difficult being alone and his isolation seems more and more artificial, even perverse. He wants warmth and companionship on this chilly afternoon and there is only one person he truly wishes to see; only one person who accepts him for what he is and reinvigorates him when he is depressed. But when he reaches her flat, Ilana is not at home.

Deflated, uncertain of what to do, he walks aimlessly in her neighbourhood, watches the round shapes of cooks behind windows. The heat of kitchens radiates out onto the street; the crunching of bones in the throats of dogs can be heard. Tired and hungry, he enters a small bar, orders a drink and a light meal. He flips through a magazine. People drift by. He draws doodles in the margins. At the tail end of dusk he walks back to her flat.

A woman he does not know opens the door. She wears an ankle length white dress embroidered with red roses that glow strongly, complementing and contrasting with her long, glossy, straight black hair and high cheek bones. The woman tells him Ilana has gone on holiday and that she is looking after the flat. Azur is taken aback. What is he to say? Disappointment at Ilana's absence floods him but the brightly dressed woman standing at the door smiles at him. He wonders if she senses his loneliness. He examines her closely.

Breaking the silence, she asks if he has known Ilana for long. He confirms that he does and explains that he is stranded in the city, unable to return to his village and unable to afford a hotel, and that he has come visiting hoping to stay the night. He trails off, unsure as to how the bright-eyed woman will react. He does not have to wait long - she shows him into the flat.

They sit in the familiar living room with its richly draped sofas and chairs. She tells him her name is Ayanda, she is from a small town and has come to the city to sell preserves. Ilana is happy to have someone stay in her flat while she is away - a spate of robberies in the neighbourhood have made it dangerous to leave any dwelling unattended.

Ayanda has long, slender hands which she places composedly in her lap. They drink coffee and eat little cakes baked by a confectionery near the main taxi rank. She tells Azur that the previous night she had slept with an old friend, a man who for many years has courted her with great conviction and with consideration; and that earlier in the day, buoyed by her change of heart, and their very satisfying lovemaking, he had proposed that she live with him. Then she adds that when Azur knocked, she was deep in thought, considering this possibility.

Azur listens attentively, comments on the peculiarities of aging, the switching of needs and desires. Ayanda tells him with a light trace of self-mocking that, in addition to his attractiveness as a person and now as a lover, this man owns a large house with a garden in which stands a small shed which is ideal for her bottling. Azur laughs, comments that people have decided to live together for far less practical reasons. Then he invites Ayanda to dinner - nearby is an intimate and inexpensive restaurant.

They set off on foot. It is an overcast night, but surprisingly chilly. On the way, they run into a roadblock - the police are searching for illegal immigrants. Ayanda is pulled aside. To Azur's consternation she does not have identity papers with her. The officer in command orders her to accompany him to a police station. Azur intervenes, pleads with the officer to check her identity number by logging onto the Home Affairs computer centre. But the officer ignores him, stares lewdly at Ayanda while handcuffing her. He instructs a soldier to search her for drugs. In desperation, Azur mentions the name of a high official in the local party structure whom he knew in the old days of the Liberation Struggle. The officer's expression immediately changes. He disappears then returns, saying they can leave.

They walk on, stepping briskly in the thick, moonless night. Azur asks Ayanda to imagine they are in a desert. He describes the call of wolves and wild dogs, the cawing of crows. Then he takes her hand, and closing his eyes, tells her he is blind and she must be his guide, and that they are walking through an arid valley hoping to find a monastery where they can find shelter. She holds his hand very tightly. They advance through Ilana's neighbourhood, smelling dying flowers and the sharp scent of camel dung. They approach the monastery - ramparts rising up towards them from over the hill, monks gathering in the inner sanctuary, chanting the special night prayer that forms the centre piece of the long fast they undertake at the start of every winter. Ayanda says the monks' singing is very pure and soulful. But soon they stop talking; only the sound of their footsteps echoes out. Eyes pressed shut, Azur holds Ayanda's hand, stepping confidently into the abyss in front of him, thrusting forward, propelled by her intact, complete presence. With each step he feels nothing can violate the love blooming between them. His breath rises and falls. Ayanda's hand is his anchor, his column of fire. They make their way towards the restaurant in the black night without stars, interrupted only by the faraway stab of a police siren transporting 'aliens' from the roadblock. They walk through Ilana's neighbourhood into the greater universe of time, denying death.

When they reach the restaurant they order a simple dish to share and a carafe of wine. They eat, holding hands, so close it seems they are one mouth, one belly that consumes the delicious stew laid on a bed of lentils and rice. Then they walk back to the flat, and this time Ayanda closes her eyes and Azur leads her over the dunes, past oases and dried out rivers, past cavernous mountains that pierce the sky, home to leopards and baboons and plants that live on dew.

They arrive back at Ilana's flat feeling exhilarated. They move straight to the bedroom, but as Azur embraces Ayanda, she says she cannot kiss him, the lovemaking of the previous night with her old friend is too vivid, and she is overwhelmed by the rapidity of the bond created with Azur and is uncertain as to how to proceed. So they lie quietly in each other's arms though he burns with desire for her and clasps her fiercely to his chest.

He barely sleeps that night. In the morning, when Ayanda suggests he stay on and help her transport preserves to a nearby market, he is happy to oblige. The day passes, they sell many bottles. What started with a walk through an imaginary desert becomes an intimacy borne of real shared experience. He asks about her old friend and his offer. She replies that she is now sure that the proposal is unsound; there must have been good reasons for her to have rejected him for so many years. Indeed, how can she suddenly change and trust a revised judgement?

At nightfall they return to the flat, tired but hopeful that their ever growing compatibility will flow into sexual consummation. But as they approach the building, they are surprised: there is light behind the curtains.

Ilana is in the living room, drinking tea. She has cut short her holiday. Her father has had a serious heart attack. She is devastated by the news. Azur tries to comfort her. Ayanda, who does not really know her, is solicitous and understanding. Ilana leans on Azur and cries. This time he does not spend the night. He leaves after dinner, promising to contact both of them as soon as possible.

He returns to the village. Weeks pass. How he longs for Ayanda! But despite this yearning, Ilana's interruption of their relationship puts him on his guard; and in a barely understood way, the memory of their walk through the desert towards the chanting monks is too powerful, too pure, for him to risk trying to embrace her again.

TODAY

"How long have you and Azur known each other?

"Twenty-two years." Pause. "Two months, and two days."

"That sounds like a cabbalistic calculation."

"It is."

"And how do you keep your love strong?"

"We do press ups and stretches!"

"And how do you keep in touch with your respective changes, your career shifts?"

"We check each others' diaries."

"What if you forget to make crucial entries?"

"We never forget."

"Are you sure?"

'Yes."

"So everything keeps rolling along?"

"On the wheels of fortune. . ."

"Good fortune in your case?"

"Without doubt!"

"Aren't you perhaps a little smug about the strength of your relationship?"

"No."

"Why do you say that?"

"Because when we first met, Azur did not find me beautiful and he spurned my love. And yet that changed."

"What changed things?"

"My becoming beautiful."

"You became beautiful?

"I became beautiful."

"You were always beautiful."

"No, I became beautiful."

"Explain."

"Plastic surgery, medication and tooth capping."

"That's how you became beautiful?"

Big laugh. "Yes."

Silence except for the slight hiss of the tape recorder.

"And you find that acceptable? That he should find you beautiful only after all that cosmetic interference?"

"Yes."

"Are you trying to defend . . ."

"Parts of my body were ugly and this ugliness buried my soul."

"But isn't that extremely superficial? How can you trust a love that depends so critically on physical beauty? I can't believe this! You tolerate a man loving you on condition that you become beautiful to him on the basis of a fake appearance?"

"Can I blame him for my having had a face that was unattractive?"

"But it's insulting!"

"Life is insulting."

"Thank you for your time. That was. . ."

"Is." Chuckle.

Click of the stop button.

TOMORROW

Azur and Ilana will see a film about a small blind boy who survives drowning because his father, after much struggle, grows to recognize his courage and love him.

HUMAN

11 February 1990

The man walking out of the high iron gate is composed and energetic. He has grey hair and a lined face. At his side is a plump, middle-aged elegant woman with rich brown eyes. She smiles self-consciously. Vaulting above them, the sky is deep and brilliant, the bright summer blue of the southern hemisphere; rising up behind them are jagged granite peaks softened by undulating green slopes. The couple walk away from the iron gate flanked by a small army of marshals. Waving their hands high in the air, they move past wire barriers towards a mass of television crews and a surging crescendo of dancing, chanting people.

One thousand five hundred kilometres away, in the low hills of the Highveld, Human sprawls in a plastic chair on the stoep of his four bed-roomed house. Despite the heat, the stoep is cool. A pile of newspapers and beer cans lie at his feet. From early morning the television has been reporting - the voices of politicians and newscasters merging into the hum of pool filters. Flicking the remote, he switches channels but each one returns him to the triumphant couple advancing towards the ecstatic, gesticulating crowds. As the elderly black man reaches a bullet-proof limousine, a security guard opens the door; the convoy of luxury cars and police riders glides away from the iron gates and disappears onto a highway.

Human lights a cigarette, draws deeply, then flicks the ash into his hand and blows it into the air. He grinds the burnt match under his foot. The convoy arrives at a jammed city square. Tens of thousands of faces vibrate against a background of palm trees and brownstone buildings. Table Mountain towers into the sky. The Parade has been brimming since early morning; it is now a heaving quilt of black, green and gold. The old man in his dark suit and ostrich leather shoes appears on a balcony. Below him stand colonial statues and a vast, overflowing sea of people. He is, at last, before them and, with eyes choked by history, raises his fist in salutation: he whose face is on their T-shirts, their caps, their umbrellas, their key rings, pasted everywhere across book covers, pamphlets and newspapers.

"Amandla!"

Thirty million voices respond.

"Awethu!"

Human stares blankly at the cypresses cutting the horizon of the paddock where a group of horses graze beside a small dam. He knows the words; he has heard them many times. He has seen the hysterical, sweating rows jiving their war dance, drowning in the drumming of hands and feet, the mobs of chanting youth burning their schools and their fathers' beer halls. He remembers the gun shots, the screams, the grinding hours of interrogation breaking their leaders.

He pushes the volume control down to zero. There is silence; then he is swamped by the buzz around him - cicadas and beetles, the pool filter. Two peacocks appear. He stares at the birds. As their diamond fans swish, a hoarse screech cuts the morning.

He does not return to the television screen. He watches the bordered shapes before him, the clear, flowing sequences.

1 May 1990

He looks at the twelve men sprawled round him. They have been squashed in this city hotel room since early evening. Now morning seeps in and the smell of garbage rises up from the back alleys that surround the building. The men are restless: it is time to sum up.

A waiter knocks. On his tray are a bottle of brandy, cans of Coke and a bag of ice cubes.

"Put it on my account!"

"Christ, man, you're the manager! Since when do managers keep accounts?"

"Shit, you know me. I'm the only honest one."

The men laugh. The 'manager' begins pouring.

Hey, Frans! You forgot the cigarettes! Go bring four packs of Gunston. Last round! Make it quick, boy."

From outside, the wail of sirens cuts in, compounds with the staccato of his voice. No one reacts. After the glasses have been filled, Human continues; clipped, half sentences. The men fall silent. The buzz of the city reaches up to them; it is the surf on which the brandy rides.

"Ons kan nie nou oorgee nie." His eyes narrow. "Wie sal dan die kaffirs keer? Kom, ons het werk om te doen. Ons sal vir hulle wys. Daar is nie tyd te mors nie."(1)

The white men empty their glasses.

14 March 1991

The bright red car swings out of the driveway, crushing the last brittle leaves still piled along the tracks. A line of trees with bare branches thrusts up; an almost full moon floats in a purple halo. The veld is yellow, even lawns and golf courses left to wither, grass highway verges scorched black by burning. The crispness is vaporous, sharpening in the throat; highveld night when the cold air is like a leopard's claws lacerating the lungs.

Human drives with leather gloves, rubber soles touching the pedals.

It is six months since Helena's departure. How many years had he waited for that day to arrive? She with pale blue eyes who after Christiaan's birth had become an anxious and highly irritating woman. But he had been patient.

No matter what happened, he was never going to leave this plot - his land with its field of mealies, rows of pumpkin and spinach, the paddock with horses, the chicken run with mesh fences in the yard. No, she would be the one to leave. He would do everything he could to set her up on her own, give her the money she needed, but he would never abandon what was his. And she had known this but ignored his wishes. Year after year, passive and dependent, her marble eyes filling with distance, she had stayed on and he had lived in bitter heaviness, made bearable only by the work that demanded his whole being, his total attention. Then, one day, very matter-of-factly, he was alone and could do as he liked. He will never forget her last night in the house: he lay listening to her breathing, the tick-tock of the brass clock his mother had given them when Christiaan was confirmed.

Now he is on the M1 North, passing the Roodepoort exit. He turns on the radio. It is the nine o'clock news. The Monster of Sebokeng, Victor Kheswa, has died in police custody. During ongoing violence in the Vaal triangle, Kheswa is alleged to have murdered over forty people, these killings made notorious by their brutality. Though a black man identified as a member of the Inkatha Freedom Party, he is also said to have membership status in the World Preservatist Movement - an international apartheid-supporting, white supremacist organisation.

Human reaches the flyover at Newtown. He slows down as the car rises and falls, bouncing on the highway's corrugations. He looks at the slender but massive concrete tower on the skyline to the east. The tower is the emblem of his first year in Jo'burg; the year after his graduation from College; that year, when he had been stationed in Hillbrow, had been central to his life. Mid-way the most promising recruits had been interviewed by a prestigious but demanding unit, and he had been accepted for specialized training. That year had seen him embark on a successful career in the security police.

He leaves the highway at the Oxford Road off-ramp and enters the green maze of Saxonwold. The red car glides down the intimate, tree-lined avenues, reaches a white house surrounded by high walls topped with electrified security wires. He stops at a metal gate and presses a buzzer. A watchman steps from a concealed side door and hands him a canvas bag. Human reverses back into the street. As he does so, the main gate slides opens and a BMW with three aerials speeds out. He drives back to the highway with the BMW keeping a discreet distance. The lanes are empty; he turns up the volume as the news ends and the phone-in begins.

Few black callers believe that Kheswa has died from self-inflicted wounds. As negotiations between the ANC and the still ruling Afrikaner nationalist government become more and more protracted, the public demand to identify and stop the wave of terror attacks on trains and taxi ranks grows stronger. There is general consensus that the State Security apparatus has murdered Kheswa to ensure his silence. Notwithstanding this, many white callers argue that the Freedom Alliance (of right-wing White parties) is a justified response to the ANC's dominance and its intolerance of political opposition.

The BMW hangs back, ever ready to accelerate. Neither the driver nor the man beside her speaks. They follow the report on Kheswa together with Human and another two hundred thousand listeners in the metropolitan area; they listen to a denial by Inkatha that Kheswa is a World Preservatist Movement member. The chairman of the Inkatha PWV Youth League denounces the allegation as an ANC smear. His statement is followed by one from Burger Oosthuizen, the WPM's president, denying knowledge of Kheswa.

Human takes the Empire Road exit and drives east. When he passes Pieter Roos Park, the BMW overtakes him then pulls over. Human draws up alongside it as the man in the passenger seat hands the woman at the wheel a package from the cubby hole. Inside, wrapped in soft grey cloth, is a silencer and bundles of money with which to pay for the War. She passes Human the package.

Tiered glass office parks banked with vivid green grass shining ahead of him, Human barely registers their glittering reflections. The BMW disappears. He circles the park. Turning at the ornamental flower clock on the north side, he brakes - a middle-aged black man is walking on the lawn alongside the road. He is alone; there is no one else nearby.

Human pulls up, activates the automatic window winder, and calls out, "Hallo, my friend, how do you get to Pretorius Street?"

Squinting, the man approaches the car, "Sorry, sorry, my baas . . . speak loud, baas . . ."

Human motions with his hand for the man to come closer, then, as the wrinkled face fills the open window, he repeats, "Pretorius Street, you know where that is?"

The man gestures, "No, my baas. I'm not from here. I come from far . . ."

Human smells the beer on the man's breath; he slips his hand under the cloth. The man coughs.

"I come see my wife. She got job in Berea, she work for white man, he won't let her go. He won't let her go tonight."

"He won't, hey? What's going on? Jigga-jigga?"

The man stares blankly then tries to smile, "I don't know, baas. I come from far but he won't let her go."

"Is she ironing? Is that what she's doing?"

Human waits, he looks around, "OK, boy. You can go now. Fok off! You hear me, fok off!"

The black man staggers back in surprise. He tries to step onto the grass and away from the tense, spitting white man at the wheel of the sleek car. As he does so, Human, with a single sweeping movement, lifts the pistol and fires. He barely hears the dull snort. The black man collapses face down onto the grass while the car surges down Empire Road.

Driving back to the house in the avenue of arching green, Human feels the trigger's magnetism curled into his finger, the iciness of the moment of action, the ease with which the bullets had sunk into the man's flesh. Flicking the headlights, he pulls up at the gate. The guard salutes.

"Buenos noces, Manuel."

The guard answers in heavily accented Mozambican Portuguese, "Buenos noces, Commandante."

Human faces the gate as car lights flash behind him. It is a patrol car with the markings of a private security company. In it are two uniformed men; one of the men jumps out and runs to him. He shakes Human's hand but waits for Human to speak.

"Net een. En julle?"

"Raai."

"Hoeveel?"

"Raai. . . "

"Kry end, man!"

"Twee mannetjies. Naby Katlehong." Human gives him the Victory sign, the man salutes. "Goed, Kolonel, ons ry maar. Sien jou Saterdag." (2)

The gate opens. Human disappears along the red-brick driveway that cuts through the grounds.

31 March 1992

He parks next to the BMW and walks to the front door. The path is flanked by a waterway filled with lilies and bull rushes and plastic crocodiles mounted on small rocks and ledges. Interspersed among the bull rushes are statuettes of mermaids and a spear-bearing Neptune. The night is still; soft soughing of leaves. For a moment he feels he cannot face the door, its heavy brass knocker shone to brightness. He is tired, deep furrows line his face. He stands outside the carved door. He does not know what to do - again the milkiness has clouded his eyes.

At first the man had been a gaunt shape breaking out from a dust track, a shambling, lumbering giant emerging from the smoke of a burning field. Then he had become a wild hand, gesturing to passing cars. Human had stopped. Without check or preparation, he had drawn the pistol from his shoulder holster and fired. The man had fallen by the roadside, blood gushing from his stomach as he tried to stand up. But he had remained prone on the tar and begun screaming - a screaming that was louder than the crackling of the burning field and the gusts of wind that cut through the trees breathing new life into the flames.

A cloud had covered the road and the black man in brown sack cloth, whose eyes glowed red in the half dark; a milky shapelessness had covered everything and the gun had almost jerked out of his hand. The cloud was very thick and quiet and he was inside it. He wanted to lie down and float in it while the car idled and the man in sackcloth lay moaning. Then a bakkie had pulled up, and a group of black men had jumped out and run to the wounded man and carried him away. One of these men had grabbed an automatic rifle from the bakkie's cabin and opened fire. The volley of bullets had hit the red car's rear window but the bullet-proof glass held. At that moment another car had come into view. It had shaved past, then left the road and spun into the bushes. Human had heard agonised cries followed by an explosion; a blast of yellowy orange, brighter even than the dry grass burning by the roadside and the polished fist of the door knocker.

Human feels a momentary dizziness; he leans against the wooden door. He rings the bell.

The door opens; a black man in starched uniform smiles. Behind him, Human sees a white woman dressed in a leisure suit. She has a glass in her hand.

"At last!" she says.

He follows her down a passage; notes the strawberry polish on her nails. They pass under the heads of wildebeest and other trophies, and alongside an antique side table laden with fruit. Then they enter a side room, their steps echoing on the parquet floor. The room is dominated by a large painting of an eighteenth-century English country scene: a brook running through a meadow, swallowed by a wood.

A red-faced man rises from a chair at the fireplace and limps towards Human. He places an arm over his shoulder.

"Go all right?"

"Of course, Ralph."

The man named Ralph turns to the woman.

"What did I tell you, Pam?"

His arm remains on Human's shoulder, but the clasp is now hesitant.

She asks, "Would you like a Scotch?"

They leave the room and move to a patio that sits aside a swimming pool. A television is placed on a low table. It is the rainy season; the northern suburbs are cool at night but moist with an almost sub-tropical humidity, each garden brimming with the lustre of blossoms. Pam reads a black, leather-bound book. Human and Ralph sip their whiskeys and watch images of a large, fortress like structure flash on the television. The camera tracks two groups of men dressed in khaki and camouflage uniforms. Each group is bunched in opposite corners of a courtyard.

Ralph is agitated. "These fools from the Boerekommando are buggering us up. For God's sake! Occupy something really strategic and only act when you're sure of success."

Human nods.

Willem de Ratte's takeover of Fort Schanskop, a forgotten and useless relic of the Boer War, is ludicrous; the broken down fort near the Voortrekker Monument has no military or economic value. But De Ratte is a hero of the Angolan bush war, a Boer with impeccable credentials. How then can one explain his stupidity? Human has long opposed the romantics. He is wary of symbols. They must make the country ungovernable so that the negotiations to hand over power to the blacks will be aborted. To do that, they must be clear-sighted and ruthless, not blindly and sentimentally ideological. For this reason he has recruited Ralph. The Rhodesian-born arms trader is not an Afrikaner but he has more than proven his worth. He deals in guns, oil and diamonds and other commodities for which there is always a black market. Pam, the steady, well-groomed woman reading by the pool, is his secretary and confidante.

Ralph reports on the International Committee's recent work. He is co-ordinating another meeting in Brussels. The network has expanded; sympathisers from all over Europe and the Americas will attend. The meeting is crucial: funding for both open and clandestine work is low - despite the many volunteers, the costs of running both types of operations keep rising. (Ralph enjoys the solidity of Brussels, the succulence of its restaurants. But as much as they tempt him, he can never forget a particular autumn day in the Old Quarter. Walking out of a cinema into a fashionable shopping arcade, a bomb had blasted a hole in the cobble stones, destroying everything in front of him, gouging his right leg, shredding his chest and arms with fragments of metal and glass.)

Pam hands Human the book. It is an old volume, printed in Hamburg in the 1930's. She has underlined sentences with a red pen. Human reads: *The White Race must fight the Jews and the Black Race because they are the Dark Force made Manifest on Earth.*

He refills his glass. The television jumps to a furniture advert. His eyes move back to the garden, to the lines of shrubs outlined by the house lights' glow. He wishes he was alone.

Two hours before, in the dark of an avenue in Randburg, he had slowed down in the red car and called out to the young woman who walked ahead on the grass, "Where are you going?" When there was no reply, he had tried to coax a response, "You want a lift? Come on, I'll take you where you need to go."

She was wearing a bright orange dress and fashionable shoes. She had turned away. Then, when he repeated his offer, she had answered very deliberately for one so young, "Leave me alone, I don't need a lift."

Human had called again, "Come with me, don't worry. I won't hurt you."

"Go away!"

But she had become fearful as he continued staring at her, chalk-faced, the car engine running almost silently alongside the grassy sidewalk.

"My mother's waiting. She knows I am coming from the shop."

The young woman was carrying a bottle of Fanta. Human had flexed his hands, one on the wheel, the other gripped round the pistol.

"Please go!"

The avenue was deserted.

After firing there was something so tender about her face. Collapsing silently, folding into herself, something so gentle about the young black girl he had shot.

Human studies his hands. The gloves were dark and inside them were fingers; the same ones he now flexes round a frosted glass swirling with ice cubes. As Ralph speaks, he sees the orange bodice, the fullness of the stain, the small breasts pushing inside: she so vibrant, so willowy, swaying with the bullet's force.

"Of course, I agree," he says. "The attacks must be stepped up."

24 June 1993

They are seated in the main study; the oak desk dominating the room is chequered with small piles of documents. Ralph has loosened his tie. The ashtray beside him is heaped with shrunken butts. He rewinds the video-tape they have been watching. His movements are raw and dispirited.

Pam sits reading in a leather rocking chair. Human drains his glass. He observes Pam through the thick, empty bottom: her close-cropped, well-styled hair, her large, even teeth framed in pink lipstick. He watches her fingers turn the pages. He waits for Ralph to replay the video. This is the third time they will watch it.

The screen flickers. Two khakied storm troopers speckled with red dust slouch on the ground, their backs propped against a pale green Mercedes. A third man sprawls along the back seat; he is already dead. Above them, gun in hand, a black soldier shouts out that the Boers have shot people at random in the streets of Mafikeng, the Boers have left markings of blood. The camera pans over the AWB man stretched rigid on the leather upholstery. The black soldier raises his rifle and aims at the storm troopers on the ground. There is no doubt as to what he is about to do. Human watches the unbelieving white men leaning against the Mercedes, plead for mercy; he watches as the fat, sweaty bodies of the storm troopers jerk with the impact of the bullets.

Next week Ralph will be back in Brussels. He will organise fresh funds. He will walk the cobbled streets of the old town as if he is still in Saxonwold's green arms surrounded by antique bookcases, coin collections, lithographs of South African birds and a stinkwood coffee table draped with the Vierkleur and a Rhodesian flag.

The disorganised AWB convoy retreats from Mmabatho.

Ralph is saying, "We can't afford this rabble mouthing off, wearing revolvers, riding white horses with blonde children holding torches."

Journalists photograph the killing. Many newspapers report it as an act of barbarism: lawless continent always birthing and throwing up shrunken cattle, slaves, prisoners, nameless peasants under choking skies, acrid continent searching for rivers, mined out, all value extracted under torture after underground explosions.

Pam underlines another paragraph in the book with the thick leather cover:

Separation of the races is in accordance with the deepest laws of Nature. Enforcement of hierarchy is a necessary condition for maintaining the harmony of both higher and lower life forms. Every being and thing has a place in the world but harmony results from knowing and living out that specially designated place.

He studies Pam's youthful, porcelain skin. She has caressed his cheek once or twice after their operations. Recently she had touched his hand in the corridor leading to Ralph's study.

The video ends. White specks splatter across the screen, white light wrapping round glitter.

Ralph speaks of the trip to Brussels, "I want you to come with me. You need a break, you're looking buggered. After the meeting we'll go to the coast for a few days, eat mussels and crab." He leans forward. "I know a restaurant right on the beach."

Human has seen travelogues showing flower markets, waffle stands, chocolate shops, guards outside United Nations buildings and gold-tipped iron railings marking the perimeters of palaces.

The screen is snow falling on the streets of Brussels; the snow is the colour of Christiaan. They had sent him to boarding school. During the holidays when he came home, he lived in the TV room, absorbed in dramas and talk shows and drawing - always drawing something on the big square pads Helena bought him: black and white sketches of tidal waves and spiders crawling over cliffs to swallow houses. Or he would be in the kitchen watching her bake, helping her sprinkle hundreds of thousands on butter biscuits.

Christiaan has soft, brown hair that falls to his shoulders. He is slender with the unnatural pallor of a haemophiliac. Year by year, Human has watched him, and the sons of other men.

Snow falls in the streets of Brussels.

Where is Christiaan? At this moment he is with Helena, helping her choose curtains for her new home in the Cape where she is remarried to a widowed fruit farmer.

Human adjusts the armchair. It slides back. Ralph switches off the video recorder. As Human closes his eyes, he again sees the pale green Mercedes.

10 October 1993

On his back, grass spearing his skin. The sky above: a coloured vacuum that reflects and acknowledges nothing - only sucks up sacrificial smoke. He is sated with braaied meat; hands greasy, a smear of mustard across his lips, he snores.

Resistance organisations have set up contingency plans, but he has gone to only one meeting and left while the volksleiers were arguing about the correct line of action. He has withdrawn to the plot, taken special leave from work. There are reports of Boer farmers setting up communities in remote parts of Paraguay.

He rolls over, burps. The coals in the mobile barbecue still give off the fragrance of lamb chops, of fat. The hangover he has carried the whole day refuses to leave him. The previous night, driving home, already surrounded by open fields, he had felt a wave of vertigo. Unable to face the quiet, locked house with its lumbering dogs, he had driven back to the city, to the place where they had taken their oath; to the hotel in Hillbrow filled with black prostitutes. In the dimly lit bar, pummelled by a shattering disco bass, he had drunk beer after beer till a hand had reached over the pile of bottles and caressed his face and, before he could resist, stroked his back - long, piercing nails trailing over his skin. Then the whore had sat on his lap and parted his thighs, and when he was aroused, had taken him up to her room and sucked him. Then before he could strip her, she had pulled her top up over her head and twisted off her panties, and he had turned her, swivelling her face into a pillow and fucked her; a violent lunging that made her shout out. Once he came, he had withdrawn and seen that the condom was broken, and he had struck her with his fists, over and over again till she cried.

He wakes, struggling to breathe. He catches sight of green-yellow leaves, mottled waving of foliage. He has been dreaming of his mother. In the dream she says, "Kom, liefling, kom drink. Daar is koffie in die kan."(3) He peers into a black pot. She brushes his hair. Once she has softened it into waves, she massages his scalp with her strong, work-hardened hands. His brother, as usual, is teasing: "Dom kaffer-korrels."(4)

Human hates him for saying that, particularly because he has said it in front of Sanette van der Merwe. But it is true - his hair is unusually curly, like Oom Sarel. Usually his mother defended him, but in the dream she was also scared of Kobus.

Human sees her grey eyes, forty years before her murder in the Stormberg farm house - her body axed in six places, gashes across her shrunken old woman's breasts. Hendriena, the family servant, brought to the bedroom to identify her, then clean up the blood that stained the bed and the breakfast tray; Hendriena who made the best bread pudding in the district, who had worked in their house since she was a child, broken now by nightmares of the murder and by the months she had spent in jail as a suspect.

He sits up abruptly. He has spilt beer on his shirt. He tugs at the wetness. The shirt rips. Sun floods his chest. It is many months since he has enjoyed the sun. Today he is drunk, lying on the lawn. Everything drains out of his fingers, swollen black sausages. A sharp pain cuts through him. The spasm repeats itself. He twists to one side. A gush of half-chewed meat and potato spills over his arm. As he coughs, more mash of half-digested food pours out of his mouth. He hears a loud screech. The peacocks are on the veranda. Human sees the sheen of their rainbows. He feels scabrous hot beaks nip at his feet. He spins.

He will not go out tonight.

6 April 1994

He stares at the scuffed wooden cupboard brought from the farm after his mother's murder. The curtains with their thick, black under-sheet keep out all light. The TV has been on for days: lines of people waiting to vote; lines and lines waiting to bury him.

He moves to the kitchen but the taps won't open. He takes a bottle of Coke from the fridge, looks for crackers; dry crackers to eat with the Coke. As he pours, the bottle slips to the floor and breaks - there is a frothing pool on the white plastic tiles. And when the doorbell rings, he doesn't move. When it rings again he wonders who could have walked past the dogs - he cannot remember hearing them bark. But he cannot hear footsteps outside. Human closes his eyes. The bell rings again.

The TV gives an election update. There have been widespread irregularities in rural KwaZulu. There has also been sabotage in the delivery of ballot papers. After the discovery of hundreds of thousands of ballot papers dumped in the veld near DF Malan airport in Cape Town, there is growing talk of invalidating the election.

He recognises the voices - the louder one is Oosthuizen, his neighbour; the fainter, lower one is Conradie, the kaffie owner at the shopping centre near the crossroads. Oosthuizen is speaking but the words are jammed by the rasping of the peacocks and the striking of the brass clock. Then he hears Conradie. There is a crash as the door breaks and boots stamp in the doorway. No, it is not Conradie. It is Isaac, the gardener, who steals the mielies and pumpkins he waters so carefully, whose girlfriends come to drink on weekends; waddling around in tight jeans, locking slyly at Human, they stagger to the blocked toilet in the yard.

Isaac is standing next to Oosthuizen. Staring over his shoulder is Christiaan, pale and small in his primary school uniform, thin arms and stumpy legs so paltry next to Isaac's calloused hands and bare feet.

"Pa! Hoe gaan dit?" The boy smiles. "Gaan dit goed? Ek kom totsiens sê."(5)

Christiaan runs and huddles on the grass near the swimming pool. There is an old car tyre round his neck. Isaac stands over him swinging a jerry can that smells of petrol.

The boy smiles again and touches the tyre.

"Dis nie so vreeslik nie, pa. Party keer gaan dit lekker vinnig."(6)

7 July 1994

The strike by over 30,000 private security guards intensifies. For three days the centre of Johannesburg has been paralysed by violent battles between militants and the police. Mounting their own protest in support of higher wages, bus drivers set up a blockade, abandoning their vehicles in the streets and creating massive rush hour traffic jams.

Thirty kilometres away, in the heart of a five-star hotel, a conference room has been booked, a podium and an ornate main table decorated with the hotel company's colours and logo stand ready, porters reserve space for limousines. The Minister's convoy arrives an hour late. His entourage sweeps into the vast open foyer filled with waterfalls and criss-crossing escalators, chandeliers dropping from a height of six storeys.

"Hendrik," the Minister says, "why do you always tell me it's impossible? Are we not paid to resolve impossibility?"

Flanked by his generals, the Minister will face the media; the room is crowded with journalists from all over the world. He places a sheaf of papers on the podium and reads his prepared statement. The text written by the head of his communications department gives assurances that the government of National Unity respects the right to strike. At the same time, without using excessive force, it will ensure that minimal disruption is caused to persons and property.

He finishes reading the statement and pauses, turns away from the journalists and looks down the line of his delegation. Sometimes he cannot believe that he is looking at these hard, florid faces under their peaked caps, these representatives of the National Police Service, the National Intelligence Service, the National Security Service. These white men have all been his enemies, have hounded him since the start of his political life. They have spied on him, threatened his friends and his family with imprisonment, forced his expulsion from university, ordered his dismissal from jobs, attacked those who remained loyal to him and, when he became more prominent in the underground structures, plotted his assassination. But the strikes must be contained, dealt with firmly, though always with maximum restraint. The President is treading a tightrope, he cannot afford a massacre. The handover of power is fragile, still in the balance. There are too many elements seeking a spark to light a conflagration.

The journalists remain unconvinced. The Minister has spoken with charm and confidence and he is accompanied by experienced top-ranking officials, but their questions hammer away: can the country afford such negative publicity? Surely the strike wave will dampen investor sentiment? Why has the government been slow to take action against intimidation and anarchy?

The Minister begins to falter. His responses become repetitions of earlier explanations and arguments. The journalists are expectant - will he finally concede the seriousness of the situation, the potential spiral of ungovernability? The Minister becomes more and more frustrated. He begins to bluster. Then, as he prepares to close the press conference, one of the white men beside him begins speaking.

"Gentlemen, I would like to assure you that the situation is completely under control. We are taking all necessary steps to safeguard law and order. We know there is always a small minority which is radical but all sides must show reasonableness. This is a difficult time we are going through but, we, the national security forces, are well equipped to deal with all eventualities. I assure you of our willingness to cooperate with responsible trade unions leaders. We must stand together to safeguard peaceful protest. South Africans of goodwill must stand together to calm emotions. Let me tell you once again, there is no crisis. Of that you can be sure."

The slow, guttural voice, so unlike the Minister's, is almost hoarse but the words carry to all corners of the room. The journalists are silenced, eyes locked on the speaker.

"Let me repeat, there is no crisis and we are able to handle all developments. I would also like to take this opportunity to congratulate the Minister on his outstanding leadership and to assure him of everyone's maximum support. Thank you, sir".

The journalists talk among themselves; a name is mentioned. The Minister is jubilant.

"Anything else, ladies and gentlemen? Any other questions?"

The Minister smiles at the wiry man with the clipped moustache, faded grey eyes; hands in his lap, fingers playing as if screwing two objects together.

"Thank you, Colonel Human. Thank you so much for your contribution."

16 December 1995

He is alone on the stoep, tired after a day spent digging round the borehole. The pump is broken; he has battled to repair it. Twilight lulls him into a half sleep. Though the abundant rains of the previous week are still being soaked up, the heat of day has roasted the earth. Now evening falls, the air begins to freshen and the sky masses with rolling horizons of cloud. This is the first time since his adolescence that he has not gone to Blood River, to the commemoration service for those early martyrs. But he cannot face the crowds; the knowledge of defeat.

Tomorrow he will not wake at five, exercise then leave for the city. He will lie in bed, rise only when the sun is high and slowly eat the breakfast prepared by the servant girl. He will look up over the rim of his coffee cup and see the cypresses, erect like green candles, horses flicking their tails in the paddock, the peacock pairs flashing fans in the shade.

In front of him, next to a rack filled with toast, will be a copy of Hustler; the magazine will lie open on a centre fold photograph of a blonde woman embracing a whip. Under it will be a document on a government letterhead: PENSION AND RETRENCHMENT PACKAGE; the numbers roll on, zero after zero.

Farms are cheap in Zambia and Mozambique; hundreds of Boer families, guaranteed cultural autonomy and cheap labour, have set up their own communities on choice land.

After he has eaten, he will switch on the radio. The news will report the granting of amnesty to another group of policemen. He will switch off the radio before the report details the acts they committed during the period of Total Onslaught. Later he will make a few phone calls, his face set absent-mindedly as different voices respond. Then he will drive to a shooting range.

Every day, in the heat of the afternoon while clouds build into banks of dark foam, he fires round after round into a cardboard target: the orange and black figure of a young woman with slender hips and round, budding breasts.

1. "We cannot handover now. Who will deal with the kaffirs? Come, we have work to do. We'll show them. There's no time to lose."
2. "Just one. And you?"
   "Guess."
   "How many?"
   "Guess."
   "Enough, man!"
   "Two youngsters. Near Katlehong. Right, colonel, we'll be off. See you on Saturday."
3. "Come, darling, there's coffee in the pot."
4. "Stupid kaffir curls."
5. "Dad, how's it going? Going well? I've come to say good-bye."
6. "It's not so scary, dad. Sometimes it goes really quickly."

154

ATLANTEAN CHRONICLES
The Life and Times of Alpheus D'Oliviera Dhlomo
For Martin Rodriguez, Herman Hesse, Doris Lessing and Jorge Luis Borges

INTRODUCTION

Dear Reader

This essay is an extremely brief synopsis of an ongoing project. It takes the form of a compilation of extracts culled from primary and secondary sources and is part of a series covering seminal historical figures, as well as the forces which gave rise to their personal and public actions. In considering which would be the most revealing selections from Alpheus D'Oliviera Dhlomo's many different works, I have had to put my literary and political judgement to its most arduous test. On this score, the selection's limitations must be laid squarely on my shoulders whereas its strengths owe much to the advice of my partner, Phillippa, whose patience and insightful advice during the lengthy editing process was exemplary.

A life as rich and contentious as Dhlomo's warrants careful and exhaustive study. No straightforward, quick evaluations are possible – or desirable. For it was a life of struggle waged against mediocrity and complacency, a life that demanded much and was prepared to contribute much to many important human endeavours; to experiment as well as to attempt to transcend the terrible costs of social exploitation, the tyranny of instinct and loss of emotional control. The legacy and the paradox of his life live on in our history; its heroic consequences are played out as we create the future.

Bongani Ishmael Lewis
Weskoppies laboratory
Atlantis

PART 1

retreat v. & n. 1. *go back, retire, relinquish a position, (esp. of army etc.); recede (retreating chin, forehead). 2. v.t. (Chess) move (piece) back from forward or threatening position. 3. n. act of (Mil), signal for, retreating (beat a retreat, abandon undertaking; make good one's retreat, get safely away); 4. withdrawing into privacy or security, (place of) seclusion; temporary retirement for religious exercises or meditation; lurking place; place of shelter.*

Abbreviated Biography of Alpheus D'Oliviera Dhlomo (2625 - 2725)
Entry in the Encyclopaedia of Earth, published by the Laboratory of Tanganani in 2987

Born 28 February, 2625 at Atlantis, Western Cape Region; mother, Thanda-bantu Beatrice D'Oliviera, Sculptor and Co-ordinator of Gymnastics and Dramatic Arts; father, Samuel de Villiers Dhlomo, Actor, Mathematician and Co-ordinator of Energy Resources. Dhlomo was a graduate of the Veldvlei Laboratory School; he achieved distinctions in Astronomy, Architecture and World Literature; for fifty years he was a Master at the Saldanha Laboratory and Co-ordinator of the Department his father had founded.

Bonded with Louise Retief Sheik, Dancer and Social Researcher (for the period, 2648 - 58) with whom a son, Themba, was parented; with Leila Hartford Shapiro, Drummer and Systems Analyst (for the period, 2659 - 68); with Lindiwe Isobel van Schalkwyk, Poet and Pharmacologist (for the period, 2670 - 73); and with Lettie Naidoo Saambou, Painter and Educationist (for the period, 2680 - 95).

Main works were the design and building of Vuyoville, the most advanced human habitat of its time (now a World Heritage site); the writing of *Terra Astra,* a mythic, poetic epic also known as *The Book of Dhlomo*; the writing of the uniquely intimate chronicle of his private and political life known as *Dhlomo's Diary*; and his compilation of Amenite thinking entitled *The Teachings of Amen.*

As a built environment, Vuyoville's unique synthesis of astronomical positioning, world architectural styles and the general motifs of archetypes in the visual arts, constituted one of the foremost achievements of the Late Atlantean Age. However, the literary and intellectual worth of *Terra Astra* has been fiercely debated. It is probable that the more extreme views - brilliant evocation versus overblown self-indulgence - are both overstatements. Whatever their differences, most readers and more specialised critics agree that it is a landmark, both on account of its sheer physical length (there are six hundred and seventy two sections each averaging thirty lines), and the fact that Dhlomo revised each section obsessively for over seventy years, working and re-working, amending, adumbrating and polishing, with the result that while this epic literary and philosophical production's dominant feature is that of the manic, the overcharged, it almost always manages to regain balance and clarity. In this quality of diligence and attention to detail, we find the same approach responsible for conceiving the planetary scale and superbly clear articulation, both in design and in construction, of the metaphysical and material environment which became Vuyoville - the crucible that so directly facilitated the flowering of the Laboratories.

Dhlomo's life, filled with great personal tragedy, soaring artistic excellence and relentless political struggle, was, as could be expected, an extremely active and pulsating one. His trial in 2695, and subsequent imprisonment, for the murder of Lettie Naidoo Saambou, was the catalyst for a remarkable conversion which, in time, became a critical act in the dissolution of the Order - this after almost three centuries of stable and unrivalled government. As an ardent and dedicated Officer of the Order and as one of the key Co-ordinators in the Western Cape Region, Dhlomo's embracing Amenism required enormous courage and conviction. There have been few examples of such a mature evolution, a more considered and exhaustive reversing of one's previous worldview. Indeed, today, with the benefit of the hindsight of two centuries, historians agree he was the major figure of that period.

Dhlomo's life sentence, obliging him to act as Internal Co-ordinator of the Helot Penal System, opened his Mind to the central contradiction of the Time: the Officers' exploitation and manipulation of a slave population while at the same time claiming to live at the highest human meditative and scientific levels. His leadership role in The Struggle, in championing the Amenite cause without arrogance and bombast, enabled a relatively peaceful dismantling of the Order, and the transition from domination to democracy.

When Dhlomo died of heart failure on the night of his hundredth birthday, the integration of the Helots was only twenty years away and Atlantis was on the brink of becoming the definitive human society in which all cosmologies, moralities, languages and physical characteristics are interwoven; the true Rainbow Society of our Planet.

Extract from the first edition of Terra Astra

Section 1.

Flaming near the Centre of Ecstatic Sun,
Molten Wings Wrapt round Creation's Higher Rungs,
Streams of Spirit Unconcerned with Us
(We, Transient Ones who Sweat and Age),
They Play with the Animals
And Others of the Divine Nature -
Dolphins Surfing in Tropical Seas,
Blue Cranes Hovering Above Green Gorges -
Creatures Still Radiant with the Mind
And Matter of the God Head.

Pristine in Form and Bloodless,
These Spirits Claim Certain Choice Companions -
Outstanding Souls, who, though Born to Die on Earth,
Defy the Deal, the Pile of Things,
The Urge to Strut, the Taste for Bile;
Few Certain Seasoned Souls,
Resisters of the Dirt and Weight of Time,
The Rack of Pleasure and of Pain;
Outriders on Passion's Pendulum
Who Walk the Thin Line and Seldom Falter.

These Few Survivors of the Gross Realm
Regain the Paradise.
But in Reconnecting with the Celestial Flame
Do not Abandon Us;
Their Compassion Flows,
They Remain Our Guides.
Indeed, between the Innocence,
The Glory of their Merged Perfection,
We Enjoy the Daily Unfolding,
The Hourly Rate of Love and Hate,
The Minute Shift that Grants Ecstasy Power
To Conquer Death's Flesh.

Extract from Dhlomo's Diary

Dhlomo's private diary was discovered after his death by his grandson, Lungile Karl Visagie, at that time, a child of nine years of age. The disk had been secreted in the jacket cover of a rare tenth century illuminated version of the "Book of Daniel". It was written in a specially coded program that took the young Lungile almost two years to decipher. The diary consisted of random entries (he did not maintain it on a daily basis); Dhlomo would move back and forth in time, commenting at random on what took his fancy or what seemed of importance. Though the prolixity of his entries and their extreme subjectivity call into question many of the perspectives put forward, the editors Elise and Elias Kunstenaar have expressed the view that as bulky and unsystematic as they are, the diary constitutes a remarkable raw record of Dhlomo's thinking and is, on that basis, worthy of perusal by students of his life and work.

8 February, 2695

"It is a quiet, bright morning, the aromas and perfumes of the spreading gardens with their exotic flowers and stretches of grass rise up over the Laboratory.

I am sitting at my work-table. It is a long, rectangular chrome sheet resting on wooden legs. Carved into the legs are eagles and snakes. I sit at a Terminal entering my thoughts. Reading the script as it appears on the screen and playing out the dances and wailing of the images, the furrows between my eyes are sharp and deep. I feel a pulse in the centre of my forehead. I move the cursor, reviewing what has been conjured.

In the afternoon, I will join the landscapers to plan the next season, to decide what should be uprooted and what should supplant them. I will ride round the grounds in a bubble car and plan for the season to come. But now facing the screen, all that occupies and possesses me are the system codes shining out in yellow; and above them, I confront the open, still empty, potential of black space."

Extract from the third edition of Terra Astra.

Section 4.

Despite the Ease and the Splendour,
String of Days and Nights Blending
Without Loss, without Panic,
The Brightest, Fiercest Souls,
Seeing Themselves in the Mirror,
Swelling with Desire to Make Their Own History,
Demanded the Field of Freedom.

God Head Emanated at the Exit,
Massive Fire-gate near the Forest of Streams;
God Head Faced Them with the Void
And they Felt the Vibration and Heard Its Voice:

"All Consequences in Accord,
Moments of the Universal Need,
Live out Your Ambition.
You have Shown no Taste for My Perfection,
But Plotted and Conspired to Create your Own.

Now as Every Creation reflects its Creator,
Your's will Reflect the Infancy of your Ability:
Predatory, Despoiling, Accumulative;
A World of Slaves Manipulating Each the Other,
And Your Other Inventions.

Though You Trumpet the Glories of your Cleverness,
Long will You Crave My State of Everlasting Ripeness,
Perfect Oneness in the Chain of Being.
Once Absolute Expressions of My Will,
As of This Instant You Are Cast Off by Your Revolt;
Now Wander, Expelled From Timelessness,
Banished from My Terrible Love.

Extract from Dhlomo's Diary

9 February, 2695

"It is only five days. At first, I was swallowed by a darkness that chewed a great hole in my stomach; but now, over the past few hours, it has steadied into a dull, hammering blankness.

I buckle under the weight of this withdrawal of love, this sudden ending of my relationship with Lettie. It is not that I have felt us, gradually and inescapably, after a long period of crises and tension, made bitter and estranged by an increasing incompatibility, lurching apart. No, all my instincts and experience tell me that we have loved each other profoundly and unreservedly during these fifteen years.

Yet now I discover that this same Lettie, this Lettie whom I adore, is not who I imagine she is. Despite the years passed together, the rich history of our shared lives, she has surprised and shocked my core: she who has concealed from me for so long her utter alienation.

What am I to do?

I know that I still love her. So much so that I cannot conceive of living without her! But how am I to persuade her to return? Reconciliation is impossible. For that to take place, we would have to meet and be together, would have to confront each other. And how can I confront her when she is absent, when she is no longer herself?

I think of nothing else. Whichever way I look at it, she is the cause of my suffering. Of course, she must live freely and independently, as she sees necessary, but I cannot accept these changes. I say this honestly. I know the contradiction but this is a question of betrayal. I have never acknowledged the right of others to live entirely as they choose. There are clear limits placed on our freedom to act. Officers are enjoined to act in terms of The Code. For us, there can be no separation between personal morality and the values contained in The Code. And yet we have always maintained the right of the Individual to explore the ramifications of individualism and free choice. How much more important for me to recognise this right for someone I love and respect! And because I expect Lettie to be more enlightened, more sensitive than others, I hold her more accountable. And so, how can I gloss over and ignore her actions which threaten our Bonding; which threaten our very Civilisation? How can I ignore this betrayal on account of my private, personal love?

All this is confused: I have to find a way to control my unhappiness. I cannot allow it to overwhelm me. Periodically during my life, the wish to die has been strong in me, but I have never felt as weak and defeated as I do now.

Can I rely on what I know?

At the time of previous crises, during breakdowns of love and respect, I experienced the same acute pain, but I transcended the emptiness, the terror of aloneness. I did so by screening my thoughts, clearing them, and at the same time, being completely honest and aware of my deepest feelings, whatever their texture and orientation. Most importantly, I was able to continue believing in the omniscience of intuition.

Till today I have implicitly known that I would crystallize an appropriate Way Forward; that I would throw up a response which would be the foundation for a successful decision. But now I have no such confidence although I know that each step I take in my relations with Lettie will have massive repercussions - both for us and for others.

It is undeniable that a defeat has taken place. It is difficult to believe that someone as dedicated and self-conscious as Lettie could do as she has done. Moreover, her actions have rocked confidence in my own judgement. What did I really know of her if such forces were able to erupt, pushing all reason aside?

Lettie has been overcome by a momentous, overpowering obsession. She has surrendered her core to a relationship that can only destroy everything we cherish - everything noble and true which we have inherited.

I have sat here for five days tortured, knowing that I cannot accept, tolerate or indulge her.

All my life I have studied the Dialectic, its Contexts and Forces. I have subjected myself to its Discipline and to the Codes of the Order. I have dedicated myself to the conceptualisation and construction of the Necessary Balance. Despite great difficulties I have never wavered. How can I now abdicate these supreme truths in the face of this most momentous challenge!

LATER: EVENING

I have spent the day alone.

Outside, the paths are still thronged with visitors. It is Open Day at the Laboratory and many thousands have streamed into the grounds. All over, groups have formed to take part in seminars and symposia. Normally I would have been in the Centre co-ordinating the whole sequence of activities, but today I have felt so demoralised that I was forced to ask my Deputy to substitute.

Lettie's image consumes me.

How could it be otherwise? Her presence permeates our home. Wherever I turn I am reminded of her. Though she has embraced an alien philosophy, my love for her is still so strong. But my love will not make me deviate from what I know to be right. For those who place their personal love above the Path of the Order can only fall into a pit of delusion. And I am painfully aware of the consequences of rash behaviour. Having analysed each aspect of the situation, I will act in defence of the World and the Values we propagate and have long worked for. But having said this, I must emphasize that my responses will be well-considered. I intend my Course of Action to be scientific and effective. Faced with this crisis, I must maintain my strength to set aside the deviations that love can cause. More than ever, I need to hone my powers of determination and resolve. There is no purpose in lamenting that such has been my life, that such have been the sufferings and heartaches which afflict me. But must I finally accept that I will never know rest and wholeness?

In all my Bondings I have inevitably known torment. Despite each having been founded on the embodiment of the Beauty of the Female Form, the subtlety and warmth of the Female Spirit, its stamina, its loyalty, its maternal cunning, I have been dazzled by sensitive, gifted, tender, passionate but often neurotic women who have immersed themselves in a great love with me and then twisted, in sudden, violent, capricious swings, out of my reach. I have, in the end, always been abandoned, remaining alone, mystified by their fierce rejections.

And now even Lettie has betrayed me."

Extract from the third edition of Terra Astra

Section 5

When the Golden Darkness, Pride,
Swelled Inside Us,
We Dared not Speak of It.
Indeed, we did not Know
We had Spoken Until after Word Formed
And was Uttered.
The Word was Guttural Yet Sibilant;
We Pronounced Ourselves: **I.**

We Stood by the Tree,
Juices of Many Fruits
Dripping from Our Jaws.
Through the Branches,
A Great Shining.
And We Began to Decipher The Light.

"How I Long to Give Body
To What I Myself Design!
How Wonderful the World
I will Make My Own!"

Then Reflections,
Memories of Astral Sweeps,
Caused Us to Hunger:
We, the Drifting, Particles of a Single,
Mobile, Incandescent, Sublime Ocean,
Moving in Waves.

But Cast Out of the Divine Field
To Manifest on Earth,
Immersed Daily in Steamy Swamps and Slime,
We Sweated for Sustenance,
Backs Bent, Planting, Harvesting,
Tending, Slaughtering:
All These According
To the Measure of Our Needs,
The Bound and Unbounded
Limits of Our Appetites.

Expelled, in Flight from Divine Anger,
Incarnating in Jungles and in Ice Caverns,
We, with Our Five Pronged Sensations,
Engaged with Disease and Decrepitude.

Extract from Dhlomo's Diary

10 February, 2695

"I feel hollow. When I face a task, I am overwhelmed by a sense of utter futility. There can be no progress. Indeed, the word 'progress' provokes a loss of strength. How can there be human advancement when in Life there is so much contradiction, so much pain and desperation?

Lettie and I have been living together for fifteen years. For me this has been so short a time, yet it seems as if we have been together for an eternity that I so much desired, and then savoured so intensely.

We had known of each other for many years but from a distance; that is to say, only through publications and our respective reputations. The first time I read one of her many essays, I knew I was encountering a superbly maturing yet light Mind. The breadth of her knowledge was vast; ranging from the technomatrix of the mouth in the forming and delivering of words, to the elliptical paths of comets as they sweep through deep space. As a painter there was the sensitivity yet force of her colourism, her dramatic evocation of darkness, and her ability to express the core of human motivation.

When she was still a child, her family had left Atlantis for Brasilia. Yet despite her youth at the time of their migration, and her being educated in Sao Paolo at the Laboratory of Our Magna Mater, she remained very Atlantean in both her speech and outward behavioural style. So while I read and digested her Work, my admiration took on a personal aspect. Indeed, while my relationship with Lindiwe was dying, I fantasized about Lettie but with the security of an ocean: that holy body of water became my moat. For I was too much in awe of her mental and physical beauty to take the initiative.

As it was, we did finally meet the year after Lindiwe and I separated. The meeting took place at a congress of the Association of Laboratories in Transamerica. It was exactly noon when we shook hands in the lobby of the Conference Centre. How wonderful that, no matter how hard one's life, there is always the hope of Romance! More enchanting is the sensation itself.

I had a strong desire to embrace Lettie as soon as Professor Rhodes made the introductions. I felt my lips on her smooth, round, brown cheeks. Her eyes still milky but sighted now after the infections she'd suffered as a child, her hair braided to form a turban of black silk, we stood in the middle of the vast, circular foyer, under the mosaic in gold and emerald-green portraying the Ten Stages of the Mean. Professor Rhodes smiled and moved away. I stood clasping her hand, overwhelmed that the moment was actually taking place.

She spoke first. "Can we meet after the symposium? I would like to show you my latest paper. I'm sure it will be of interest to you!"

Her eyes sparkled; there was no trace of arrogance in her tone. I had no doubt that she was fully tuned to me and I was overjoyed. Her work was reaching maturation, transcending all previous research in the field. She pressed my hand again. I stood by her side. My isolation was finally broken! I had felt so depressed during the last three years with Lindiwe.

Of course, there were those who sniggered at our age difference. But generally the Laboratories welcomed our Bonding. After all, Lettie was the most inspired Educator of her generation, a young woman of great charm and intelligence, and I was an honoured, if slightly fatigued, Co-ordinating Officer with a history of meritorious service and brilliance.

What no one could deny was that we were in love and nothing could check our combined energy. We converted a cluster of dilapidated farm buildings into a suitable Habitat. In keeping with her fascination for antiquity, Lettie painted the walls with the Signs of the Egyptian Zodiac and I built a rudimentary but functional observatory on the flat roof of a store-room. We grew our own Wafer as well as vegetables.

I do not believe it to have been merely fortuitous that these past fifteen years have been among the most productive of my life. I at last began to deepen my knowledge of Chemistry, Sociology and the general patterns of Spiritual Transformation. And my physical strength, which had begun to slacken, was restored. Taken collectively, all these positive forces gave me a new Balance and Sense of Purpose. More importantly, in experiencing this reinvigoration, I realised just how advanced had been my imperceptible decline into a jaded Lassitude, and that any real motivation to continue the Struggle for Perfection was slowly seeping out of me. (I am not speaking of adolescent Utopianism but of mature energy which coheres when the sense of Mortality becomes truly personal and the abysses of Indolence, Nihilism and Destructiveness have been stared down).

There were many Projects that Lettie and I jointly undertook, and in all of them we created new norms and targets. There was a rare inventiveness and originality in our preparation and execution. The most notable of these projects was the utilization of Alpha Energy to enter Sleep Depth; and in so doing, to slow down the particles and enable the recording of dreams.

The recording of dreams so that they can be observed, reflected on, explored, analysed – is an age-old Project that had defeated many Generations. To have such access to the Sub-Conscious is to grant intervention by a Conscious Party so as to heal malignancies, distortions and other psychic abscesses.

The power of the Technique we invented was such that each Subject is able to study his or her Self without a sense of shame, and without the obvious pressure of outside Judgement. This intimacy is vital; the facility to observe and follow the shifts and fancies of the Sub-Conscious must be kept completely confidential in order to preserve Confidence and Self-Belief for Healing. It was therefore imperative to design an extremely secure system for entry to a Subject's Dream Stream. As a result, we constructed a unique Access Code based on the Subject selecting any Form, Word, Numeral or Image as a Key. This Key changed on a daily basis in that the dominant symbol in the Subject's most recent Dream became the new Key; as such the chances of keying in to someone else's Code were negligible.

As there had never been a reported case of this occurring, it was with shock, that one day, while Lettie was away, and I had entered her Sanctuary driven by some blind impulse to feel her Spirit, that standing by her Terminal, I glanced at the Monitor, and there on the Screen was a giant, pulsing volcano erupting into a sea of glowing, red, dissolving lava. Instinctively, I knew that this Image was Lettie's Code - all I had to do was proceed and ENTER.

Little did I know what was to result from this Violation! But how vivid and unfathomable were Lettie's dreams! I soon began to spend hours viewing those sharp, bright sequences of colour and motion. And how could one fathom the fact that each time I stood in front of Terminal the latest Key was open to view. Hour after hour I spent viewing her Dream Stream. Indeed, I was so utterly drawn into them that my other hours were passages of Dead Time, mere waiting until the opportunity to again slip into her Sanctuary and gorge on those unforgettable Images presented itself.

Apart from the hours spent working together on Projects, the most intense moments of our Joined Life were those consumed by lovemaking. I revelled in her softness, her muscularity, her rhythms and her fragrance. How fortunate I was to have met and attracted such a glowing woman! How bitter that today all those hours are burnt up, rotting memories and the ties knotted between us have been so brutally cut!

LATER: MIDNIGHT

I must declare something.

Among Lettie's varied Dreams were strips of mad, feverish couplings and saco-masochistic acts involving partners of different and the same sex - more shocking were the acts involving animals.

The first Dark Dream being unlike anything I had ever understood to be in Lettie's Nature, I was at first incredulous, then disgusted; but almost immediately, stimulated by their brilliant configurations and energy, something new stirred in me. I soon became obsessed to the extent that I would leave the Laboratory early so as to get home before she arrived and Key In.

Let me be frank: the heat of our first years had passed. Despite my optimal physical condition (my health has always been good and I have maintained a high level of stamina), I was growing older and my sexual power was inevitably waning. All this was taking place while Lettie was growing into maturity as a woman, becoming more passionate, more open in expressing a range of sexual preferences and needs. As such, it did not take very long for these Dark Dreams to begin to fuel our love-making; indeed, they plunged us into a phase of Abandon that both shocked and fascinated us.

I traced my initial attraction: surely the truth was that this Abandon had always been within me, albeit in a semi-conscious way: the Phallus driven mad. And then in considering Lettie, there was the example of her consumed by the Life of the Body, when an expression of instinctual, unmediated carnality would inhabit her face.

Another remarkable aspect was that I began recording the Dreams in my Diary. The third or fourth time that I did so, I found myself spontaneously writing out both a description and an interpretation. I did so in verse; free-running verse stanzas that were very tight and concise but simultaneously elaborate. Afterwards, before I fully appreciated what was happening, I began to habitually enter each Dream as a stanza in "The Book". Every evening I would return to my Terminal, eat a Wafer, and write them out in all their stark cycles. I must emphasize that they were not just sequences of debauchery, mere twisted, violent battles to reach Orgasm; perversions, in that only supremacy and humiliation are able to bring satisfaction. Many were variations of myths of the Very Beginning - ancient sciences which had been woven into stories, cosmologies laying out the foundations of human thought and understanding.

I know that Lettie was never aware, nor suspected, that I had access to her Code; at no point did she ever intimate so, either by word or by gesture. Nevertheless, after the first entry, I was tormented by guilt. This was the first time that I had invaded Inner Space: I knew only too well that the consequences would be severe. Unforgivably, I was now living with her in a way which precluded her equal participation; she was the passive one, feeding me, but unaware of what I was taking in, on what I was being nourished. And, in addition to the calamitous Sequence I knew would unfold the longer I continued to be a voyeur, there was another perspective: The Code punished such Invasion by stripping the Violator of all Responsibility and all Honour. He or she was removed from Office, then taken to a Place of ReLearning and again inducted into the Code, this time not gently as if he or she was a child, but remorselessly as the accepted manner of dealing with an erring adult who had broken down in the face of Temptation and buried all Moral Sense in pursuit of some unworthy goal and now needed to be "shocked" out of False Consciousness.

I knew that I was guilty, and without even the slightest mitigating circumstance to soften my responsibility. Invasion of a stranger would have been bad enough. How much more damning that the victim was my Partner, my Lover, my Muse! Again and again, I vowed to reveal everything to her so that she could secure another Code and block me out. But wearing the Holoscope, whirling in her flamboyant abstractions and abandonments, it was always tomorrow, tomorrow...

Finally, midway through the third year, I began to admit to myself that I was happy to ignore the question of Morality: I was addicted. I could not live without Lettie's Fantasies. And it was clear that any resolution to cease keying in could not keep me from her Sanctuary for an extended period. In fact, three weeks was the longest stretch that I was able to withstand the Need.

It filled me with shock that many Dreams focussed on a young girl who was always enslaved, and that many were filled with a mass of almost faceless, gleaming, muscular torsos who preyed on her. But it was not as if they were all violent: in all her dreams there were composites of strength and generosity as well as morbid, self-destructive characters. And not once did I see myself; that is, visualised literally. And there were rarely older men who could have represented me.

After six years tormented by this fixation, I could no longer live with myself. I retreated to the Masakhane Healing Centre near Ceres. Seven months of Meditation and Gymnastics quietened me. Then slowly purging my being of the images and my responses, and distancing the Power Madness, the licence that boiled in me, the lust and the love of Bright Shining that imbued Lettie's dreams, transmuted into an unextinguishable need for forgiveness. ·

I returned to the Laboratory to confess to her that I had inadvertently stumbled across her Code. However, I told her that I hadn't keyed in - even at that point, I was too ashamed to be completely honest. Another serious evasion was that I said that I had discovered the Code only that day. How great was my fear that she would be utterly dismayed by my betrayal and leave me! So I allowed the cancer of fear to dominate me. Now the wheels are turning and I feel so low, so defeated. Why should our brief lives not be glorious and joyous?"

Extract from the fifth edition of Terra Astra

Section 6

Strapped to the Rock of Nature,
Living in a Web in which Our Juice is Sucked,
A Web, Stronger, More Beautiful
Than any Other Construction,
We who Fled the Failed Paradise
Of a Failed Creator,
Stumble in a Wilderness:
The Wastes of the Body and its Pride.

We Stagger through Deserts of Carrion
Chewing Shanks and Livers
And Other Intestines.
We Throw Bones at Each Other,
Smeared with Blood,
Chanting as the Moons of Planets Revolve,
Tugging at our Insides.
We Expand and Contract
Under Multi-Coloured Satellites -
Our Creator, Imperfect,
Creator of Our Imperfection,
Creating Us to Struggle.

Desperate for Blissful Endlessness,
Wounded Souls Falling,
Blinded by both Darkness and Light,
Chance and Certainty Meet,
For Consequence Creates
Further Consequence,
And no Moment is without its
Ancestry.

Extract from Dhlomo's Diary

11 February, 2695

"I've chewed another Wafer. This is my third today and it's not even noon. The crisis has affected me like no other, worse even than the deaths of my beloved mother and father. For how does one explain this rupture, its coming so suddenly, so unexpectedly, just after we had spent three extraordinary, perfectly balanced and mysterious weeks together?

It was towards the end of the Cycle, before the Day of Reflection when we observe the Purification. How could one fail to be moved by the earnest solitude and silence of those unique days? When everyone cleanses, examining the slate of the soul, accounting for all thoughts and actions, and culminating in the annual State of the Order debate led by the inner core of Bright Ones. Lettie and I were to travel to our Purification Place, the site we had designed and built on the beach at Cape Point. We reached the clearing just as the sun dipped away. As dusk draped a dark blue film over the waves and sand, a chestnut horse galloped over the dunes, dogs snapping at its hooves. Lettie was carrying provisions and I had the Tools and Instruments on my back. The clearing was almost as we had left it. But then it is rare for Purification Sites to be tampered with. Occasionally a disturbed or malevolent Soul will smash the Landing or the Fireplace. Since the New Period, such acts of destruction have become rare. Those who are unable to keep Balance have been given the opportunity to enter the Chemical Realm and to remove themselves from Psychotic Consciousness.

When we arrived, Lettie swept the leaves and gathered the branches which covered the Polar Places. I laid down our sleeping mats, redug the fire-place and scented the latrine with a natural essence. As backup should there be rain, we set up an Energy Stand. This was to be used only if the making of Fire was impossible. The rolling in of waves became louder in the stillness. We watched sea-birds cross the expanses of dune to land along the ridges of wooded growth. After many years of intense work, Life's Work, the final stages of our Personal Projects were at hand. As we stood in the perfectly shaped alcove we had pruned into the thickets, the sun, a burnt-red stub over the ripples of ocean, we sensed each of our excitements and fears - so much depended on our success."

Extract from the ninth edition of Terra Astra

Section 4

Each Manifestation
Unique, Significant,
Yet Temporary;
Mere Version, Adventure in a Series,
Struggling with Memory;
Curious, Arrogant,
Capturing Fire,
Sounding and Spelling out Language;
Hurling and being Hurled
Into Scarcity then Satiety,
Always Agonising
For the Whole of Paradise,
But Driven beyond That Infinity,
To Produce its Own Forms -
However Primitive, Brief, Dumb,
Incoherent, Flat, Inverted, Brash,
Deformed.

Extract from Dhlomo's Diary

12 February, 2695

"I opened a container of Water. Lettie spoke the Words to purify the Chalices.
I filled them. She sprinkled drops around the perimeters of the Polar Places
then refilled the Chalices so we could drink our fill. On each of the fourteen
days of the Purification we repeated this ceremony, at dawn and at dusk.
She had decorated the clay receptacles with the Yin and Yang, using black
and white on the unglazed reddish surfaces. The chalices had been made by
a blind potter, an old woman who lived in the great Blouberg Sanctuary. Her
vessels are prized for their simplicity and purity as well as their strength.
We faced the ocean. Lettie led us in the Breathing; we steadily reduced our
pulses. Soon I felt the Glow begin in my midriff, then spread outwards, a

slow, persistent, grand flowering of warm vibration simultaneously spreading from my centre to my feet and my hands. Reaching its crescendo, it rose up into my head. The Field held then rushed, shooting through me as I connected with the Root-Energy of the surrounding trees and the varied vegetation massed around the clearing. The sky lifted. The darkness, impregnated with radiant particles, became visible. The flow intensified, sub-matter articulating forms of consolidated fields to emerge, flare, cool and die. How one loves the Glow as it pulses in us, livening as no other experience, when we Humans enter into the realm of Godhead, leaving our gross material form, transmuting into purer Energy!

Several hours later we returned to the Polar Places. It is always so exhilarating to perform the Breathing in the still, transparent beauty of the Beach and Forest! Though we try to sustain our Openness in the Laboratory, there are so many distractions! And, of course, there is the sometimes negative over-intensity of our Work, application to those Tasks with Total Commitment.

My Poem is in its seventh draft. The initial outlines are cohering even as they extend themselves, each facet beginning to shine with the force it needs for full realisation; the poem is filling and swelling with itself, moulding itself from quirks and fragments of Idea. From the start, I set myself the highest and most difficult Task: that of integrating the experience of my Generation, my Epoch, with the unique and direct nature of my Moment in the Universal Ocean. The past two years have witnessed me working with exceptional intensity and discipline. My editors, the brother and sister, Elias and Elise Kunstenaar, have become more and more effusive in their praise and excitement! They believe my best work is now emerging.

Elise and Elias spend their mornings sifting through the writing I do in the evening. At noon each day, they hand me their annotations and comments. Then I evaluate the original text as well as their suggestions, and begin sculpting, polishing, rinsing each line in the waves of my thinking.

Alone, at my Place in the heart of the Laboratory, I sit before the screen upon which my thoughts travel: the Epic advances and I am drawn deeper and deeper into that World.

Lettie's program has also been progressing. The children being educated for advanced leadership are in their tenth year of Development. They seem blessed with energy and vision. Lettie is full of admiration for their clarity and purposefulness. She says they are stronger than we were at that stage of Incarnation.

How fortunate that this is the case! These children will have to counter the Great Despoilation as Forms disjoint from their contexts to become frozen, stale, obstructions to the Flow. And in so doing they will have to take decisions whose outcomes will fundamentally affect the continuation of the Incarnations we currently know on our planet.

Lettie has a highly perceptive and genuine understanding of her pupils. She felt they will soon be competent to make useful, well-articulated proposals to the Local Councils. Both the young men and women respond to her positively, affectionately; she is universally respected as an exceptionally gifted and sensitive teacher.

So it is that both our Works are bound up with integrating the many millions of Incarnations since the beginning of Primate Time; countless histories as each sinew expanded, flowered, despite the solitariness, the misery of struggle, after the first inkling of self-consciousness expelled us from the primal state of undifferentiated inertia. But now with The Millenium so near, the Plague has bred suffering and death. Hysteria is spreading amongst the masses of Helots. There are reports from many Inspectors that they flock to participate in obscure, crude ceremonies conducted by demagogic charlatans; preachers, both men and women, who wear white head-bands, simple gowns of linen and purple capes, who carry staffs topped with silver pennants. They promise a Way Forward, this movement of ascetic but crazed revolutionaries founded by a lapsed, renegade Particle Scientist named, Amen.

I knew him well. For Amen was one of us, an Officer. While researching the Morphosphere, he performed certain experiments around whose findings have developed various theories. But without exception, these theories (which soon codified into a set of doctrines) have been exposed as a sham, as misguided and unsubstantiated. In particular, the celebrated Laboratory of the Boland, one of our key Knowledge Centres, after an exhaustive and cross-referenced check has dismissed them as "ill-conceived, overly emotive and tainted by utopian primitivism".

It has always been the case with The Bright Ones of the Laboratories - whilst never denying the importance of Intuition, which they consider to be a necessary but subordinate feature of Creativity, it is the Discipline of Analysis which is the unshakeable core of Enlightenment.

The irrational outbreaks of fervour amongst the Amenites are ancient in character and represent throwbacks to the earliest days of Automatic Consciousness; those times when violent, orgiastic tribal hordes were gripped by superstition and impulse. But, however much the Dialectic explains the Unity of Opposites, it is nonetheless shocking for an Officer to witness the abandonment of the Helots; their surrender to the grosser levels despite their pretensions to the contrary.

Yet I write this in the full and painful knowledge (which is wholly shared by the Convocation of Laboratories) that the current crisis of the Amenites is nothing less then an appropriate response to our Imbalance: we are too measured, too calm, too still and reserved. However, we are also wise and astute appraisers of history. Accordingly, we appreciate that we are in decline, that our vision has failed to fully Uplift and that, as a result, we have passionate, brutal throwbacks like Amen challenging our legitimacy, our structuring the Way for the Masses.

Like every organism, we are tiring. Still trapped in the Gross Process, we cannot Brighten ourselves further in order to fully Enmind; we cannot reach further Forms of greater complexity and synchronicity. Yet our Knowledge prevents us from destroying Amen - we know he would merely be replaced by some other instrument to perform the task of hastening diversion and the decay. The pendulum has swung. Though our Way has guided Earth for many hundreds of years, it now faces an altogether new kind of challenge; pressures that seem to be increasingly insurmountable.

Of great concern is the fact that no new direction has been conceived in the Laboratories to restore the Balance of Forces. Stricken by the Plague, the Masses show psychotic tendencies. The Amenites have consolidated cells in the largest cities; only in the smaller towns have we managed to uproot them. The security situation grows tenser even if it is not yet critical. Fortunately, despite their eruptive, passionate rituals, they have remained true to their oath of Non-Violence: the promise of a New Way has not yet led them to defy us. More dangerous, are the signs of our precariousness - in particular, the intellectual breakdown and emotional confusion shown by leading Officers. With hindsight I now realise that Amen was but the first to break Discipline. Today, further grievous betrayals occur.

My Lettie is a living example.

(At this point in the original text, Dhlomo drew the outline of a woman's face; slender yet full features expressed in about seven or eight deft lines).

SEVERAL HOURS LATER

From our mats at the Polar Places, deep in the pulsing of Meditation, we could hear the spouting of whales in the bay before us, the low squealing of seals. Last light ebbed after sunset; a strident but comforting solar blaze touched down in the centre of the Place, in the middle of this thicket which we had staked out many years ago while walking over the dunes; discovered and cherished, our most profound Home.

For months, we had searched for such a location. Every Bonding requires its Place, beside the ocean or in a forest, on a high ledge cut into a mountain or beside a river; every Bonding needs its Place to consolidate and purify, removed from the turbulence of social and political life, quiet in the depths of the Binary Pulse, full with the spirit of Other Worlds.

Lettie returned into Automatic Consciousness before I did. When I too, returned, she was looking at me, her eyes radiant yet filmy, exactly as I remembered them from our first meeting.

After orgasm her eyes shine like that, but thicker, more tenderly. This glow was more focussed: dawn-light after rain has fallen and there is a perfume of soil mixed with minerals, salts and flowers, oxygen enriched by plants; the tide of orgasm surges, then withdraws into tranquillity, whereas this vibration is light.

When she reaches such a state of clarity and intensity, the manifestation enraptures me. I love her again as I loved her in the conference foyer: hair high and towered, her lips like mulberries.

The morning after our first meeting, alone in my room, bathed in sunlight, I sat covering my eyes, picturing her. She had said how much she treasured my poems, as well as the various features (whether articles or programs) which she had encountered on me in various media.

The most recent interview appeared in the annual survey of major Laboratories conducted by a team from `Transcendence', one of the foremost Stations. The focus was on my attempt to delineate the foundations, the key starting points, for the development of Symbols. Another subject was my work as Habitat Co-ordinator for the Western Cape region, in particular after the breaking away of the Peninsula. This period, immediately after the great flood of 2112 when the city of Cape Town was washed away and Atlantis, its orphan child, stuck in low scrub and dunes up the West Coast, became the new Capital and flourished, giving birth to our Order and its Sacred Way, was the High Point of my Architectural Life.

For centuries this has been the core of Atlantean understanding: no intellectual or artistic Life can be properly balanced if the Creator is not also involved in the economic and technical spheres. So following the example of my beloved Father, Jason Vusimuzu Dhlomo, I volunteered for, and was appointed, Regional Co-ordinator responsible for Architecture, Energy Usage and Land Allocation.

After the last conference session of the day, Lettie and I met again in the foyer. She took my arm and led me to the bus which drove us back into the Old Quarter; we were staying at the same Hospitality Centre near the harbour. Lettie was bubbling over with energy. She suggested we have dinner at a small restaurant - an old wooden house lit with human-size candles overlooking the Langebaan Lagoon.

We ate calamari with chips and salad. (For many years we would celebrate this anniversary by dining on this same menu!) Later that evening, we went down to the beach and lay on the sand and looked up at the stars, listening to the tide come in. Still later, in the dark of her aromatic room, we consummated the passion and curiosity generated over years of experiencing each other's Minds. Never before have I ever experienced such depth and force of passion! Lettie sat on her mat glowing. I faced her and we remained breathing, lulled by the drag of waves. The moon rose, white, cratered, bulging up from the north-east. Lettie sighed then rose. I followed her. (She always led me in the Purification). She began the next Exersize. I waited to test her mood, her speed and timing as we performed the gymnastic element - the Exersizes that were first to be done in the clearing, and then those that were to be performed along the dunes. The last set was kept for after we had pushed deeper into the thickets towards the Head, then we would trek up towards the stony summit of the low hill which guards the bay. I followed her movements. Suddenly she motioned to me to stop. I remained sitting, knees pushing into the earth. Just beyond the trees to the side of the clearing, I heard foot-steps.

Section 1: Summary Extracts from "The Teachings of Amen" as selected and introduced by Alpheus D'Oliviera Dhlomo, Co-ordinating Scribe of the Order of Solaris and published in 2664 - almost thirty years before his own conversion to Amenism.

Introduction to the Selection

Several factors have guided my selection of extracts from The Teachings and from the canon of interpretative essays. Naturally, the most important is based on my special scope of Interest: namely, the stripping away of Amenism's mythology so as to reveal the tawdry core. But I have also tried to be impartial; that is, to describe those of its aspects of Amenism which genuinely fascinate, beguile, amuse, shock, and above all, hold attention.

In addition, it has been my intention to add limited sections which cast historical light on the Movement, in terms of biographical details pertaining to its founder and his disciples, and their disintegration through various psychoses, as well as to examine its fragmented splinter sects with some of the main heresies which survive and imagine that they challenge the Order and our institutions. The central themes covering these sects are those of haphazardness, wilful distortion, circuitousness and malevolence. Amenism's malevolence towards the Order cannot be dismissed as an eccentricity - it is the critical glue holding Amenites together. If the student is to gain an accurate understanding of this Moment in History and its consequences, it will be necessary to include the mass psycho-dynamics which have contributed to its slow but steady burst to prominence. All this despite the fact that Amenism is a raving lunacy similar to the great libel, Protocols of the Elders of Zion, or the Stalinist tirades against Leon Trotsky, or the writings of Abbot Clement of Nongoma as encapsulated in his work, The Satanic Web as Woven by the Machine Minders.

Chapter 1

from the Beginning there was no beginning   light and dark are light and dark   light and dark are light and dark when there is light and dark light becomes dark when light becomes dark and dark becomes light when there is light   many bees make a hive of honey
the Officers are cold hypocritical oppressors who have enslaved us   they force us to provide and serve their needs while they engage in irrelevant intellectual activities   all their efforts are directed at conceptualising and perfecting new and more sophisticated techniques to keep us downtrodden ignorant submissive   why do we not all experience the Training? why should only those selected by the Order have freedom of choice? the Officers are corrupt   many of them abuse us for personal gain though that is the greatest heresy an Officer can commit   there is also sexual abuse but when cases are reported they are covered up by the Co-ordinators
     we have no opportunities for privacy where we can know the comfort of Love which the Officers claim for themselves through their Bondings they have exploited us for generations   their grip shackled us since the Great Crashing of 2129 when the economies failed and war raged across the continents   they rule us with their Enmindings   their computer driven Humanoids
            these creatures planted among us to expose any attempt at revolt they cannot be dematerialised   they disintegrate when their parts fail   we are kept in research camps near the Laboratories   they perform their experiments upon us   but now we have begun to mobilise against the Officers   from the black depths of these unsanitary and violent camps no   longer will we tolerate suppression   we will use our forces of Compassion to disarm their tyranny   in order to achieve this we must first purge ourselves of all excess all desires   in the Stream of Time we exist as particles appearing and reappearing in different forms and incarnations

the forms created by   Consciousness carry their own forms of consciousness those who would be Amenites must know hunger and pain and sorrow must bleed with the agony and bitterness of the massacred the rotted the stripped the deluded   then they must find their Balance in the Way of Things their bowl for rice carved with images of great birds and fishes   we wear our organic garments to show all eyes the simplicity of this Way as opposed to the Officers and their Power Suits   we carry our staffs to reconnect with the soil Our Mother our dust her dust   we will only reach beyond our Solar System if we complete the Return to Deathlessness   if we are genuinely able to Enmind even as the Officers attempt   no one being will serve another   no one being will require the subjugation or exploitation of another   there will be fair and equal exchanges   the Officers control us because they need a stock of our Genetic Pool for their experiments   they breed us with their robots their synthetic constructions   they have set up institutions where they take certain of our young ones and train them with their Humanoids   they claim these children will be able to undertake indefinite voyages into this material galaxy and into at least one Parallel Dimension   the Officers are deluded   they have not created more advanced Humans   they have created thuggish cyborgs who terrorise us after the Officers have attempted to enmind have eaten the water   the males become more and more perverted   their sexual satisfactions increasingly sadistic even as they achieve higher levels of understanding into the Nature and into our Place   we the last slaves at the mercy of their obsessions

Extract from Dhlomo's Diary

13 February, 2695

I stood in the conference foyer magnetised by Lettie's presence. I had for so long fantasized about her.

What was the essence of my fantasy?

Her superb intellect? Her insight and delicacy? Her smooth oval face? Her rich brown skin? Her expression of composed joyfulness? Her voice that filled me with alternate sensations of lust and gentleness?

Until that point, I would not have said that I had a conscious sense of seeking out the unique image of an Ideal Woman. But when I met Lettie, I knew there was a fusion of sensual, visual experience and a very deep sub-conscious resonance on the emotional, aesthetic and erotic levels: all these combined to form my Perfect Partner. In other words, had you asked me to describe my Ideal, I could not have done so as eloquently as Lettie was herself that manifestation; her glowing presence under the interacting epic figures representing the Ten Pleasures and Pains in the emerald and gold mosaic that filled the giant arching foyer.

I have often wondered if this spontaneous bonding, this state of Sublime Love, is an element we can ever pass on to the Masses. We have tried so hard to Uplift them yet they defy every effort. How many of the most gifted, most patient, Officers like Lettie, have devoted their lives to cultivating in them even the faintest signs of sensitivity. How tragic that The Wars bred a renegade gene which has proliferated uncontrollably. We have struggled to contain those unfortunates who carry the fatal Program and have placed them in enclosed and protected areas. This has been done with the greatest reluctance and only after long and persistent failure to de-energise their violence and savagery and make them able participants in Free Society. In addition, we have failed to prevent their excessive multiplying. Now they burden our Nutrition System and Habitat.

The smile which radiated across Lettie's face was the stimulus that revived my love for her even after the most upsetting, difficult periods. And to be honest, I must admit to a number of other crisis points. In particular the time, five years ago, when she had a brief but very intense relationship with her Co-ordinator Educator, a woman named Rochelle. This relationship almost broke our Bonding. I was thrown into a deep distress and confusion. Today, after careful reflection, I understand there were three aspects to my reaction. The first, and least important, was that her new lover was a woman and not a man. The second was that for the first time since our meeting in Rio de Janeiro, she was freely giving of her most intimate self to another person. And the third, and most distressing, was that there was a serious possibility of my emotional collapse.

I couldn't control my anxiety. Was it conceivable that this friendship could lead to her leaving me? The awfulness of this possibility was the essence of my panic. Over and over again I asked myself what had been my key limitation. What was so grievously lacking that Lettie had chosen another partner? Had I failed her as a lover? Was I unimaginative, weak - too crude? But no matter the answer, the fact was that Lettie's departure from the Known stirred me to a high pitch of erotic fantasy.

During the first few weeks after she had told me of her passion for Rochelle (this was before she actually moved out of our home to live with her), I found myself hoping that she would agree to share Rochelle with me. Though I had for many years played with this fantasy, of being with two women, I had never dared openly express it to her. Now she herself had taken a step that could make it a reality. If I was open to her and did not carp or complain, if I was light and friendly, concealing my pain and distress and also hiding for the moment my secret desire, perhaps she would still make love with me and I would win back her attraction but not to the extent that she would want to abandon Rochelle. No, desiring both of us, she would contrive a meeting at which we could explore the new situation. So as much as I feared losing her to Rochelle, I shivered with anticipation of the possible sexual benefit.

Rochelle was highly independent and competent. A senior member of the Regional Education Board, she was more than a little inhibiting. There were the obvious qualities of confidence, self-worth and humility. She was the epitome of the one who serves others, and serves gladly, but who serves with a masking of her own self, her own needs, her own satisfactions. Rochelle seemed so well-poised, collected and unaffected, so energetic in the face of challenge, that I could understand Lettie's liking and admiration for her.

But what had suddenly prompted sexual attraction?

Before meeting me, Lettie had been involved in two short-lived Bondings; on both occasions with men. It was my feeling that neither of these had reached the depth and intimacy of her relationship with Rochelle. Surprisingly I never knew why these earlier relationships had failed, and both times abruptly, for Lettie would not speak about them. This was the only issue about which she refused, or perhaps could not, communicate her deepest emotions. And I accepted this limitation on our intimacy, albeit under duress, for I did not want to force her to lie to me. I reasoned it was better to leave the memory to fade than to risk confrontation. When she became involved with Rochelle, I again did not want to provoke her refusal to express her feelings. Better withdraw from the Field Of Action than fatally undermine any chance of reconciliation. In any case, if she returned to me for negative reasons, for example, if Rochelle rejected her, my pushing for information and emotional disclosure could only undermine her confidence in my love; she would be jarred by my niggling interrogation and even more clearly see our continuing relationship as a poor substitute for her preferred but ill-fated partnership with Rochelle.

It is difficult to live with someone who spurns you, yet remains with you for ulterior, pragmatic reasons. One offers love but the other merely perpetuates a material union.

As much as I loved Lettie, I could not accept that.

Fortunately I was spared.

Lettie left Rochelle after four months. We never made up a sexual triangle. When she returned to me, she was as affectionate as she had been before. I

believe she initiated the break with Rochelle but we never spoke about what
had happened. Her love in the following years never seemed to diminish.

Extract from the thirteenth edition of Terra Astra

Section 8

We, Who Agitated to Leave the Paradise,
Brightest of the God Head's Creations,
Living Deathless in the Garden,
Bathing in Waves of Acoustic Zero,
Full but Empty with the Paradise:
Why is the God Head Controlling Us?
Why is the Oneness so Puissant?
We, Egos in the Ether,
Fan the Splinter of Being
To Flame Ourselves Fully Divine;
Each of Us Aspiring to Become One,
We Followed the Brightest,
The Most Splendid, the Boldest.
Shining with the Sheen of Deep Darkness
We followed at the Edges.
Then Soaring with the Self Belief Born
Of Conscious Achievement,
We Gathered at the Edges of the Fire Stream:
And the Emanation Appeared:

There is Only Light,
There is No Darkness.
There is No Darkness,
There is Only Light.
There is No Sleep.
There is No Sleep,
There is Only Dream.
There is Only Dream,
There is No Waking.
There is No Waking,
There is Only Illusion.
There is Only Darkness.

Extract from Dhlomo's Diary

14 February, 2695

Lettie turned in the direction of the footsteps she had heard along the edge of the Purification Place. I picked up the swish of sand, the brushing of twigs. It was the final mottling of dusk. I caught the outline of a face; a woman stepped into the clearing. She was flushed and sweating and she stopped as she saw us. Lettie looked at me enquiringly: the woman was dressed in the garments of an Amenite.

Let me make an aside: During the time of Upheavals, when the Order was wracked by the first of several Schisms, notably that between the Laboratories of the Highveld and those of the Kei concerning the Nature of our Stewardship over the Masses, Lettie and I would intersperse work cycles of fourteen days with cycles of meditation. As a result, we managed to retain some Existential Balance. Those who were too immersed in the day-to-day manoeuvres of each faction, soon burnt out under the pressure: yes, it must be admitted, there were factions (this term must be understood in the crude, polemical, propagandistic sense): many Officials degenerated to the level of Charlatans consumed by personal ambition and sensual temptation, by breaking the aesthetic of austerity and indulging in satiation of the gross senses.

We would leave Cape Port in the early hours of the morning when it was high tide, and sail in our skiff to the Point. As we put out to sea, we would feel the frustrations and tensions of the fortnight recede as the city lights fell away and we rounded the range of Apostles, those toothy mountains along the back of the peninsula towards the Sentinel, and on past Noordhoek and its estuary to the white sands at the base of the finger that jutted into the oceans, at that Point where the hot and cold currents of the Atlantic and Indian swirl together. Mooring the boat on the beach, we would traverse the dunes to our clearing.

Extract from Dhlomo's Diary

15 February, 2695

Lettie raised her arm as the robed figure entered the Clearing. The woman who stepped forward must have been walking swiftly - sweat ringed her forehead. She stopped abruptly and turned to us.

Nothing could have prepared us for the mass of scars and ulcers that made up her face. She was a coagulation of blood and puss and her features were alternately too low or too high, squeezed out of human proportion so that her mottled brown eyes were irregularly spaced, her nose was a narrow slit which travelled half across her cheek to one ear, her mouth twisted up at its sides in a grotesque curve and, when she parted her lips, I could see a large gaping cavern with stunted teeth all decayed into brown and yellow streaks.

Lettie, however, did not react to this grotesque set of features. She inclined her head in greeting. (Only now does it strike me how strange it was for the Amenite woman to have taken the initiative: with that one action she broke the barrier. However, despite registering the extreme deformity of her features, what shocked me more was seeing someone openly dare to wear the Amenite robe. Though Amenites were known to have built secret sanctuaries in the area situated higher in the dunes, and I had heard rumours that the Stabilisation Units had not succeeded in finding and destroying all of them, I had never before seen one of these sanctuaries in the many years since we had selected and frequented our Purification Place).

There was the sound of waves breaking and withdrawing along the beach. The woman looked back at us, a careful but confident expression. Any other Helot would have reacted with shock, for it was expressly forbidden them to enter our Purification Places. One could only assume that in the dark, she had not seen the white ribbon defining our perimeter. Now she stood inside the Clearing, with an attitude which was neither aggressive nor submissive and bowed to us, not obsequiously but with decorum, almost in the manner of an Officer, but graver and lifted her face. The waves rose, sucking at shells and pebbles. She spread her hands, as if to say: I am here but I do not know what to say to you.

I wanted to break the Meditation Silence and set her at ease but I reasoned that she should be fully aware of why we did not speak and would not expect us to break the Vow. After all, the Amenite teachings regarding Seclusion and Fasting were adapted from our own. Then I noticed there was blood on her gown, dark stains which were caught by the moonlight. There were also traces along her legs and arms. I moved forward to inspect her more closely. She rocked back on her heels as if to retreat but I motioned to her to remain where she was. Before I could take her hand, Lettie burst between us. The woman cried out as Lettie held up her arm. There was a deep gash running along her shoulder and across her back; the cut was fresh and still bled copiously.

The woman made as if to speak, then very deliberately covered her mouth, nodding her head as if to say, Yes, I know I must not break your Silence. Then she ran her fingers over her shoulder and neck exposing the cut, motioning with her hands, tracing the stab of a knife. I felt myself grimace. She smiled, bowing her head again. Lettie left her and ran to fetch water. She filled a Purification Chalice. I was surprised that she did not instead use one of our ordinary bowls; this was a serious violation of the Code. I gripped her wrist, pointing vigorously to the chalice. Without show of emotion, Lettie stared back at me and presented the Sacred Vessel to the Amenite woman.

I looked up. The moon had drifted clear of a cloud-bank. A heavy, distended not quite full moon with black wrinkles. The breeze which had dropped after sunset now picked up. The trees round the clearing whistled and swayed. It was forbidden to give one's Purification Chalice to anyone except one's Partner. Why had she chosen to foul hers? The woman had probably been injured in a drunken clash with a man. Why show her any sympathy? It is common knowledge that, though obliged to abstain from alcohol, the Amenites were susceptible to their Helot deficiencies. Alcohol was still their most common dependency, their most widespread form of self-abuse. Indeed, many Amenites came from alcoholic families so the cycle ran deep notwithstanding their elevated intentions.

The woman drank greedily, water gushing over her lips. Lettie stood beside her, the jar poised for refill. I thought of walking back to my Place. Instead, without knowing why, I pulled Lettie to me, but she turned away and moved closer to the Amenite woman and remained doggedly beside her while I faced the two of them. Pausing, I was caught in the silence; we stood - the three of us - buried in the pounding of waves. Then the Amenite woman began to drink again with her cupped palm, water dripping from the sides of her mouth. She was clearly very tired and caked with sand. Still heaving from her half-walk, half-run, she brushed back her hair with tapering fingers. She wore a rough woven robe, scuffed white, around which ran a purple border. I was familiar with their priestly colour, a beige sash draped across her breasts. There was neither servility nor defiance in her attitude, and though I scrutinised her fiercely, she seemed unafraid. But why should she be afraid? What would a Bonded Pair of two senior Officers, in the quiet and serenity of their Purification Place, do to a woman, irrespective of the Class to which she belonged? At worst, they would indicate to her that she should move away. At best, they would give her water, allow her to rest, bind her wounds and evaluate her, especially her eyes and mouth, and her way of carrying herself. Lettie seemed totally absorbed in ministering to her. I decided to maintain an exterior calm and wait. The Amenite woman lifted her arms, trying to remove the cloth that clung to her wound. Blood still seeped along her hem. As she lifted them, the moon rose and filled her face with light. She stretched. I caught the sway of her breasts. She was slender in the waist, yet fuller than Lettie. Lettie stood jug in hand ready to pour her more water, but after some moments, turned to her, and led her to her mat. The woman stood stiffly. Lettie motioned that she should lie down and remove her robe. When a startled look crossed the woman's face, Lettie repeated the same movements, stepped forward and raised up the hem of her robe and lifted it over her head. Then she carefully set the garment aside.

The Amenite woman lay naked on the mat with the moon shining on her and Lettie gently washed her wounds. She seemed so very soft, yet her whole being radiated firmness. She shone with the Goddess, the binary completion; corruscating sheath, breathing in hot waves for the swelling spear, wombing frenzy, copulating corn and breeding of blood. She began to relax as Lettie massaged her neck and her shoulder. The Amenite woman smiled in acknowledgement of what she saw in our eyes: from her neck down along her torso and thighs and legs, her body was perfect.

Extract from the sixteenth edition of Terra Astra

Section 13

I Heard a Nightingale
In a Rubbish Dump,
A Song Made of Air and Raw Nerves -
A Nightingale from Cairo.
I Lay with my Lover,
And We Listened;
My Love and I
Under the Skin of Ancestors,
Nomadic Intelligence;
Listening to a Song Springing
From the Heart;

In a Rubbish Dump,
On a Rusted Tank,
Bald Nightingale
Thrilling Us.

Extract from Dhlomo's Diary

16 February, 2695

I am so distraught at what Lettie has done. But while I struggle with all the strength and self-discipline in my being, it seems I have no choice but to come to terms with her betrayal. The fact is that Lettie must have long been an Amenite sympathiser; must have planned her crossing over many months before doing so.

I understand now that a woman was sent to collect and guide her back to the Colony; but that while making her way in the dark towards our Purification Place, she slipped and fell onto a rock and was injured. I also know that once she came to her final decision, Lettie requested the Amenite leaders to permit her to spend the two week Retreat with me as a final leave-taking.

The Amenite Council agreed to her request. For how were they to know that the escort would deliberately leave the Colony two weeks early, and would contrive to spend the entire two week period with us by exaggerating the extent of her wounds?

And how ironic that those two weeks should have been so idyllic! The three of us, always silent, bound by the Code of Purification, united in moments of stillness; whether during the quiet, white minutes before dawn or at sunset when the sky was torn into deep reds and yellows and the waves endlessly lulled us into Astral Motion.

And, of course, there were the nights.

PART 2

advance (-vah'-) v. 1. v.t. move or put forward; promote, help on, (plan, person); bring forward (claim, suggestion); bring (event) to earlier date; pay (money) before it is due; lend (money); raise (price); so ~MENT (-sm-) n. (esp. of promotion of plan or person). 2. v.i. move forward; make progress; rise (in price); (in p.p.) far on in progress (the work is well advanced), ahead of the times (advanced ideas); ~d studies (in higher branches of a subject). (M.E., f. OF avancer f. Rom. *abantiare f. L.L abante in front f. ab away + ante before)

The following is an extract from Dhlomo's Introduction to the first Edition of "The Teachings" published by the Swartberg Laboratory Press in 2695. This edition was published at the start of his murder trial. The most persuasive argument advanced to explain the timing of publication, which Dhlomo had steadfastly postponed, was his desire to present his poetic and sensitive nature to as wide an audience as possible, as opposed to the common public perception of his radical and, at times, seemingly over-zealous defence of the values and systems of the Atlantean Polis in the face of what he perceived to be betrayals or deviations.

Dhlomo was, of course, also attempting to reach the widest possible audience for his solutions to the moral and institutional crisis faced by Atlantis. But if he was harnessing public attention to make a political state-ment, it was not without remorse - his suffering was acute and open. At no stage did he attempt to gloss over his profound sorrow at having killed the woman he had loved and yet ceased to love. What he did, was to explain the context and the reason for his fatal lapse, his momentary but irrevocable loss of control. At the same time, he carefully presented the extreme provocation to which he had been subjected.

His Introductions for later Editions were superbly insightful and articulate reflections on the processes and ordeals he underwent over the twenty years following his sentencing to be the Internal Co-ordinator of Prisons during the course of which he, himself, embraced Amenism. As Internal Co-ordinator, though technically still a prisoner, responsible for the proper running of the penal settlements, Dhlomo came to know the Helots as he had never done as an Officer. This intimate exposure aroused in him a deep compassion and sympathy. The definition of `criminal' included those interned for economic, sexual and political crimes against the Polis, the

Officers and against other Helots. Many prisoners were Politicals; Amenites being the majority although another Tendency, the Human Liberation Army, which consisted of small, highly disciplined cells engaging in economic sabotage, had a strong core.

The radical reforms of the penal system, which he championed and some fifteen years later implemented, were outstanding contributions to the ultimate undermining of Officer authority over the Helots and provided a clear example for those living in more enlightened times who contributed to the Movement for Transcendence whose essential feature is Classless Consciousness - the conceptual advance which finally emerged as a mass practical reality in the first half of the twenty-sixth century. Contemporaneous with the elimination of political and economic inequality were explorations of Inner and Outer Space, all being very ripe fruits on the tree of Dhlomo's planting.

19 October, 2699   Elgin Place of Detention

To you, Dear Reader (whoever you are, wherever you are, whatever you think),

I greet you as a potential comrade but know, full well, the probability that you are hostile. Why hostile when I cannot claim to know YOU? Why assume negativism, suspiciousness and sourness on your part? Arrogance, stupidity and insecurity are manifestations of immaturity. Emotionally we continue to battle with these characteristics. I claim no special knowledge beyond that garnered through fifty years of, what have been, unceasing and relentless Struggle. But despite my years of study and experience, I must admit to ignorance of the underlying foundations and trajectory of even my own destiny, never mind that of our species and ultimately of our planet. (I concede that DESTINY is a term not many in the Order may recognise as a valid category. However, the poetic and scientific meanings of the word need not be eternally keep apart. In the following paragraphs, I hope to show why). Decades ago, The Order agreed that we were trapped in doldrums; suspended in our attempts to create autonomous and self-reproducing artificial intelligences. Our continuing failure to build such effective androgynous beings showed that the difference between human and human-made intelligence is finer and more difficult to bridge than we have presumed, and that the products of our work in the most fundamental of ways have not equalled ourselves, let alone proven transcendent.

Despite this self-evident failure, we were perplexed: why were we failing to develop beyond a "memory" when we had uncovered so many of the key sources of Energy and allocated such massive resources for further research? Despite being able to plan and execute an enormous range of functions, the circuits we have created cannot reproduce the subtlety and evaluative powers inherent in our own Genetic Computing. Our "artificial intelligences" cannot live out their own dynamic, quite apart from being able to reproduce themselves as a higher order of organism. They remain dependent on us, their creators, like recalcitrant children who refuse to leave home. And was it not "coincidental", that in parallel to the frustrations of this failure, there arose a sociological phenomenon - over time, despite all attempts at prevention, the Order became physically constituted almost exclusively by the sons and daughters of existing Officers.

The Selection Boards, made up as they have always been by Officers, have for decades selected fewer and fewer children of non-Officers for our required education. The result has been elitism and an inbreeding which has led to the irresistible growth, over many generations, of the current crisis. We now have an insurrection by the Helots, who though restricted to certain areas, to certain occupations, deprived of real choice or self-determination, have achieved a high level of counter-organisation and have launched, not only a moral, non-violent revolt guided by their Speaker, Amen, but a far-reaching challenge to our entire civilisation, the Atlantis of the Officers.

The gravity of the Crisis, the proof of their superiority, is borne out by our knowledge of their success in addressing their own emotional and intellectual primitivism. How ironic that the dregs of the Centuries of War, the atavistic rabble groomed for bestiality, who could not be removed from our Gene Pool, and which we detained in places of safety for its own sake and for the sake of others, has now challenged its own brutality on the strength of the teachings of a core of revolutionary preachers! And now our beloved Atlantis is threatened by a moral force which it as a decaying elite, cannot resist.

Already many Officers, the most perceptive, the most compassionate, the most intelligent and noble are abandoning the Order and joining the Amenites. They recognise that the inevitability of this conflict flows from its innermost Nature: all Imbalances in the Present must give way in their Future to their Instabilities. So what are we to say to these Officers who abandon us? Are they traitors or are they heroes to be followed?

Those who would defend their privilege and their comfort will reject these musings as an unwelcome and irrational assault. But those who are familiar with the old nineteenth and twentieth century socialist texts with their emphasis on the moral struggle in addition to class struggle will recognise the echoes which have resounded in the Amenite teachings, and will recognise in this ebb and flow, the concept of Dialectical Necessity - when a particular Moment gathers up its contradictions and suffers them. In addition, the narrowing of the Officer base has had serious repercussions. In less than six hundred years, the proportion of Officers to Helots has dropped by seventy-seven percent. Once the Helots were a criminal minority - they are now a massive majority. And as the potential pool of Officers has shrunk, we have seen a weakening of our intellectual and physical powers in that inbreeding invariably creates a higher probability of defective genes.

If all these factors taken together constitute the political crisis of Atlantis, I would now like to propose is a program which, while recognising the Immanence of Contradiction, seeks to effect syntheses which advance our unfolding destiny as favourably as possible. We are yet to succeed in our program for the construction of superior humanoids: not mere robots but organic creations whose intelligence and powers far supersede our own.

We have wished to create these new children for the exploration and research of both the Inner and Outer Universe. The need for this development lies in the knowledge that our physical bodies cannot survive the rigours of travel in Deep Space. Developing a mutant whose physical self can be easily reproduced and extended, and whose emotional self will not be subject to the same extreme shifts from which we suffer (for even the most developed, disciplined, and wisest of the Officers' struggles with the mood changes to which our species is prone, our `highs and lows', our moon-led perturburations), this was our Task.

Faced with this liability, this outmoded conditioning, we embarked on experiments with the Helots. These involved the grafting of synthetic materials onto their bodies as well as genetic cloning. Tragically they have only resulted in deficient imitations of our Selves - sometimes in the producing of truly gross monsters. Now our program is at a standstill. Vast expenditures and millions of Mind Hours have failed to improve on the current prototypes. More than ever we must ask: do we continue or do we stop to reflect on the reasons for our failure?

I suggest the first understanding will be that all research and endeavour must from now on be solely directed to perfecting travel in the Seventh Dimension - the dimension of Particles. The insistence on transporting our bodies on a spatial axis must stop. The experiments which are in progress must be terminated and all our efforts placed in Dematerialization research. Now if we accept that this is the case, we will naturally arrive at the second main question: how can we continue to physically confine members of our own species for use in experiments whose results have largely been to deform and degrade? Particularly since these experiments have had as their objective the pursuit of deeper knowledge and the extension of human vistas. This central contradiction must be resolved. It should also be noted that it is decades since experimentation on animals was made unlawful, and many decades more since the consumption of animal meat was banned. How ironic that we now only exploit our own, having full regard to the rights of animals!

This demands that, while still maintaining authority, we reconsider the position of the Helots. We must devise a means to gradually reduce their numbers through population control and through more intensive integration into our own Nurturing Systems. We will have to prepare for some confusion in our own community but I am confident that we have the resources and discipline to deal with this. The alternative is to allow Amenism to slowly win over both a significant Helot majority and our own Officers. Openness on our part can save the most valuable, the eternal features of The Order, and at the same time strengthen the sublime in Amenism.

Lastly, let me mention how much the writing of this Work has meant to me. As a child, in the company of my parents and their friends, who were at the forefront of the literary renaissance of the Thirties, I read voraciously. The `home' readings organised by my mother were famous for their vitality and daring. Poets and dramatists knew they were sure of a genuine welcome. How often artists who were completely unknown would turn out to be gifted and passionate! Many beautiful evenings were spent in the small amphitheatre my father designed, enraptured by unexpected performances. It was for such occasions that I composed my first works. Writing `The Teachings' has been a continuation of those precocious efforts. But I hope, with greater discipline and insight at my disposal, that the results are more powerful, more comprehensive and valuable. Of course, only you, the reader, can ultimately judge the extent of my achievement. And I do not use the word lightly - I so much hope that what I have produced is an achievement. I would not want to believe that these quite agonising efforts have been wasted - not out of a sense of boastfulness, but from knowing how I wrestled with myself, fighting my persistent mediocrity, my banality, my arrogance, my pigheadedness, my dullness, night after night for these thirty demanding years.

And at the same time, I know full well that authorship is a dubious notion. The experience that constitutes any Work must acknowledge the whole canon of human endeavour. If I claim anything, it is the satisfaction of knowing that I put my nose to the grindstone, that I did not shirk the Inner Call. Whether the results give pleasure and enlightenment to others that must remain my hope. Dear Reader, you hold my Life in your hands.

As a child, my supreme ambition was to be a writer. I dreamt of writing a seminal work which would be one of such brilliance and insight that it would stand with the giants of world literature. But why was I still fascinated by 'literature' when the notion of written articulation has all but faded in favour of direct experience and the charged anti-expressionism of meditation? As such, this was a romantic ambition, perhaps even a noble one - but hardly a popular one. My father always stressed that isolating the source of Creativity still eludes us; that, as much as the State of Happiness. He encouraged me to experiment even though the Laboratories frowned on the writing of poetry. The Order demanded instead the construction of programs. and at most begrudged the penning of moralities. To safeguard myself, this book therefore began as a classic, Officer didactic. It was only after two decades of consistent writing that I felt strong enough to veer off into a discouraged, forbidden Mythism.

As a student, I began work on it in the mornings during the breaks between lectures when others were concentrating on Systems Analysis and Meditation Technique. I would write in the evenings, alone in my room, window open to the night-sounds, music chosen by the moment's intuition, hand cupped under my chin, swimming in the blue depths of my Terminal. I would write of my ideas, my attitudes, my projections. I would write about people and things I had seen, sensations I had experienced. I would write about everything that filled my world, everything, that is, except my feelings. These I would shift and evaluate, censor before recording for fear that an unwelcome reader would break into my Screen and discover how inwardly possessed I was, how filled with a momentous passion that could not be realised. I was in love with a fellow student and she was refusing to meet me. My heart was filled with adoration and hatred, and my testicles, how I remember the unbelievable adolescent agony, swollen with unconsummated desire!

Now, I leave you, dear Reader, to consider these issues, in the face of difficult, painful but unavoidable decisions.

Extract from the thirteenth edition of Terra Astra

Section 9

Beyond the Border,
The Darkness Now
Not that of Projection,
We Were in the Darkness
But We did not Mourn.
We Stood Holding
The Weight of Darkness,
That Hole of Space,
Cold, Constant Sense of Death.
And We Joined Our Selves -
One Joining the Other -
And Found a Connection.

Weighty in the Light
Of Feathers and Foul Wounds,
The Drunken Wanton
Coughed Out Mystery to Us,
The Dormant and the Blind,
Blacking the Prism,
Embracing Those who Grab
With Perfumed Hands,
The Hands They Hire,
For Their Bidding:

Children Prone before Idols,
Vague Manuscripts,
Instructions Framed with Gold,
Till Noon Becomes Evening,
Evening became Night,
And Night becomes the Island
On which Day must be Planted.

But Day Refuses to Dawn,
Plans become Lies,
And Lies become New Promises.

Extract from The Teachings of Amen

Chapter 2

the Officers are wont to abduct Amenite women and force them to submit to a sexual cult that derives from a belief in the Primacy of the Orgasm as
the Highest Wave within the scope of human cosmic sensations   in experiencing its state of overwhelming bliss, completion and intimacy Humans rejoin the Instant of Timeless Creation   world of immediate everlasting cosmic fusion

the Officers preyed on our women comrades   they did so shame-lessly

none more so than Alpheus D'Oliviera Dhlomo, Chief Co-ordinator of the Laboratory of Atlantis, Western Cape

Extract from the Third Introduction to the Book of Dhlomo, as written by Alpheus D'Oliviera Dhlomo, in the fifteenth year of his sentence as Co-ordinator of the Helot Stations.

My Dear Reader

Once I lived only in the World of the Order - I was an Officer and a Senior. Now for the past fifteen years, I have lived entirely in the World of the Helot. But my status, both as an Interned Officer and as Co-ordinator of the Penal Colony, has given me a unique opportunity to enter all areas of penal life and to experience the world of the Helot as it unfolds in the context of an Incarceration. And so, without directly making it apparent, this has allowed me to penetrate the veil of Amenism. For I found, to my great surprise and later joy, that the Amenites welcomed me and opened their temples and their study groups to me. They ushered me into their Community and made me feel that I was a brother to each of them. They have a Means to achieve this State in a way, and with an intensity, of which the Wafer is a soulless substitute. And so, for the first time, I was able to experience the true Sympathy of Souls of which the Order speaks much but is unable to generate. Yet how unjust, how terribly cruel, that the catalyst for my being able to open myself to all Strata, thereby healing myself and reaching the State of Fullness of the Amenites, was the death of my beloved Lettie! Only an event as shattering, as traumatising as her death could have placed me in my current Position. (How tragic that in order to facilitate human change, there is almost inevitably a taking away, a loss, a dimunition before transcendence is achieved).

Today, however, I refuse to allow this self-reproach and horror to overwhelm me. I stand up to it and use it to make me stronger and fitter for the challenge we face: the struggle between a decaying, oppressive Order and the fresh moral impulse and clear scientific bearing of Amenism. I am comforted in knowing that if we secure this triumph, it will be the result of the sacrifice of one of the Officers most sincere and uncorrupted members, my dearest Lettie. And I do not judge myself so easily: it was an act of despair, that of someone who had been driven beyond his limit. Maddened by the prospect of losing her, I lost control. I simply could not face living without her - she was my True Partner, my most intimate companion.

I realize now that though throughout the last Purification period that we spent together I was not to know of her intended departure, nor to have any knowledge of her past relationship with the Amenite woman, she did this because, despite her whole-hearted conversion to Amenism, she needed to cleanse herself for Self-Reconciliation.

She felt that she had to part with me in an exemplary way so that I would not be bitter and hate her. This period was also the most intensive preparation for making the final momentous move from the settled Life of the Order to the hazardous underground existence of the Movement.

For many years, in addition to her Education work with the Officer children, Lettie had been involved in the Experiment. Humanoids were created by grafting synthetic circuits and limbs onto the core bodies of certain Helot prisoners. Because of their origin, neither organic not inorganic, there was a pattern of their being abused by both Officers and Helots on account of their extreme manifestations and characteristics: gross physical or mental deformity combined with either superior intelligence or physical beauty. And as a result of being cast out, many of them joined the Amenite Movement.

There was a sense of rightness then: that Lettie, as passionate and courageous as she was, should fell in love with a humanoid woman who was seconded for experimentation to her Station; and under this woman's influence, decide to abandon the Order and join the Amenite Movement. But at the time of her imminent breaking away, for a multitude of reasons, she was unable to immediately leave me and the Purification Place. The peacefulness and rawness of the surroundings, the spare, clean ritual, and perhaps the knowledge that never again would she be living with me, made her postpone her departure. It is surprising, with hindsight, that I was ignorant of all these plans and intentions although at every other Level my awareness was of the almost immediate fusion of our three selves into an unparalled triangle. The most perfect weeks of my life - those two weeks of silent meditation and fantasy, though each night the passage of the stars told me the Period was shortening. On the last evening, I signalled to Lettie that despite the unique holiness of our Connection, we must separate from the Amenite woman and return to the Laboratory. Lettie looked back at me very intently, very intimately, yet with a new and strange component in her eyes. Then she walked out beyond the white ribbon marking the border of the Purification Place.

I looked on in amazement when, from inside her Purification Gown, she took out a folded Amenite robe, similar in design and colour to that of the woman, and throwing off the gown replaced it with the robe. Then she told me of her decision to leave the Order. She gave me a brief explanation and begged me to allow her to depart peacefully. I was to report her death from drowning and the subsequent disappearance of her body under the waves.

By a supreme effort of will, I remained calm. The Amenite woman crossed over beyond the ribbon and stood by her side. My heart was in tumult but my Understanding told me to respect her wishes; her judgement though clearly disoriented was surely genuine and sincere.

Alone, I returned by boat to Atlantis. But I could not bring myself to inform my fellow Officers of her death. Instead, I said that I was not well, had eaten something disagreeable and needed to recover. I said that Lettie had decided to stay behind for a further week. Consumed with anger and sorrow, I remained closed up in our house.

I had lived in a Paradise but those days were too few. Again and again, I saw the three of us, side by side on our mats, vibrating along the tips of our bodies as the Dimensions began to tune. The presence of the Amenite woman was sublime - she sang more sweetly than I had imagined possible. Memories flooded through me doubling my anguish. By noon of the following day, I was on the brink of a total breakdown. I refused to accept that this was the end of my life with Lettie. I shuddered in an agony of bereavement: she was dying for me; she was going where she would be denied me; yet others, enemies of the Order would harvest the glow of her presence.

I decided to return to the Point and take her by force. She and the Amenite could not have gone far. In fact, I had an intuition that they might have stayed on at the Purification Place, trusting that I would never betray her. I set out from Langebaan harbour in the late afternoon, expecting to arrive before midnight. As I crossed the dunes and reached the Purification Place, I saw the glow of a fire through the trees. I approached quietly. Lettie and the Amenite woman were seated on mats beyond the Place where they had built a fire. They were eating. I squatted in the bushes holding back, then tormented by desire and anger, I watched as they embraced.

There was no doubt, Lettie truly loved her. I had lost her and I had lost her partner, whose face inspired such a terror of ugliness but the remainder of whose body had stoked in me a powerful heat.

Suddenly I leaped up, ran in and grabbed Lettie. She resisted my grip. I felt myself throwing her down to the earth. I watched in horror as her head struck a rock; I watched incredulously as her head was cut open, and a deep, throbbing spring of blood gushed forth. The Amenite woman was immobilised, first shocked by my wild entrance, my manic strength and then immediately afterwards by the sight of Lettie's wound. But before either of us could act, Lettie made a loud gurgling sound and her head abruptly twitched from side to side before stopping and becoming deathly still. The Amenite woman gave a pitiful cry, and sobbing uncontrollably, ran out onto the dunes.

I did not follow her. Instead, I returned that night to the Laboratory with Lettie's body in the boat and immediately reported what I had done. Tried by a Special Tribunal, made up of the most senior Officers, I was sent to govern the Helots, to discipline them in the name of the Order, to break their most hardened, resourceful leaders - in short, I was given the task of crushing the Amenite Movement. Today, of course, it is clear that another Mission was destined: instead I joined the The Movement and helped create recognition by the Order that the Penal Stations have, in fact, surpassed the Laboratories and become extraordinary Communities of the free-thinking and free-acting. Indeed, the Penal Stations have now achieved what the Order itself has long tried to achieve and sustain!

Negotiations recognising the civil rights of Helots and recognising Amenism as a legitimate Way are now far advanced. Soon the Order will be dissolved in favour of a single, common society. I need not repeat the founding principles of this new society, they has been expressed many times over these past few years. What I would like to emphasise is that the Black Flag of Amenism, while related to its historical predecessors, is a qualitatively advanced expression of Human Liberation. And I have made it my Work, in memory of Lettie Naidoo Saambou who died at my hands, but whose murder proved my salvation, to propagate this new spirit, this fresh manifestation of faith, this great rebirth of human hope. For, finally, the time when we subjugated and denied each other, creating hierarchies of power, is passed. And those who built empires of sensual obsession, those who dispossessed others of land or water, those who amassed great fortunes through the servitude and the misery of others, and those victims who trembled under the yoke of captivity cut off from their language and their music, those and even those snared in the images of surfaces, all of us, at last, ready to magnify our lives.

GLOSSARY

amabulu	Boers, Afrikaners (derogatory)
amakhulu	Indians (derogatory)
Amandla	power (Zulu)
awethu	it is ours (Zulu)
baas	boss, master (Afrikaans)
baba	father (Zulu)
bakkie	pickup truck
bangbroek	coward
bliksem	bastard (lit. lightning)
blouetjie	blue pill (amphetamine)
boere	Afrikaners
boeremeisie	Afrikaans girl (lit. farm girl)
boesman	Coloured person (derogatory)
boeta	buddy
boykie	little boy, little chap
Bushie	Coloured person (derogatory)
Civics	township organizations formed in the 1980s to deal with local government matters
churrah	Indian person (derogatory)
dief	thief
die Volk	the (Afrikaner) nation
doek	head scarf
doos	cunt
dorp	country town
fokken	fucking
fris	strapping, strong
gaan aan	carry on
gemors	mess
gevaar	danger
hoosit	how's it
ingozi	danger
inyanga	traditional African doctor
jalabiah	traditional robe (North Africa and Middle East)
jigga-jigga	sexual intercourse (slang)
kak	shit
kakstorie	shit story, rubbish
kafferboeties	negrophiles (lit. 'kaffir' buddies)
kaffie	local corner shop
kierie	stick with a knob at the end (traditional weapon)

koppie	hill
laaitie	youngster
lappie	dishcloth
lekgai	how are you
lekker	nice
liefling	darling
makgosha	prostitute
mal	mad, crazy
mfo	brother (slang)
meneer	mister, sir
moegoes	fools, nincompoops
moer	beat up
moerse	helluva
moffie	homosexual (derogatory)
the Movement	African National Congress
my china	my pal (slang)
naaied	screwed (vulgarism)
nee, wat	no, not really
oupa	grandfather
pondonkie	small hut, hovel
Onse Jan	Jan Hofmeyr, early champion of the Afrikaans language under British rule (pun in this instance)
pap	stiff (usually maize) porridge, a staple food
pilletjie	lit. little pill, capsule – in this instance, a drug
pozzie	place, pad
sangoma	African diviner
sies	ugh, yuk
sisi	sister
slap chip	lit. limp chip (as opposed to crispy fried chips)
skop	kick
soeking	looking (for trouble)
Sowetan	popular black working class newspaper
tsotsi	(township) thug
umlungus	whites (derogatory)
vark	pig
Vierkleur	lit. 'four colours', flag of Paul Kruger's South African (Boer) Republic
volksleiers	the Afrikaner Nation's leaders
waar's die	where is the . . .
waar's djou	where is your (slang)
wors	sausage

Also by Allan Kolski Horwitz

Fiction

Out of the Wreckage
Meditations of a Non-White White

Poetry

Call for a Free State
We Jive Like This (with the Botsotso Jesters)
Dirty Washing (with the Botsotso Jesters)
Greetings Emsawawa (with the Botsotso Jesters)
Saving Water
There are Two Birds at My Window

Drama

The Pump Room
Comrade Babble

Children's Literature

Blue Wings